About the Author

Claire Boston fell in love with romance and romantic suspense at eleven when she discovered her mother's stash of Nora Roberts novels. Like Nora, she writes series set around families or groups of friends with a guaranteed happy ending.

She loves travelling and learning about new cultures and interesting vocations which she then weaves into her writing.

When Claire's not at the computer typing her stories she can be found creating her own handmade journals, swinging on a sidecar, or in the garden attempting to grow something other than weeds.

Claire lives in Western Australia with her husband, who loves even her most annoying quirks and is currently learning how to knit. You can find her complete book list on her website www.claireboston.com/books and can connect with Claire through Facebook and Twitter, or join her reader group

(http://www.claireboston.com/reader-group/).

Also by Claire Boston

Romance
<u>The Texan Quartet</u>
What Goes on Tour
All that Sparkles
Under the Covers
Into the Fire

<u>The Flanagan Sisters</u>
Break the Rules
Change of Heart
Blaze a Trail
Place to Belong

Romantic Suspense
<u>The Blackbridge Series</u>
Nothing to Fear
Nothing to Gain
Nothing to Hide
Nothing to Lose
Shelter
Shield
Harbour
Protect

<u>Aussie Heroes: Retribution Bay</u>
Return to Retribution Bay
Trapped in Retribution Bay
Escape to Retribution Bay
Secrets in Retribution Bay

Non-fiction
<u>The Beginner Writer's Toolkit</u>
Self-Editing

Return to Retribution Bay

Aussie Heroes: Retribution Bay

Claire Boston

BANTILLY
PUBLISHING

First published by Bantilly Publishing in 2021

Return to Retribution Bay: Aussie Heroes: Retribution Bay

EPUB format: 9781925696745
Mobi format: 9781925696752
Print: 9781925696806
Large Print: 9781925696813

Cover design by Mayhem Cover Creations
Edited by Ann Harth
Proofread by Teena Raffa-Mulligan

Chapter 1

"I'm getting out."

Sergeant Brandon Stokes jolted, ripping his gaze from the two attractive women across the crowded bar in the army mess hall. He looked for his best friend's tell-tale lip twitch to prove he was having him on, but the lighting was too dim. "You're kidding me, right?"

Sam shook his head. "It's time, mate. That last tour to Afghanistan…" The despair in his eyes didn't need to be spoken. They'd both been there. "Besides, Izzy's due any minute and her partner's walked out. The kid's going to need his uncle. I've done my time."

As if the army was a prison sentence. Perhaps for some it was. For Brandon it was penance. He clapped a hand on his friend's shoulder and while he wanted to shake some sense into him, he couldn't argue with his reasoning. The prospect of not signing on for another four years had crossed his mind more than once in the past twelve months. But unlike Sam, he couldn't face his family. Not after what he'd done.

He forced a smile. "So how much longer have I got to put up with you?"

"Another couple of months. Brass want me to spend

time with the younger recruits, take them through their paces." Sam smiled.

Not long at all. It wouldn't be the same without Sam. "What are you going to do with yourself?" Brandon sipped his beer. Whatever it was, it wouldn't be sitting behind a desk pushing paper.

"Not sure yet. I've got enough saved to cover me for six months and I reckon Izzy will need me for at least that long if the baby doesn't sleep."

Brandon ignored the pain in his chest. His own sister, Georgiana was about Izzy's age and he hadn't seen her in over a year, not since she'd finished university and moved back to Retribution Bay. She sent him a chatty email every few months, but it had been a while since he'd heard from her.

"So, what about you?" Sam asked. "You re-enlisting?"

He shrugged. "What else would I do?"

"You could go home."

Brandon shook his head. "You know I can't."

Sam studied him as he took a long mouthful of his beer. "Mate, don't you think it's time? We're not getting any younger. I'm sure they've forgiven you."

That wasn't the problem. Brandon could never forgive himself. He tapped his middle finger on the bar. "Leave it."

"That last tour almost killed us both—"

"I'll think about it," Brandon interrupted. His chest constricted at the memory. The intense barrage of ammunition, the race through the streets. They'd made it out. Just.

"What are you two moping about? You promised me a good time if I dragged myself out." Arthur "Sherlock" Hammond stood stiffly at the table, as if the military posture had fused his spine.

Brandon grinned. "About time you showed."

Sherlock didn't know the meaning of 'at ease', and rarely came out, always working on some extra task for the military, always trying to get ahead. "Sam's just saying he's not re-enlisting." The absolute disbelief on Sherlock's face made Brandon chuckle. The only way Sherlock would leave the army was in a body bag.

"Why?"

Sam shrugged. "I've got my sister to take care of."

Sherlock flinched. "The army needs men like you."

The words could have come out of Major Hammond's mouth. Sherlock always parroted his father, only Brandon wasn't convinced he believed what he said. The one time Brandon had cracked that stiff, duty-bound shell, he'd discovered an emotionally vulnerable man underneath.

"You're staying in, aren't you?" Sherlock asked him.

He nodded as his mobile rang and he grabbed it, glad for the distraction, even if it might be his brother, Darcy trying him again. It wasn't.

Major Hammond. Not good. "Major."

Across from him Sam raised his eyebrows and Sherlock stood even straighter.

"Sergeant Stokes, I need to see you in my office immediately."

"Yes, sir. I'm on my way." There was no other answer even though it was seven at night and he was off shift. Brandon stood as he ended the call.

"What's that about?" Sam asked.

"Major Hammond wants me to see him in his office."

Sam frowned. "I'll wait for you here."

"Does he need me as well?" Sherlock asked.

Brandon shook his head.

As he walked out of the mess he ran through his activities over the past forty-eight hours, but nothing stood out that would get him into trouble. He zipped his jacket closed as the wind whistled past him. Summer was a long way off down here in Perth. Even after twelve years living south of the Tropic of Capricorn he still hated the cold.

The major's office was across the field from the mess, so Brandon broke into a jog, partly to keep warm and partly not to keep the major waiting. He wasn't a patient man and had extremely exacting expectations.

Brandon hadn't broken a sweat when he arrived in front of the building. He unzipped his jacket as he walked into the heated room and approached the major's office. His team leader, Lieutenant Colonel Dobson, affectionately known as Dobby, was also there, along with a padre and a woman he didn't recognise. They all looked solemn.

Shit. This couldn't be good. He saluted.

"At ease, Sergeant," Major Hammond said.

The woman clenched her hands together and looked at the padre, who shuffled his feet, but it was Dobby who cleared his throat and spoke. "There's no easy way to say this, Brandon," he said. "We had a phone call from your brother, Darcy. There's been a car accident."

The breath left his lungs. "Where? Who?"

"I'm sorry, Sergeant," the major said. "Both your parents were killed."

"No." The denial was instant as the bottom dropped from Brandon's stomach to be replaced by a deep numbing pain. The last clear image he had of his father was his look of disgust when... He squeezed his eyes closed. "I've got to get home." Too late for a flight and driving would take over thirteen hours, but if he left now he'd be there by morning. He turned to go.

"Wait, Brandon," Dobby said. "The RAAF are flying supplies up to their base tonight. We've got some equipment going up for our next training mission. Maybe they can fit you on." He glanced at the major, who scowled but picked up the phone to call. He hated anything personal getting in the way of the military.

Flying was the fastest way to get there. He should have answered Darcy's phone call earlier. How was he coping? Georgie would be a mess. Had Ed made it home yet? "My youngest brother's in Perth, too."

The major inclined his head, phone to his ear. "Call him. I'll see what I can do."

Brandon dialled Ed's number, but it went straight to voice mail. Shit. What to say? "I just heard the news. Might be able to get a flight with the RAAF to Retribution Bay. Let me know if you need it." He hung up and noticed the missed call from Darcy was from around midday. Chances were high Ed had got the afternoon flight home.

The padre watched him carefully as if waiting for him to break down. Wasn't going to happen. He had a mission—to get home as soon as possible. "What happened?"

"Darcy said your parents were heading into town," Dobby said. "The car rolled and both were dead by the time anyone found the wreck."

Brandon closed his eyes. The stretch of road between the family sheep station and the main road into the Bay didn't get a lot of traffic. Had his parents survived the crash and been waiting for help?

Major Hammond hung up. "You've got a flight if you can get to the airbase within the hour."

"I'll be there." Brandon saluted and strode out of the building. The cold hit him, penetrating his thoughts, reminding him to focus on something other than his parents trapped in their car. He jogged back, already planning what he needed to take with him and by the time he arrived at his car, he'd packed everything in his mind. Sam and Sherlock were waiting for him.

"Dobby called," Sam said. "I'm so sorry, mate. I'll

drive you to the RAAF base."

Sherlock shifted uncomfortably. "I'll catch you when you get back." He didn't do emotions well.

Brandon nodded and jumped in the car with Sam. They detoured past his place only long enough for him to throw some things in a bag and then headed east towards the RAAF base.

"What do you know?" Sam asked.

Brandon stared out at the street, the darkness his friend. "Car rolled when they were heading into town. They were dead by the time someone found them."

Sam swore. "Call me if you need anything. I can probably get time off to attend the funeral."

Always had his back. Sam knew how hard it was for Brandon to go home. He was the only one he'd ever confided in. It had been during a moment of weakness on their first tour together when Brandon was certain he was going to die. "Thanks."

They pulled into the airstrip and were directed to a plane on the runway. Sam parked and got out, coming around to hug him and slap his back. "Take care, mate. Keep me up to date."

Brandon nodded. He grabbed his bag from the back and strode across the tarmac, greeting the airman at the base of the plane. Not long after, he was in the air on his way home for the first time in twelve years.

He stared at the floor in front of him. Home. Memories stampeded him; barrel racing at gymkhanas, playing pranks on his brothers, taking Georgie across to the bay so she could swim. Every moment revolved around the family he'd destroyed, the ones he'd failed. He'd only seen his niece, Lara once, but she had to be ten by now. He'd failed to be there for Darcy.

How would they react seeing him again?

The plane landed just after ten. "You got someone to

pick you up?" the officer in charge of the flight asked.

"I'll sort something out." He wasn't calling and waking his brother. The station ran on daylight hours which meant they were usually in bed early to be up with the sun. Besides, his family had already had a shit day and the station was a good hour's drive away. He'd walk over to the public airport and hire a car. Then he'd have his own wheels and could leave whenever he wanted. They wouldn't want him staying past the funeral anyway.

He slung his bag over his shoulder and walked with the other men across to the hangar. Several uniformed officers were inside but it was the man leaning against one of the walls, dressed in jeans and a blue checked shirt who caught Brandon's attention. Despite the fact that the sun had long since gone to bed, a brown Akubra shaded his face. Shit.

Darcy had grown up. He was no longer the lanky teenager who had been by his side through all their adventures, always the one to add a little caution to their plans.

The man pushed himself off the wall and strode over, his forehead furrowed, eyes narrowed, and a glare so bright it would give away his position on a battle field. This reunion would be as bad as Brandon had expected.

"Darcy." He nodded a greeting at his younger brother. Two years his junior, he stood a good two inches taller than Brandon.

Darcy's blue-grey eyes darkened. "Couldn't be bothered to return my call?"

"Figured I'd see you soon enough." The whites of Darcy's eyes were bloodshot, evidence of crying. Brandon's heart pulled. "How'd you know I'd be here?"

"Your lieutenant colonel called me back, said you were hopping an air force plane."

What could he say to the man who used to be his best friend, but who he hadn't seen in the twelve years since he'd joined the military? How could he convey the devastation hammering away in the part of his brain where he'd locked it? "You got a car?"

Incredulity swept across Darcy's face. He shut it down. "This way."

Brandon waved to the officer and followed his brother out of the hangar into the warm night air. This far north and this close to the coast, it never got too cold. Such a contrast with the city.

As they exited the air force base Darcy drove away from town, the darkness of the night swallowing them immediately. Only the high beam spotlights illuminated the road, giving them early warning of kangaroos, emus or feral goats.

Brandon swallowed the lump in his throat. "Where'd it happen?"

Darcy glanced at him. "Hangman's Bend."

The only real bend in an otherwise straight road. Legend had it that sailors on the Retribution had mutinied when their ship was wrecked in the bay and the mutineers had eventually been hung from a tree in the area.

So not on the station. "What happened?"

Darcy sniffed and cleared his throat. Brandon didn't dare look at him. If he saw tears in his brother's eyes, he'd be a goner. "They were taking the day off. Georgie had arranged for them to go out on her boat, do a whale shark tour, so it was pretty early in the morning. When they didn't show at eight, she called to make sure they hadn't forgotten."

His mother never forgot a thing.

"They'd left plenty early enough. You know mum never likes… liked to be late to anything."

Brandon bit his cheek at the past tense and tapped

his finger on his leg.

"I jumped in the ute and found the car on its roof. They were already dead."

Fuck. "Jesus, Darce, I'm so sorry."

"Don't." The word was a bullet. "You don't get to say sorry. You haven't given a fuck about this family for years."

"That's not true."

"Isn't it? When was the last time you visited? When did you last talk Georgie down from one of her crazy ideas? When did you last chat to Dad about the station and how it was doing? When did you sit and have a cuppa with Mum?"

Each question pounded on the wall he'd built to protect himself. Cracks began to form.

"I've got commitments," he managed. It was his standard response. The military as a mistress had been a damned good excuse over the years. He was deployed over Christmas and Easter regularly. His family didn't know he'd requested it.

"Bullshit. It wouldn't have taken much time to call Mum. Once a year on her birthday didn't cut it. She made excuses for you, but I could see in her eyes she was disappointed."

Brandon wanted to press his fingers into his ears and block out Darcy, but his brother was on a run now.

"Did you know Georgie tried to visit you when she was at uni?"

She'd stopped by a couple of times, but he didn't spend much time at his house. "Shut up, Darce. You don't know shit."

It was the wrong thing to say, but as Darcy drew in a breath to retort, they rounded the bend.

His parents' four-wheel drive was still on its roof, the ute's headlights reflecting off the white surface, the body crumpled, windscreen smashed and police tape surrounding it. "Stop the car."

Darcy pulled over without comment, turning the car so the lights shone on the wreck.

Brandon fumbled for the door handle and got out. On the rear window was a faded sticker proclaiming *I love horses*. He took a closer look. Shit. It was the same car they'd had when he'd left, the car which had taken them to many gymkhanas, and now it was destroyed. For it to be that far into the bush it had to have rolled a few times. He could imagine his mother's screams as it did. The same anguish he'd heard in her voice only once before. No. He squeezed his eyes shut. Don't go there.

Behind him the car engine stopped, and a door closed. Footsteps crunched over the red dirt as Darcy joined him.

Silence. Deep and endless.

"Who was driving?" His question was almost offensively loud in the night.

"Dad."

Brandon frowned. That couldn't be right. "He wouldn't have been going that fast around the bend." It was the one thing his father had droned on about when he'd taught Brandon to drive. Bends were often deceptive, always approach with caution. And with decades of experience on this road, his father knew every inch.

"Maybe he was worried about missing the boat."

"No signs of a 'roo?" He slid down the gravel decline and walked closer, saw the blood around the door frame and clenched his teeth, looking away.

"None."

It made no sense. "What did the police say?"

"Priority was getting Mum and Dad out. Major Crash Investigation are coming up from Perth tomorrow."

He'd be interested in what they had to say. He ran a hand across his cropped hair. Darcy's face was in shadow and his arms wrapped around himself like he was cold.

He couldn't imagine what it would have been like finding the crash. He stepped closer. "Darcy, I'm sorry you had to find them."

Darcy spun around, strode back to the ute. "You can look more in the morning."

Silence stretched between them for the remainder of the drive. Brandon's skin prickled as they drove through the wide gate, passing the sign Charlie had made weeks before he was killed. *Retribution Ridge.* An angry looking ram staring out at them.

Nausea swelled and he fought the urge to jump out and walk back to town. Darcy pulled up in front of the farmhouse, a solitary porch light illuminating the verandah. His mother had always left the light on for him on the odd occasion he'd gone into town to meet friends.

"The house is full. You'll have to sleep in the shearers' quarters," Darcy said as he closed the car door. "Just don't take the first two rooms. They're occupied." Without another word, he headed inside, closing the door quietly behind him—never mad enough to forget the others who would already be asleep.

Brandon sighed and trudged the short distance across the yard. In the dark he could make out the shape of the machinery shed, and behind that, the sheep pens and shearing shed. He used the torch on his phone to ensure he got the right room and dumped his bag on the floor. The single bed was unmade and there was no linen in sight, but he'd slept in more uncomfortable places. He kicked off his shoes and lay down. After over a decade he was back at the Ridge.

The ceiling stared back at him, dark and judgmental.

He shouldn't be here. He didn't deserve to be here. His family didn't want him here.

He inhaled deeply. Red dirt and lanolin.

Home.

His chest constricted and a tear escaped down his face.

Chapter 2

Amy Hammond's head throbbed like she'd been on a twelve-hour bender the night before. Sunlight stabbed her and she groaned, dragging her sunglasses over her eyes, but they offered little relief. Her steps dragged across the red dirt heading for the farmhouse. If only it was an alcohol binge that had made her feel like this and not... she blinked back the tears and took a moment to breathe.

The ute was gone so Darcy was probably already taking care of the animals. Maggie, the joey Bill had saved after its mother had been hit by a car, lazed under the shade of the trees over by the sheds. Nearby a couple of the sheep Lara had named, and adopted, roamed freely. Darcy's policy was they couldn't send the sheep to slaughter after Lara had named them. Luckily Lara wasn't aware of the policy, otherwise all the sheep in the flock would have names.

On waking, Amy had hoped yesterday would prove to be just a nightmare, but Georgie's blue car still sat in front of the farmhouse bringing the truth with it. Beth and Bill were dead.

She squeezed her eyes closed, willing away the tears. A terrible, tragic car accident had taken Amy's employers far too soon. She wiped her eyes and kept walking. Employers was such a blah word for what Beth and Bill had meant to her. They'd welcomed her into their home, had made her feel part of the family, the first real family she'd had since she'd left home at fifteen. She'd had only a few months with them before they were taken.

As she controlled her tears, she gazed around the yard for anything which might distract her. Someone walked around the side of the sheds and Amy braced herself, not really wanting to speak with anyone this morning. As the tall, lean man walked closer, a camera around his neck, she recognised him as one of their camp guests, Lee. He was up early. She lifted a hand in greeting and he shaded his eyes from the sun and then waved back and strode over.

Quickly she pressed the tears away.

"Got some amazing sunrise photos," Lee said. His black hair was neatly parted down the side and his clothes were clean and tidy despite the fact he'd been camping for the past month with few luxuries.

"That's great, Lee." She forced a smile. The last thing she wanted was to be chatty, but that was her role. "What are you up to today?"

"I thought I'd drive to the national park. I've heard there are some great photo opportunities at Charles Knife Canyon, and I figured the family probably needed some space today."

Her stomach clenched and she nodded. "Thank you," she said. "You'll enjoy the drive to the canyon. Make sure you take plenty of water though. It's going to be hot."

"Will do." He headed for his tent and Amy continued to the farmhouse, her emotions firmly tucked away for the time being.

The first time she'd seen the house, she'd fallen in love. It sprawled in that way old houses did, the ones where rooms had been added haphazardly over the years, yet still had a wide verandah around two sides and a high corrugated tin roof. A small garden offered the only real lush greenery in kilometres, with a small patch of grass and a selection of tall trees. The red bottlebrush had almost finished blooming but was still a magnet to the white butterflies dancing around it, looking like snowflakes. The idea of snow in the outback made her smile.

Entering the house via the kitchen, she wasn't surprised no one else was up. It had been a long, tiring day yesterday. Lara had been inconsolable, Darcy had lost all of his usual warmth, and then Georgie had arrived with their brother, Ed who had flown in from Perth as soon as he'd heard the news. By the time she'd gone to bed there'd been no word from the prodigal son, Brandon, a military man.

Amy shuddered. She almost hoped he was in some Middle Eastern hot spot and wouldn't get word of his parents' death until after the funerals, until after she'd left on her quest to find some other work. Military men were rigid and regimented. She would know. She was related to two.

She filled the filtered coffee machine and set it to heat. Normally they offered fresh coffee and cake to the half-dozen people who camped on a patch of ground near the main house, but she'd been around yesterday to tell them what had happened to Beth and Bill and some had decided to move on out of respect. Only two campers remained–those who'd been at the Ridge for over a month–and this morning she'd put a no vacancies sign out so they didn't get anyone else calling in.

Would Darcy carry on with the campground experiment after the funerals? It had been his idea, but perhaps he wouldn't want strangers on the station so soon after his parents' death. And if he didn't continue, she was out of a job.

Not that it mattered in the scheme of things. She always found something new, but Retribution Ridge was the first place which felt like home in the ten years she'd been travelling around Australia. She hadn't even realised she'd been looking for home until she'd arrived here, and been so warmly welcomed, surrounded by a family who genuinely cared for one another. She'd started thinking about staying permanently, maybe buying a house in town.

Now that was all at risk.

She collected the empty mugs and a bowl of half-eaten chips from the table. Last night none of them had cared about cleaning up before they'd stumbled to bed in a daze. Today they would have a whole heap of people dropping in to give them condolences and she wanted to be prepared, take as much work away from the Stokes family as she could.

The fly screen door slammed and she jumped, whirling around. A tall, stocky man stood there, his dark hair buzz cut short, a deep frown on his face. His posture was military rigid and even after ten years, her immediate reaction was to straighten her spine and pull back her shoulders. Her skin tingled as her mind shouted danger. He wasn't one of the campers she'd spoken to yesterday. She crossed over to put the table between her and the man. "I'm sorry, we've got no vacancies."

He frowned. "Vacancies?"

"The campground has no vacancies," she clarified.

The man glanced around as if not sure where he was.

Calm and friendly was the best way to deal with conflict. She'd learnt that very early after she'd left home. "Sir, you'll need to leave. The family had a tragedy yesterday and we'll be closed for the next couple of weeks." She forced a smile.

"What the hell are you talking about?"

It was her turn to frown. She rubbed the sides of her eyes in the hope of clearing some of the ache from her head. "You're not after a place to camp?"

"No."

"Right. Then maybe you should tell me why you're here."

At that moment Georgie stumbled into the kitchen mumbling something about coffee. She stopped when she saw the man at the door and her eyes widened. "Brandon!" Her shriek was loud enough to startle a whole flock of cockatoos. She flung herself into the man's arms.

The shock on his face would have been comical if not for the grief that quickly followed it. He buried his head into Georgie's neck.

Understanding filled Amy. The prodigal son had returned.

She swallowed hard as the emotion threatened to overflow again and made herself busy cleaning the coffee mugs. Such a coward for him to return when Beth was no longer here to greet him, to discover why he'd stayed away so long. He'd been a constant ache, an emptiness in his mother's heart for over a decade and Amy had hated seeing the devastation in Beth's eyes when she spoke about it.

Amy tempered her instant dislike of the man. Beth would have been thrilled he was back, would have welcomed him with open arms, a cup of tea and a batch of her famous scones. When the siblings separated, Amy held up a mug in question to Georgie who nodded.

"Did you just arrive?" Georgie asked.

"Got in last night. Darcy picked me up. What's with the blue hair?"

She grinned. "Felt like a change. Darce didn't mention you were coming. I thought he hadn't got hold of you."

"Called his boss," Darcy said as he strolled inside with barely a glance at his older brother.

Brandon stiffened. Talk about cutting the tension with a knife. Amy didn't know the full story, only that Brandon never came home, but Georgie always said he was the greatest thing ever. She'd bragged about him being in the army and fighting overseas. Though Amy understood the sentiment, in her experience, army life made people lose their humanity. Darcy obviously didn't share Georgie's high opinion. Hoping to distract them all, she asked, "Who wants coffee?"

With three affirmative answers, she poured the drinks, placing milk and sugar on the table for them to help themselves. As she placed a mug in front of Brandon she said, "I apologise for the misunderstanding. I'm Amy."

"Brandon."

"Amy's our guest liaison officer," Georgie told him.

Brandon raised an eyebrow. "What guests?"

"A lot has changed since you were last home," Darcy said.

Georgie rolled her eyes. "We opened six campsites over by the shearers' quarters this year. People can book in advance and spend a few nights here. It's a way of diversifying our income."

"I suggested that years ago."

"Yeah, well Dad's stubborn like you," Darcy growled.

Amy cleared her throat before the brothers could

snipe at each other further. "Does anyone want breakfast? I could cook porridge or some eggs and bacon?" No one had eaten much the night before.

"Can I have porridge?" The quiet question came from the doorway where Lara stood, still dressed in her Wonder Woman pyjamas and clutching a well-loved teddy bear, her chocolate brown hair sticking up in all directions. With her was Bennet, the family blue heeler, who trotted over to sniff at Brandon. His tail wagged a couple of times as Brandon patted him.

"Sure, honey," Amy replied. "Take a seat. Would you like a hot chocolate too?"

The girl nodded and made a beeline to her father who pulled her onto his lap and held her tightly. "How are you today, pumpkin?"

"Sad."

Georgie reached out and squeezed Lara's knee. "We all are."

As Amy poured the oats into the pot, Lara whispered, "Who's that man?"

"He's your uncle, Brandon," Darcy responded.

She glanced over in time to see a flash of guilt cross Brandon's face. The remorse made her soften a little towards him. Her father didn't know the meaning of the word, but at least some military men could feel. It couldn't be easy coming home because his parents died.

"Do those cockatoos ever shut up?" Ed, the youngest brother flopped into a spare seat at the table. "Hey, Bran."

Amy placed a mug of coffee in front of him and gave the hot chocolate to Lara. "Thanks, Ames."

She smiled. She'd met Ed when she'd first started at the station and he'd been visiting his parents. A sweet guy who had spent most of his time with his mother in the kitchen, or star-gazing with Bill at night. He'd mentioned on multiple occasions that wrangling animals was not for him.

"They just want everyone to know its morning," Lara told him.

He took a long sip of his coffee and made a contented sigh. "Morning in my world doesn't start for another half an hour." He grinned at his niece and she laughed. The sound brought tears to Amy's eyes and she turned to stir the porridge. Her emotions were all over the place today. If she wasn't careful, she'd be a blubbering mess. She had less reason to cry than the five people sitting at their family table who were holding it together far better than her.

She turned off the stove and divided the porridge into six bowls. Now she knew who Brandon was, she saw the resemblance between him and Darcy. His hair was the same chocolate brown and though his gaze was more shuttered, his eyes were the blue-grey of both Beth and Darcy. In contrast, the two younger siblings had taken after their father with fair hair and brown eyes. Darcy and Georgie both had a sun golden colour to their skin but Ed's pale skin showed he hadn't been outside much lately.

Amy added honey and milk to the table and then hesitated. Normally she ate with the family, but it didn't seem right today, not with everyone back home. They probably had things they wanted to discuss.

Darcy glanced at her. "Sit down, Amy. You're part of this family too."

The words stabbed her in the gut. She shouldn't want it so much. She'd sworn she wouldn't rely on anyone again, wouldn't be vulnerable. Still she could hardly walk out now. She managed a watery smile and sat next to Ed at the far end of the table.

Silence fell as they ate. She shifted, uncomfortable but not willing to be the first to speak. It wasn't her place. Normally Beth would ask what everyone had planned for the day, and Lara would regale them all with stories of school. Sometimes Darcy and Bill would talk farm stuff and she always enjoyed learning about what it took to run a quarter-million-acre property. When they'd first told her the size of the land, she could barely fathom it.

Lara spoke first. "Am I going to school today?"

"Not if you don't want to," Darcy answered. "We're going to plan Granny and Grandfather's funeral, and you can help if you want, or else you can hang here."

"I'll stay with you," she answered. "How do you plan a funeral?"

The grief in Darcy's eyes made Amy bite her lip. "I don't exactly know, pumpkin. We'll have to find a funeral director, somewhere."

"There used to be one in Carnarvon," Brandon murmured.

Silence again and Ed and Georgie exchanged glances.

"Will Sergeant Dot want to talk to you again?" Lara asked.

"Probably. They'll have some people look at the crash site."

"Why?"

"It's standard procedure, pumpkin. They want to figure out why Granny and Grandfather crashed so they can try to stop it happening again in the future."

"Oh." The answer seemed to satisfy her as she ate another spoonful of porridge.

Amy cleared her throat. "Is there anything you want me to do?"

"How about we deal with food?" Ed suggested. "We're going to get a lot of visitors as news spreads."

"Everyone will probably bring food with them," Darcy commented. "But if you could help us deal with the visitors that would be great. Georgie, are you working?"

She shook her head. "Jimmy told me to take the week off. I'll find us a funeral celebrant."

"Do you want a hand?" Brandon asked.

"No, I'll be fine. I know everyone to call."

The phone's shrill ring made Amy jump. Darcy sighed. He'd spent most of the day yesterday talking to people about what happened, but this wasn't something she could offer to do for him.

Darcy answered and from the sound of the conversation it was the police. When he hung up, Brandon demanded, "What did they say?"

Darcy ignored him and instead looked at the rest of his siblings. "Major crash investigations will be up on the morning flight. Dot said she'd call before they headed out to the scene."

It was nice the family was being kept in the loop, but Georgie had mentioned it was how they did things up there. Retribution Bay was pretty isolated out on the north west peninsula in Western Australia and towns were few and far between anywhere north of Geraldton.

"Dad, where did they take Granny and Grandfather?" Lara asked.

Ed's hands tightened around his mug and Georgie focused on the table in front of her.

Darcy winced. "They took them to the hospital. They'll keep them there until the funeral."

"Can we see them?"

More grief crossed his face. "No, pumpkin. I'm afraid not."

Amy didn't want to imagine what state the bodies were in. The phone rang again, and Amy gathered the dirty dishes to wash. Darcy carried the phone into Bill's office and Ed made himself scarce mentioning something about a shower.

"La La, shall we go for a horse ride before it gets too hot?" Georgie suggested.

Lara glanced down the hallway after her father, then sighed. "OK." They went to change, which left Amy alone in the kitchen with Brandon. He clasped his coffee mug in both hands and stared at it as if it was a crystal ball. She wasn't entirely sure what to say to him. She was the outsider here, not him, but she had the urge to welcome him like Beth had welcomed her. She huffed out a breath. She was good at small talk. Moving around so much meant she had to be. "Are you staying long?" She winced. That hadn't come out right. "What I mean is, I can prepare one of the shearer's rooms for you. That's where Matt and I stay." Georgie and Ed were already sharing the spare bedroom in the house and it was too early to suggest he use Bill and Beth's bedroom.

"Darcy's already got me in there. Some linen would be nice though."

Her mouth dropped open. "He made you sleep there without any blankets?"

"Yeah. It doesn't matter. I've slept rougher places."

She shook her head. "Of course it matters. Beth would give him a good talking to—" Her words died and sorrow replaced them.

His sad smile was full of understanding and she felt a low tug in her belly. He no longer reminded her of a military man, but simply a man.

She cleared her throat. "I'll make up your bed as soon as I've finished the dishes." She turned her back on him and ran the hot water in the sink. Beth hadn't believed in dishwashers.

His chair scraped back, and he grabbed a tea towel from where it hung over the oven. "So how long have you been here?"

"Since February."

"And what is it you actually do?" He seemed a little bewildered.

"I'm in charge of the campgrounds. It's my job to take reservations, show people around when they arrive and be on hand to answer any questions. I'm working on ideas to keep the guests entertained and to attract more, and I run the Ridge's website and social media sites." That had been a learning curve. "It hasn't been overly busy yet, so I've also been helping Beth around the house. The plan was for me to take over the cooking at shearing and help all the temp workers if they need it."

"How long have the campgrounds been open?"

"We had our first guest in March." How much did he know about Darcy's plans and Bill's reaction to them? "From what I gather it's a trial. Just six unpowered sites over by the shearing shed. The guests share the shearers' bathroom. If it works out, they'll expand it to more sites next season."

Brandon grunted as he placed the dry bowls in the cupboard. "Anything else new I should know about?"

How was she supposed to know? "You'll have to ask Darcy."

Georgie and Lara returned to the kitchen dressed for riding and Lara grabbed the two water bottles Amy had filled for them, tucking them into a backpack.

"Thanks, Amy." Lara slid the backpack on her shoulders, and they headed out the door.

"I can't believe how big she is," Brandon muttered.

"When was the last time you saw her?"

He shook his head. "When she was about this high." He held his hand to his thigh. "Mum brought her to Perth when she helped Ed settle into university."

Probably more than five years then. No wonder Lara hadn't recognised him. "Kids tend to grow fast." So why hadn't he been home? From experience she knew military men did get leave, did get to come home to their families every once in a while. Far too often for her liking.

Pushing away the memory of her father, she retrieved the flour from the cupboard, and then milk and lemonade from the fridge. If they were having people around, she'd make a batch of Beth's famous scones and then perhaps some biscuits.

Ed came in, his hair damp from the shower, wearing an astronomy related T-shirt and a pair of shorts. He examined the ingredients. "Scones?"

She nodded.

"Great. I'll make the choc chip biscuits." He grabbed the ingredients he needed and turned on the oven.

In no time they'd have the kitchen smelling like baked goods, just the way Beth liked it.

Amy swallowed her tears and got to work.

***

Brandon wasn't needed. He was basically in the way as Ed and Amy baked in preparation for the influx of people, but he couldn't stop watching Amy. She moved with confidence and a familiarity with the kitchen, sweeping her frizzy blonde hair back into a ponytail before she even began to get the ingredients out of the cupboards. She didn't reference any recipe, but soon turned dough out onto the floured table. Such precision. The scents of the flour and vanilla reminded him of his mother and suddenly it was too much.

Saying nothing, he strode out the door and into the warm morning. He inhaled the clean air and listened to white cockatoos screeching from a couple of nearby trees. Across the red dirt by the horse yard, Georgie and Lara mounted two bay horses. He stopped as shock pierced him. The horse Georgie rode looked like

Charger, the horse who'd helped him win many a barrel race. Was it possible he was still alive? Brandon itched to stop them, to ask the question, but he didn't want to interrupt. Lara seemed uncertain of him, as she probably should be of a strange man sitting in her kitchen when she woke.

He sighed and continued walking across the yard. The sheep pens with their rusty red metal fences stood empty, and the occasional puff of wind swept little clouds of red dust into the air. The sheds were still an eclectic collection of buildings full of the same vehicles. The emergency water tanker sat ready with a full tank in case of a bushfire, the truck with its red cab, nicknamed Red Riding Hood by Georgie, and the battered ute he'd learnt to drive in. He knew his father didn't like to spend money but surely an upgrade had been required.

In the opposite direction, behind the shearing quarters was the first sign of any real change. An army green tent was set up next to a long caravan. Two four-wheel drives were parked next to them.

Campers.

He'd suggested the idea to his father over a decade ago, before he'd left but Bill hadn't been interested then. Didn't want strangers on his land. What had Darcy said to change his mind?

It wasn't any of his business. Not anymore. He moved towards his room, but the idea of being shut inside those four walls made his chest constrict. He needed to do something, anything except sit on his bed and drive himself crazy with thoughts of his parents and his family. Instead he turned towards the red sand dunes behind the farmhouse. It was the highest point of land next to the farmhouse and gave him a view over the property. Before he left, he'd borrow a horse and head up to the Ridge which gave the property its name. That view always inspired him.

A trail showed him the way to the dunes, a narrow path worn there after years of use. Small animal footprints crossed the track and when he reached the smooth slopes of the sand, footprints of all sizes criss-crossed the area, proof there was far more wildlife around than could be seen or heard. One of the Baiyungu people could probably tell him exactly what they were. He remembered the elders giving him bush tucker lessons when he was younger. His father wanted him to know what plants could be useful in case he'd been stuck out in the bush alone.

At the top of the red dune he stopped and surveyed the land. The large metal cattle pens to the east of the dunes sent a cold shock through him. What the hell were they still doing there? Surely his father would have packed them away, got rid of them years ago. No one wanted to be reminded of that day. He certainly didn't. He squeezed his eyes closed, blocking out the screams which would forever haunt him. He'd spent the past decade *trying* to forget, without any luck.

He turned his back on the scene of his crime and looked out at the farmhouse and sheds peeking up in the distance. What was he doing here? No one would have cared if he hadn't turned up.

He shook his head. He was lying to himself. Georgie's greeting had figuratively knocked him on his arse. He hadn't been expecting a joyous greeting from her. But Georgie had always been the little ray of sunshine of the family—optimistic, enthusiastic and full of forgiveness. Even if he'd been a shit brother. Ed's greeting was about as good as he'd hoped for, but Darcy's had hurt more than he wanted to admit.

They'd been best friends once, full of plans of what they wanted to do with the station.

Now Darcy could barely stand him.

Brandon deserved his disdain. He wasn't needed

here. They could cope perfectly well without him as shown by the fact he was the only one without a job to do.

But the people he really owed, the ones he'd let down, the ones he'd devastated and whose forgiveness he didn't deserve, had never earned, were gone. Dead. There'd be no making it up to them.

His legs gave way and he slumped to the ground, not caring if the sand filled his shoes or crept up his pants. He'd let down his entire family.

The wall in his mind crumbled, letting out all the memories he'd sealed up tight in his attempt to forget.

His mother's kitchen still looked exactly the same with its long wooden table and many seats, and it smelled like baked goodness. He'd done a double take when he'd first seen Amy, her back to him and putting on the coffee like his mother had every morning. Foolish, because it couldn't be his mother, and a second later he'd registered the frizzy hair, and the slimmer, curvier build, but still a part of him had hoped until she'd turned around and her green eyes had widened and her lush lips had parted in surprise.

He blew out a breath. So clearly not his mother.

Beth could more often than not be found in the kitchen, preparing enough food for an army though there'd only been seven of them. Content to feed the family before she attended her farm duties for the day. Always the reminder, 'don't forget your water bottle', or 'here's your snacks for the day' and the big grin as she'd hugged them all before they left. He hadn't been allowed to leave the house without a hug, that was her one rule.

The tears leaked out, slowly at first, like a trickle of water in a dry riverbed after it had first started to rain.

His father always had a smile when his wife was near, always loving and at one with the land. It had been in the family for generations, since the ship Retribution carrying European settlers had crashed in 1871 and stranded the Stokes ancestors in the bay.

He remembered being in the ute, his father showing him the land, telling him it would all be his one day. That it was his heritage, his heart. It had been the perfect place to grow up, riding horses or motorbikes all over the Ridge with Darcy and Charlie. No, he couldn't think of Charlie now. That was too much.

All the family had been together, had been part of one whole. The land was part of their soul.

Now, he couldn't remember the last time he'd spoken to his father. The guilt and shame had always been too much. He'd done the one thing his father told him never to do and paid a tragic price. It had been his mother who had emailed him, called him, stayed in touch. She had wanted him to come home, but how could he when he could still remember the absolute anguish in her scream when she'd realised Charlie was dead? He'd caused her grief.

It was impossible to see through the flash flood of tears. He buried his head in his hands and wept.

A soft clink of metal and squeak of leather warned Brandon someone was coming. Shit. He wiped his eyes on the bottom of his T-shirt and stood, brushing the sand from his pants. Georgie and Lara rode along the bottom of the dunes, not far away. Lara spotted him and he lifted a hand in greeting.

Georgie's wave was instant, but Lara's was a little more hesitant. What did he expect? He was a stranger to her. Bracing himself, he walked down to greet them. "Have a nice ride?"

"Yeah, it was lovely," Georgie said. "We saw some emus. You should come with us next time."

He hadn't been on a horse in years and the urge to

agree was strong. Lara screwed up her nose, but he said, "Yeah, sure." He examined the horses. "That's not Charger is it?"

Georgie shook her head. "No, it's Wesley. Matt usually rides him. Charger died a few years back."

Not surprising. He'd been gone a long time. Before he could ask who Matt was, Georgie said, "Whatcha doing out here?"

"Taking it all in, it's been a while."

"It has. Don't take so long to come back next time. We missed you."

He had no words. She might have missed him, but she was the only one. "Heading back now?"

"Yeah, it must be about scone time," Georgie said.

His mother's scones were legendary, soft, fluffy and oh so good. He'd never have them again. He rubbed the ache in his chest. "Lead the way."

Lara turned her horse and they rode back to the yard with Brandon following. When they arrived a couple of unfamiliar cars were parked out the front and as the girls dismounted a dirty white ute drove into the yard. A dark-skinned man in his mid-twenties got out. He might be from the Baiyungu people. Lara beamed.

"Uncle Matt! You're back!" She dropped the reins of her horse and ran to the man, flinging her arms around him. He picked her up and swung her around. Brandon ignored the stab of jealousy. To have a relationship like that with his niece, he had to be around.

"Hey, La La. Did you miss me?" As he put the girl on the ground she burst into tears.

"What's up?"

Georgie dropped her reins and joined them. "We've got bad news, Matt." Her voice cracked. "Mum and Dad died in a car accident yesterday."

"What?" The man stepped back, his face full of horror and then seemed to process the news. "Christ,

I'm so sorry." He dragged both girls towards him in a hug. They clung to him.

Brandon was glad they had someone they could turn to even if it wasn't him. He gathered the reins of the horses and the man looked up, tears in his eyes. "Hey, Brandon."

Crap, who was this guy? Georgie pulled out of the man's arms and said to Brandon, "You remember Charlie's best friend, Matt. He's a station hand for us now."

Of course. He should have recognised him, should have remembered his mother had mentioned employing him.

"Sorry to see you again in these circumstances."

Brandon nodded. "Yeah, likewise. Why don't you three go inside and I'll deal with the horses?"

"You sure?" Georgie asked.

"Yeah, is everything still in the same place?"

She nodded.

He waited until they went inside before he led the horses into the yard.

The tack room hadn't changed, still full of clean and polished old saddles. His father had always insisted they keep everything clean, shut all the doors in his war against the red dust, which he constantly lost. The dirt squeezed through any gap, got in everywhere. They tried to keep the equipment clean because out here, spare parts were scarce and if something broke, it could be days, sometimes weeks before a replacement was found and sent up from the city. You took care of what you had. His family motto. The one he'd failed.

Blocking out those thoughts, he focused on his task, uncinching the saddles and placing them on the rail, replacing the bridles with halters and brushing both horses until their coats gleamed. When he returned the brushes to the tack room, an old poster advertising a gymkhana caught his eye. He stared at it. He'd won his first trophy at that event, had felt such pride at being a good horseman. So long ago.

Heading back to the farmhouse, voices reached him first. Loud chattering and then a female voice rose higher than the others. "Amy, just three dunks of the tea bag, a teaspoon of sugar and a dash of milk."

A smile crept onto Brandon's face. He'd recognise that voice anywhere. Mrs Fredericks, his primary school teacher and his mother's best friend had her tea just so for as long as he'd known her. All the Stokes children knew how to make it, understood how much trouble they would be in if they got it wrong, but she loved to remind them, with a smile on her face, a cheeky glint in her eye. He tapped his finger on his thigh. He hadn't considered all the people he would face. All the judgement he would receive.

His footsteps slowed. Going inside had little appeal now, but if the military had taught him anything it was that sometimes you had to face enemy fire. He took a breath and strode inside.

Chapter 3

Amy handed Jenifer her perfectly made tea. Personally, she had no idea how the woman could drink such a weak brew, but she always insisted on a tea bag over tea brewed in the tea pot.

"Thank you, dear."

Brandon walked into the kitchen like he was walking into a minefield. His movements were slow, cautious, and his gaze darted from Jenifer, to their neighbour, Danielle and then to Ed, Georgie and Lara. Poor guy. It couldn't be easy.

"Brandon Stokes, I can barely believe my eyes," Jenifer shrieked and stood, placing both hands on his arms and studying him with an intensity that made Amy squirm. Brandon had more control, no squirming for him, but his entire body twitched the minutest amount, before he casually answered, "How are you, Mrs Fredericks?"

Wow. The warmth in his tone hid his tension, but it was there. The casual observer might miss it, but Amy had learnt the art of reading people when she'd drifted from place to place as a teen. It had kept her from making some bad decisions.

"Oh, you're too old for such formalities," Mrs Fredericks said. "Call me Jenifer. Now take a seat and tell me what's kept you from Retribution Bay for so long."

His mouth narrowed for a split second and he shifted backwards.

Their neighbour, Danielle, who was of the same generation as Beth and Jenifer, perked up with interest. Amy winced as she exchanged a glance with Ed. Now wasn't the time for dirty laundry. "Would you like a scone, Jenifer?"

"No thanks, dear. Got to watch my waistline. I'm not as active as Beth." Her face fell and her bottom lip trembled. She cleared her throat. "You know what I mean."

Amy squeezed her shoulder. "We do. Tea, Brandon?"

"Please, and I'll have a scone if there are any spare."

"They're fresh out of the oven." She gave him the scone she'd offered Jenifer and then poured the last of the tea from the teapot.

"Mum's recipe?" he asked.

"Of course. She taught Ed and me how to make them when he was last here."

"I told her I was desperate for something decent to eat in Perth and she took pity on me," Ed added.

The scone recipe was a family secret and Amy had felt blessed to receive it. She'd sworn an oath never to tell a soul. She smiled at the memory. Beth had always done little things like that to make a moment special, or to include Amy.

Brandon sat at the far end of the table, close to Georgie and Lara, away from their guests. Not to be deterred, Jenifer plopped into the spare seat next to him.

Damn. They hadn't distracted her enough. Amy

filled the kettle ready for a new pot of tea, and said to Jenifer, "Thank you for bringing the casserole."

"You just tell me what you need." Jenifer turned to Brandon. "Have you decided on a date for the funeral?"

He glanced at Georgie. "Not yet. We need to find a celebrant."

"I'm going to make a few phone calls as soon as I've finished my tea," Georgie said. "Do you know who I should call?"

"I'll ask a couple of friends," Jenifer replied.

"Do you need a hand on the station?" Danielle asked.

Brandon looked completely lost by the question. This time it was Matt who saved him as he strolled into the kitchen. "Not right now, Danielle," he said. "Darcy and I have a plan, but we'll call you if something comes up."

"Matt, do you want some tea?" Georgie asked, standing.

"No thanks, Freckles. I need to check some fences."

Amy bundled some biscuits in with a couple of bottles of water and handed the insulated bag to Matt.

"Thanks, Ames."

When she turned back to the table, Brandon was staring at her, a grief-stricken expression on his face. What had she done? "Are you all right?" she asked quietly.

He cleared his throat. "Yeah, ah, Mum used to pack us a lunch like that."

Sadness battled her reserves. "She taught me what to do for her men."

He didn't answer, simply turned away, but she noticed the slight tremble in his hand when he picked up his mug. She wanted to stay angry at him for rarely answering Beth's emails or phone calls, but looking at him now, she couldn't. Whatever had kept him away was eating at him. He didn't deserve her judgement.

"If you want the rest of your campers to leave, we've got room at our place," Danielle said.

"They're actually no trouble," Amy told her. "They've both been here a while and know where they're allowed to go." She'd pop out a bit later to clean the bathroom. "Do you have many at your place?"

"Not at the moment."

Amy had heard from other campers that Danielle's place wasn't very welcoming, and she'd checked the reviews, wanting to figure out what Retribution Ridge could do better. She'd proposed they have regular communal dinners to Beth last week, and she'd said she would run it past Bill. Not going to happen now. Later, if Darcy kept the campgrounds open, Amy would suggest it again. She had a long list of ideas she'd been working on, but she hadn't wanted to overstep her role.

Bennet barked as another car pulled in and Danielle stood to say her goodbyes. Amy walked her out. "Do make sure you call if you need help," Danielle reiterated as she climbed into her four-wheel drive. "Beth and Bill wouldn't want you struggling."

Amy nodded, unable to speak. She waved and then braced herself to greet the women from Beth's bridge club. They all had red eyes and signs of tears on their cheeks. Amy smiled a little harder, because if she let it slip that would be the end of her. "Thank you for coming."

The three women hugged her.

She held the kitchen door open for them. "Tea, anyone?" Her stomach protested at the thought of more tea. By the end of the week she might never drink the stuff again.

But if that's what she had to do to help the Stokes, then she'd do it. Anything to make it easier for them.

She remembered with sharp clarity how she'd prayed

for someone to help her when her mother had died.

But the help had never come.

***

Forget about water torture, tea torture was far worse. If Brandon drank another cup he would be sick. Amy had kept the teapot full and the cakes coming as friend after friend arrived to offer their condolences and see if they needed any help. Both Ed and Amy were amazing, chatting to the guests and answering questions. Amy was particularly adept at distracting people from their inevitable questions about where he'd been. It was almost as if she anticipated the question before it could be asked and changed the subject. It was fascinating to watch, and he was immensely grateful. He'd have to thank her later.

Darcy passed through the kitchen. "Pumpkin, I've got to go out for a couple of hours. Are you going to be all right here with Amy and Ed?"

Lara grabbed her father's hand. "You're not going into town."

Conversation died as Darcy crouched beside his daughter. "Yeah, I am. I'll be careful though."

Tears glistened in her eyes and the fear shining in them ripped through Brandon's defences. "I'll go with him," he volunteered. "Keep an eye on him. Two sets of eyes are better than one."

Lara studied him and some of the fear faded. "OK."

Darcy shot him a look which was part annoyance, part thanks and then hugged his daughter. "I'll be home before dark."

"Could you get a few groceries?" Amy asked.

Darcy nodded and she scribbled a list and handed it to him.

Brandon followed him out. "Where are we going?"

"Into town."

Well duh. He didn't bother questioning further. Hopefully he'd be able to convince Darcy to stop at the crash site so he could get a better look at it in the light. "Let me grab my wallet." He jogged over to his room, uncertain if Darcy would leave without him. His bed had been made, and would pass any military inspection. Amy must have come in here while he was at the sand dunes.

He shoved his wallet and phone in his pocket, and when he returned, Darcy had the ute's engine running. Apparently his promise to his daughter was more important than his dislike for his brother.

Brandon got in. Hoping to stop some of the awkwardness he asked, "What have you been up to this morning?"

"Going through Mum and Dad's papers. They've got wills somewhere in the mess."

The realisation hit Brandon like a nine-millimetre slug. They were gone which meant they had left the station to someone. "Do you know what was in them?"

Darcy glanced at him as he turned onto the bitumen road. "You mean do I know who they left the station to—no, I don't."

"Didn't they have a safe?"

His brother grunted. "Yeah, but I can't find the key. I'm hoping it will be on Dad's keyring, which is why I'm heading to town. The hospital has their personal belongings."

Brandon stiffened. The bodies would be at the hospital. Did he want to see them? No, he'd seen death before and he'd rather remember his parents alive. "Georgie have any luck with a funeral director?"

"Options aren't great. Bastard doesn't want to make two trips to us, so we can go to him, or arrange the details with him via email and then he'll come up to run the service."

"What about in Karratha?"

"Same deal. Mum and Dad both wanted to be cremated so at least we can have the service on the station."

They would have wanted that. "We can probably arrange the details ourselves," Brandon said. "You'd know what they want."

Darcy didn't comment.

Brandon changed the subject. "Where are we at with the sheep?"

"About ready to lamb next month."

He'd miss it. Shearing had been his favourite season at the Ridge, but lambing had come in a close second, watching the babies toddle unsteadily on their feet, and then prance and leap as their confidence grew.

They drove in silence, the red dirt and scrubby bush flashing past the window with nothing else in sight until they reached the crash site. "Pull over." Darcy glanced at him and he added, "Please."

The ute slowed and pulled onto the gravel shoulder. "You've got ten minutes," Darcy said as he turned off the engine.

Brandon nodded and pushed open the door. The soft ticking of the engine as it cooled was the only sound. In the bright light of day the crash was all the more horrific. All the windows were smashed, the white paintwork was scratched and dented and the doors had been cut to get access inside.

Images of his parents bloodied and broken flashed into his mind. Darcy had been the one to find them. He could see Darcy charging to the car, desperately hoping they were still alive. His heart pounded against his ribcage as his steps crunched on the ground. What did he expect to find here? Why was he doing this to himself? Despite the questions, his steps still drew him nearer to the overturned car.

The passenger side had a brown smear. Blood. There must have been a lot of blood.

Images flashed into his head of another time, another place, but also blood everywhere. Sherlock had been hit and blood had painted his hands and clothes. Brandon swallowed and moved around the car. Unlike Brandon's parents, Sherlock had survived.

The driver's side was worse. The steering wheel was far too close to the seat and the airbag dust was tinged pink. He shouldn't be torturing himself this way, but he deserved the pain. This was the last memory he would have of his parents.

A particularly long scrape down the side panel made him frown. It ran horizontal to the ground, but if the car had flipped multiple times, it wouldn't make a scrape like that. It was reminiscent of a parking accident.

At the sound of cars approaching he headed back to the ute. A police wagon and a hire car pulled up and a policewoman got out of the wagon. Brandon recognised Dorothy Campbell immediately, despite the dozen years since he'd seen her. Her glossy black hair was cut pixie short now, but she still had the wide brown eyes and determined strut of the girl he'd dated in high school. As she neared, he read her badge. Sergeant of Retribution Bay. She must be in charge.

"Hey, Dot."

"Brandon. Long time, no see. I'm sorry it's in these circumstances." She hugged him and then narrowed her eyes. "I hope you haven't touched anything."

He shook his head as Darcy got out of the car and joined them. "It's not as if it's a crime scene."

Dot pursed her lips, her eyes flicking to Darcy and back to Brandon.

His instincts went on high alert. "What aren't you telling me?" The officers from the hire car were already setting up equipment.

"It's all theory at this stage," Dot said. "No point upsetting anyone."

Brandon narrowed his eyes. "I can take it."

Dot hesitated and then nodded to the road. "Notice anything odd?"

He followed her gaze. The road was a normal, unmarred bitumen road, no pot holes, no kangaroo carcasses... "No skid marks." His father would have braked if he was trying to avoid a 'roo.

Dot nodded. "I remember your father giving me a driving lesson out on the station. He *always* drove to the conditions and under the speed limit when the wildlife was most active."

Brandon blinked. He'd forgotten about those lessons. He'd been driving around the station since he was old enough to reach the pedals, but Dot hadn't been confident, so he'd invited her out to practise where there was little she could crash into. His father had been happy to help.

That was the kind of person he was. "Could Dad have had a heart attack or something?" It was the only thing that made sense.

"Dad was the fittest of us all," Darcy said.

"They'll do a post mortem to check," Dot told him.

But if it wasn't a heart attack, or avoiding wildlife on the road, what else could cause his father to lose control of the car? The horizontal lines on the front of the car came back to him. "Did Mum or Dad have an accident lately?" he asked Darcy. "Something that scratched the front of the car?"

Darcy shook his head. "Dad cleaned it the day before and it was sparkling."

"There are marks on the front." He moved forward, but Dot placed a hand on his chest.

"Where?"

"Front driver's side panel."

"Stay here." She waited until he nodded and strode over to look, calling one of the crash investigators to her side. They had a few words and then Dot returned. "They'll investigate it."

"You think something side-swiped them and didn't stop to help?" Darcy said. He didn't look surprised.

"We can't jump to conclusions yet. Leave this to the experts and I'll call you as soon as I know more."

What the hell was going on here?

"When they're finished at the site, John will tow the car into town," Dot continued. "He's busy helping tourists who got stuck out at Yardie Creek but he said he'll come as soon as he was needed."

The local mechanic had been a good friend of his father's. Everyone in the town was.

"Go back to the Ridge, Darcy," Dot said.

Brandon wanted answers from his brother. "Come on, Darce." He placed a hand on Darcy's shoulder and he immediately shrugged it off.

"Make sure you call me," he demanded. When Dot nodded, Darcy strode back to the car.

Brandon followed more slowly, mulling over what he knew. Someone must have clipped his parents' car while passing them, or maybe swerved to their side of the road, and then hadn't bothered to stop when the car had rolled.

"I don't like this," Darcy said.

"Why don't you think it was an accident?"

Darcy didn't answer and Brandon's gut clenched.

"Who would want to hurt Mum and Dad?" The silence stretched. "Darce? What aren't you telling me?"

"We've been getting hassled to sell," he finally said.

Like that would ever happen. The land was family. "Who by?"

"Some company called Stonefish Enterprises. Dad

told them he wasn't interested but they kept increasing their offer."

It wouldn't matter how much they offered. "Did Dad explain to them the land has been in the family for generations?"

Darcy nodded. "But—"

"But what Darcy?"

Another silence and Brandon clenched his teeth to stop himself from demanding an answer. He had no right to demand anything.

"The Ridge hasn't been doing well for the past five years." The words were quiet like a confession.

Brandon frowned. "Define not well."

"Another poor season and we'll be bankrupt."

Shock hit him. "What? How?"

"More sheep are being slaughtered by wild dogs and dingoes," Darcy said. "I've been trying to convince Dad to switch to cattle for years, even found a company this year who could supply at a reasonable price, but he refused. The money from the campgrounds is keeping us afloat for day-to-day things."

Brandon wanted to be sick. They both knew why their father had been so against the cattle. "Mum never mentioned it in her emails."

"She didn't know. Dad swore me to secrecy."

"Then you should have said something."

"When?" Darcy demanded. "During one of those chatty phone calls or emails we had? Oh, that's right, you never answered any of my attempts to contact you. You wanted to be as far away from your family as possible."

Inwardly Brandon cringed and he tapped his thigh. "I had my reasons."

"Bullshit. You just stopped giving a shit." Brandon opened his mouth to dispute this, but Darcy continued, "It doesn't matter anyway. You wouldn't have been able to get Dad to change his mind. He was a stubborn git, that's where you get it from."

Brandon exhaled, squeezing his hand to stop tapping it against his thigh and went back to the purpose of this conversation. "So the farm was in trouble, a company was offering Dad a lot of money for it and he kept saying no, despite the financial troubles he was in."

"Right. I found a couple of emails while I was going through his papers and they were offering double what the farm is worth."

"Why do they want it so badly? There are other stations around."

"That's what I wanted to know, but Dad refused to speak with them. When they came around a couple of weeks ago, the guy mentioned something about having a connection with the Retribution."

The ship that started it all. "I guess that makes sense." Their connection to the land came through the ship as well.

Darcy snorted. "I offered to show him the site of the wreck, take him out to the island, but he made excuses not to go."

"That's odd."

"Yeah."

"So what happened next?"

"Dad got angry, kicked him out and told him not to come back. Said he'd never sell the property while he was alive."

They glanced at each other and both swore. "You should tell Dot," Brandon said.

"Yeah."

The glistening blue ocean appeared to the right of them like a mirage in the red dusty plain. He jolted. This land was such a contrast of harsh conditions and eye-watering beauty. "It never gets old," he said.

"What?"

"The awe of seeing the ocean after kilometres of red plains."

"Do you miss it?"

Something in his brother's tone made Brandon study him and answer honestly. "Every single day."

"Then why—?" Darcy pressed his lips together, not finishing his sentence. Instead he pointed to the right. "They've upgraded the harbour since you were last here."

Relieved to have been given an out Brandon asked, "What have they done?"

They spoke of town changes until they reached the hospital. Both studied the single storey building, with its low roof and garden beds filled with Australian natives. Inside were his parents' bodies and the last things they'd touched. He didn't want to go inside, didn't want the confirmation his parents were dead. It all felt so final.

Darcy was the first to get out and Brandon followed him into the building. The walls were white and informational pamphlets about diabetes and mental health covered a corkboard. The young, dark-haired receptionist looked familiar and it took him a second to place her as a school friend of Georgie's. She stood and hugged Darcy. "I'm sorry, Darce."

"Thanks, Tracy. We're here to pick up their stuff."

"Let me call someone for you." She spoke into the phone and then covered the receiver. "Do you want to see your parents?"

They both shook their heads. A few minutes later a nurse arrived holding a small plastic bag which she handed to Darcy. "This is their jewellery and what was in their pockets," she said. "Their clothes... weren't salvageable."

Darcy nodded, blinking, his hand shaking. Christ. Brandon couldn't handle Darcy breaking down. He stepped next to his brother, put a hand on his back. "Thanks." He used a little pressure to get Darcy to turn and they walked outside. Brandon sucked in a lungful of air while Darcy made a beeline to the car, the bag clutched tightly against his chest.

Brandon followed a little slower, needing to get his own breathing and tears under control. Darcy stopped and leaned his head against the arch of the window frame, his body shaking.

Shit.

Acting on instinct, he wrapped his arm across Darcy's shoulders.

Darcy shoved him away. "Don't! Don't fucking pretend like you care." He dashed the tears away from his eyes. "You left when we all needed you most." He yanked open the car door, forcing Brandon to step back. The fury on his face made Brandon tense, ready for attack, but Darcy slammed the door, fired up the engine and drove away.

Brandon placed his hands on the back of his neck and stared after the ute, his gut swirling with nausea. There wasn't a damn thing he could say to defend himself. Darcy was right. He had abandoned his family... for their own good. He couldn't ever explain the truth though. They'd kick him off the property so fast he'd have whiplash.

The ute disappeared around the corner.

What now? He tapped his thigh. Amy had given Darcy a shopping list and Darcy wouldn't go back to the Ridge without getting what was needed.

Which meant Brandon was likely to run into more people he knew, more questions about where he'd been.

His muscles tightened. He deserved it.

With a sigh he headed to the main street and the small shopping centre located there.

Chapter 4

Retribution Bay had hardly changed. Brandon walked from the hospital to the small shopping complex in the middle of town, detouring down a side street to check out the district high school. So many hours spent there playing football on the patchy oval, or trying to impress the girls. So many friendships he'd left behind when he left the town. Except for Dot, he didn't know what any of his high school friends were up to now. Who had stayed in town, and who had left the moment they could?

What did it matter? It wasn't as if he was staying around to rekindle old relationships. Darcy wouldn't welcome him back to the Ridge permanently. If their parents hadn't died, he probably wouldn't have let him back at all.

Several cars were parked at the shopping centre and he spotted Darcy's white ute immediately, the *I love horses* sticker on the back was something Lara must have stuck on and reminded him of the four-wheel drive. At least he didn't have to find transport back to the station. As he walked towards the independent supermarket, he checked out the other shops in the complex; Brown's newsagency was there, probably still selling a mixture of newspapers, magazines, books, stationery and souvenirs. Next to it stood a camping and fishing store, then there were a couple of dive and tour boat shops. The one where Georgie worked had a nice welcoming feel with bright colours and an open door to welcome people in.

Across the way, another building housed a bakery and a cafe. The cafe was now called Coral Connections with an ocean themed display so it probably wasn't still owned by Anna who had always given them an extra cup with their milkshakes.

Brandon entered the supermarket to find Darcy at the checkout with a half dozen bags already packed. He barely glanced at Brandon as he paid, however the woman behind the cash register shrieked. "Brandon Stokes, aren't you a sight for sore eyes." Her smile faded. "I'm so sorry about your parents."

Brandon floundered around his brain for a name. The woman had owned the supermarket for decades. Grey now streaked her blonde hair and her skin had more wrinkles but aside from that she was still the small strappy woman she'd always been. Darcy waited for his answer. Not going to offer him any help like Amy had this morning. Unable to find the name, he smiled. "Thank you. How have you been?"

The woman waved her hand. "Same old, same old."

Darcy gathered the shopping bags. "We've got to get back, Lindsay. I'll make sure Georgie calls you with the funeral details."

Lindsay nodded. "Thank you. Take care, boys."

Brandon grabbed the remaining shopping and followed Darcy out to the ute where they put the bags in a couple of insulated crates in the tray.

It was a silent ride home and Brandon didn't have the energy to fill it. Bridging the chasm between them seemed like an impossible feat. Nothing could change the past. The best thing for him to do was to get the hell out of there as soon as the funeral was over and let them get back to their own lives. He wasn't needed or wanted here.

It was early afternoon when they arrived and the sun beat down, shrouding everything in its dry heat. Brandon could feel its rays on the back of his neck as he got out of the car. The baseball cap he wore was useless against the attack. He'd forgotten how harsh the sun could be up here. Was his old Akubra around somewhere? He didn't dare ask Darcy if their mother had kept any of his things, but maybe Georgie would know.

He helped carry the groceries inside and breathed a sigh of relief to find the kitchen empty. More people would come, but the break was welcome. Amy wandered in. "Do you want a hand with those?"

Darcy answered. "Yeah. Where are Lara and the others?"

"In the lounge. They're going through photos to make a slideshow for the funeral."

He nodded and strode out without a word to Brandon.

Amy started unpacking a bag full of pantry items. "You two still not talking?"

He shook his head, biting his tongue rather than asking her if she had any advice. She'd only been here a few months. How well could she have got to know his family in that time?

"He'll come around. Darcy's too nice to hold a grudge."

Once upon a time Brandon would have agreed with her. Darcy had always been the peacemaker, the most easy-going of them all, happy to do whatever anyone else wanted to do and particularly content when they were on the station. Now he was like a complete stranger.

Amy shifted away from the table at the same time as

he moved to put milk in the fridge and they collided, her soft breasts pushing against his chest. The couple of buttons on her polo shirt were undone, giving him a view of her smooth skin underneath. The campgrounds shirt hid her lush figure pressing against him. She glanced up, eyes wide, and the urge to hold her there was strong. They stared at each other and she was the first to lower her gaze and step back. "Sorry." She detoured around him and he was left missing the warmth of her body.

He shook his head. Get a grip.

They finished packing away the food and Amy put the empty bags in the pantry. He hesitated at the door which led further into the house. Would he be welcome in the lounge? Was he ready to revisit some of the memories the rest of the rooms would contain?

"There are plenty of photo albums to go through," Amy said from behind him.

He turned and her smile of encouragement hit him right in the gut, but part of him rebelled against it. Who was she to be so comfortable with his family? Darcy had called her family at breakfast. She knew everyone who had visited, all his mother's habits, and Lara was comfortable with her. But she was still an outsider—

He clenched his teeth. He was the real stranger and the effect on him was deep, disturbing. The coward in him wanted to accept it and move on, but another part, softer, like it was hidden way back in the recesses of his mind, chafed against it. This was *his* family. He might not deserve them, but they were all he had.

He moved into the cool interior and walked into a memory. The paisley carpet in the hallway had been there since he was a child, and the walls of the corridor were a gauntlet of family photos. His footsteps slowed as he reviewed his family's history. His parents' wedding photos with both of them beaming, his father wearing a boxy black suit while his mother, with an enormous perm, was in white with gigantic puffs of fabric on her shoulders.

Then came the baby photos, each child as a newborn being cradled by both parents and then with their siblings as the family had grown. The first day of school photos were next. The yellow and brown uniform and over-sized backpack. Charlie and Georgie were grinning in theirs, but Ed and Darcy had tear-streaked faces. His was so serious. He remembered being scared of catching the bus and meeting a whole bunch of strangers. They hadn't gone into town much when he was young. His mother had her hands full with four kids under the age of six, so any trip had been left until his father was available to help too.

Lara's photo was there too, beaming, the next generation of Stokes added to the wall.

He moved on to their thirteenth birthday photos. His mother had always made a fuss about them becoming teenagers. Here there were only four photos.

The jolt of pain ripped through his chest. Charlie died only a few weeks before his birthday. He hadn't had a chance to live. Wouldn't be in any of the other photos on the wall.

Brandon took a moment to breathe past the nausea and then studied Ed and Georgie's photos. He hadn't been there for those birthdays, having left town as soon as he was old enough. They were both smiling proudly. Georgie already had traces of the woman she would become, whereas Ed was still a kid yet to reach puberty.

The final photos were graduation photos; high school graduation as well as Ed and Georgie's university graduations. He was so proud of both of them for following their hearts, doing what they loved—Ed with his IT stuff that Brandon didn't really understand, and Georgie with her marine biology. She'd always been more drawn to the ocean than the land. She used to beg him each weekend to take her to the patch of beach which bordered their land. She would have swum for hours if she'd been allowed. Had Darcy taken over that task after Brandon had gone?

So much he didn't know about his family, and it was his own fault. He hadn't been brave enough to face them.

Now at the end of the corridor he had no other way to procrastinate. He headed into the lounge. They had enclosed the large fireplace since he'd been away and it now had a door, making it more of a pot belly, and there was a slightly more modern television, but otherwise the room was the same. Long brown couches formed a U shape around the room, big enough to fit all the family. Bookshelves full of books, DVDs and the occasional console game lined the walls. His family sprawled through the room: Ed reclined on the sofa flicking through an album, Lara and Darcy sat side by side while Darcy pointed out who was who in photos, and Georgie was surrounded by loose photos on the floor.

"This is nice." Georgie handed a photo up to Ed. "This must have been one of our last family photos with Charlie."

Brandon couldn't enter the room now, not if they were talking about Charlie. None of them had noticed him yet and he could come back later, or maybe not at all. He shifted, ready to leave when Lara looked up. She gave him a hesitant smile and then turned to Georgie. "What was Uncle Charlie like?"

Crap, he couldn't leave now. He'd seem like a complete bastard to the young girl.

Georgie groaned in mock pain. "He used to tease me relentlessly and if he caught me, he'd tickle me until I screamed."

"He was even messier than you, La La," Ed joked. "We shared a room, and his stuff was always over my side."

Darcy was silent a little longer, examining the photo. "He was good at everything physical. He'd run circles around me."

Brandon's gut twisted and he forced himself to breathe through the pain as he walked into the room. "He was the prankster and the most adventurous of all of us." Brandon focused on Lara, but was conscious of his siblings' eyes on him. "He loved riding fast—horses, motorbikes, it didn't matter. And he had the most infectious laugh and this enthusiasm that before you knew it, you were caught up in his capers." All of them had taken the blame at some point for something Charlie had thought up.

"He sounds like fun," Lara said.

"He was," Darcy said.

Georgie sniffed. "I'd forgotten about his laugh."

Brandon still heard it in his head regularly. It was one of the last things he'd heard before things had gone horrifically wrong. Swallowing, he mimicked the laugh, the sound ripping at his soul, but it had the effect he'd hoped for. Both Ed and Georgie laughed and even Darcy cracked a smile.

Georgie patted the floor next to her. "Join me. You can take that pile."

He hesitated. Did he really deserve to be here? No, but he wasn't cruel enough to reject Georgie's offer. He lowered to the floor and Georgie hugged him. "Thanks," she whispered.

The pain in his gut eased a little.

"Do you remember the time he mistook that ram for Rocky?" Ed asked.

Darcy laughed. "I think he broke the land speed record that day."

Rocky had been their affectionate pet ram who wouldn't hurt a fly. Not so some of the other rams. The memories stung, but being surrounded by his family was like a balm soothing the ache that had been part of him for over a decade.

"Here's a photo of Mum and Dad all dressed up," Ed said. "Anyone know where they were going?" He handed the picture around and both Darcy and Georgie shook their head.

Brandon took the photo and stared at it. "It was their twentieth wedding anniversary," he said. "Dad had arranged a night at a resort, and they left me in charge of you all." Total disaster.

"Was that the night of the pea and ham soup fiasco?" Darcy asked.

Brandon pressed his lips together and nodded, still remembering the mess and the fear of his father's anger.

"I don't remember that," Georgie said.

"You were the only one I'd got to bed," Brandon told her. "You must have been about seven."

"Back when you used to do what you were told," Darcy added. Georgie stuck her tongue out at him.

"So what happened?" Lara demanded.

"Charlie happened," Darcy and Brandon said at the same time. Their eyes met and a glimmer of understanding shone in Darcy's. Brandon gestured for Darcy to tell the story.

"We were in the kitchen making popcorn for a movie marathon," Darcy started. "Mum had put pea and ham soup in the slow cooker so we had something for lunch the next day and Charlie was messing around with the lid lock. Next thing we knew there was an explosion and the soup sprayed all over the kitchen— ceiling, floor, cupboards, everywhere."

"I remember that!" Ed said. "It stank so bad."

"And Charlie burnt himself on the soup so I put him in a cold shower." Brandon took up the story. "Then the three of us cleaned up the mess. By the time I went to check on Charlie, he was sitting on the couch in a fresh set of pyjamas swearing he couldn't help clean because the burns were too painful."

"And sucker that Brandon was, he believed Charlie," Darcy said.

He'd felt too guilty about Charlie being hurt to push the point.

"It took us until midnight to finish cleaning. Charlie had watched the movie and gone to bed."

Lara laughed. "That's so naughty."

All three brothers grunted in unison.

The phone rang and as Darcy stood, Amy brought the phone into the room. "It's Dot."

Brandon stiffened and Darcy took the phone. "What news?"

His expression darkened at her answer and his eyes shifted to Lara before he walked out. Brandon followed him. He found Darcy in their father's office, pacing the short length of the room. "You're sure it was deliberately cut?" Darcy asked.

Brandon's skin prickled, and he clenched his hands to stop himself from ripping the phone from Darcy and asking for more details. Darcy eyed him, the fury on his face for once not directed at his brother. "There's a company who was trying to buy Dad out," he told Dot. "Dad told them he'd never sell the place while he was alive."

Dot said something and Darcy answered. "Stonefish Enterprises." He shuffled some papers on the table until he found a business card. "Our contact was Tan Lewis." A pause. "I haven't seen him around since he was here maybe three weeks ago." Another pause and then Darcy said, "Yeah, I'll ask the others and get back to you." He hung up.

"What was it?"

"Brake lines were cut," Darcy said. "Explains why there were no skid marks."

Horror warred with confusion. "Surely Dad would have noticed before then." Hangman's Bend was halfway to town.

"Not necessarily," Darcy disagreed. "The car was parked out front and Dad always crawled on the roads outside the farmhouse to stop the dust. He would have been able to see there were no cars coming on the bitumen road so the first time he had to use the brakes would have been that bend."

Still the brakes not working wasn't enough to send them hurtling off the road. His father would have started slowing early, would have noticed the brakes… Brandon froze. The marks on the front panel. Someone had deliberately forced them from the bitumen, had caused the car to roll. His hands tightened into fists. "Did Mum and Dad argue with anyone else?"

"Not that I know of." Darcy sighed. "Let's go tell the others." He headed out the door.

Brandon took a moment to control his anger. His family needed him to be calm and supportive, not a ball of fury. He wanted to gear up and fight, but his foe was unknown. Reconnaissance was required first. As he blew out a long breath he made a vow.

He wasn't leaving the Ridge until he found out who had killed his parents.

***

Brandon followed Darcy down the hallway, determination singing in his veins. He wasn't letting his family suffer any longer. He was so caught up in his thoughts he almost crashed into Darcy who'd halted just outside the lounge. Darcy ran a hand over his face.

"Do you think Lara should know?"

Shocked his brother was asking him for advice, he took a moment to consider it. "It was deliberate sabotage," he said. "Whoever did it might be satisfied, but if not, then she should know to keep an eye out for strangers."

"You're right."

They walked into the lounge where Amy sat on the couch next to Ed, flicking through photos. A few strands of her frizzy blonde hair had fallen out of her ponytail and draped down her cheeks. She showed Ed a photo and he smiled. She seemed at home there, but his comment to Darcy about strangers clanged in his head. Did he need to consider her a suspect? He knew from experience that the enemy often sent people in ahead of the main attack to find out more.

Amy murmured something and Ed laughed, the sound so normal, Brandon's heart ached. Surely she had nothing to do with his parents' accident.

Georgie moved from the floor to the couch as they walked in. "What did Dot say?"

Darcy wrapped an arm around his daughter. "It's not good news." He started coughing, and said, "Pumpkin, can you get me a glass of water?"

"Sure." She ran out and the moment she was gone, Darcy continued, "The police found the brake line on the four-wheel drive had been cut, and it looks as if another car might have pushed them off the road."

Amy gasped and covered her mouth with her hand. "Who would do that?" The horror in her eyes was real.

"We need to figure that out," Brandon said. "Can you think of any strangers hanging around?"

"Only the camp guests," she said. "I can put together a list of names."

"Do that." He turned to Georgie. "Anyone in town been annoyed at Mum and Dad?"

"Not that I've heard. I'll ask around."

"This is stupid," Ed burst out. "Why would—" He paused as Lara walked back in, and handed Darcy the glass of water. "They've never done anything to hurt anyone," Ed continued.

"The police are still investigating," Brandon said. "They're looking into Stonefish Enterprises."

"Who?" Ed and Georgie asked.

Darcy winced and shot Brandon a dirty look. How was he supposed to know they hadn't been told about it?

"A company came by asking Dad to sell the station," Darcy said.

"They obviously don't know Dad then," Ed said.

"Yeah, but they've been pretty insistent."

"What happened, Dad?" Lara asked.

"The police want to know if we've seen any strangers around the farm lately."

She frowned. "Only the camp guests. Why?"

"They're being thorough in their investigation. You tell me if you see anyone you don't know, all right?"

She nodded slowly, her eyes wide. "Did someone hurt Granny and Grandfather?"

Darcy sighed, and squeezed her. "We don't know yet, pumpkin. The crash might have been an accident."

Amy cleared her throat. "I know it's not my place to ask, but have you read their wills yet? Do you know who they've left the station to? The company might approach them next."

"Not yet," Darcy said. "I haven't checked the safe."

"We should do that now," Georgie said.

Brandon studied Amy. It was a bit of a leap to go straight to questions about the wills. Unease filled him as he followed his family and Amy into the office where Darcy tried a few keys from his father's keyring in the safe lock.

"Maybe Amy should take Lara into the kitchen," Brandon suggested.

The safe opened with a clunk and Brandon shifted to block Amy's view. Inside was a wad of cash, a few small jewellery boxes and some documents.

"No. Amy can read the will as an objective bystander." Darcy retrieved the documents and shuffled through them before he pulled out two sealed envelopes, slightly yellowed with age. He handed them to Amy and then sat in the office chair, pulling Lara onto his lap.

Brandon scowled. He hoped he was being paranoid, because if she was working with Stonefish, she'd have all the information she needed. Perhaps years in the army had taught him to be suspicious of everything.

Amy took the two envelopes and glanced at the siblings. "Are you sure?"

"Yeah, we all trust you," Georgie said.

Brandon pressed his lips together. Better he stay silent.

"Which one should I open first?"

"Mum's," Georgie said.

Amy picked up a letter opener from the desk and sliced open the envelope. The paper inside was thick and she unfolded it slowly. "'This is the last will and testament of Elizabeth Jane Stokes'," she said. "'I nominate Jarred Palmier as the executor of this will'." She glanced up.

"Jarred died of lung cancer five years ago," Darcy said.

"So what does that mean?" Ed asked.

"I don't know. We'll get legal advice I guess." Darcy gestured for Amy to continue.

"'I leave all my worldly possessions to my husband, William Reginald Stokes. Should he predecease me, then I leave my estate to be divided equally between any children I have'."

"Including the station?" Ed asked.

Darcy flicked through the papers he'd taken out of the safe and then read one. "The station lease is in Dad's name only." He nodded to Amy to open the other will.

Brandon had a sudden urge to stop her. He didn't want to know what was in his father's will. It would be the proof he didn't want that his father had disowned him. He clenched his teeth together as Amy spoke.

"'This is the last will and testament of William Reginald Stokes'," she read. "'I leave all my worldly possessions to my wife, Elizabeth Jane Stokes with the exception of the lease to Retribution Ridge station. The lease I leave to my son, Brandon Reginald Stokes, to be passed on to his heirs'." She continued reading but Brandon tuned her out, the shock making his mouth drop open.

It wasn't possible. "How old is that will?" he demanded.

"It was written in 1992."

Before the rest of his siblings had been born. It had to be a mistake. "Is there a newer one?"

Darcy's face was pale, but slowly his mouth closed and his eyes narrowed. Of course he would be pissed off.

Lara's quiet voice asked, "Do we have to move, Dad?"

Darcy glared at Brandon. "I don't know, pumpkin. We'll sort something out."

Hell. He didn't want this; he didn't deserve this. Georgie went through what was left in the safe, and he prayed she would find another document.

She turned. "There's nothing else here."

"Dad mentioned once that the station passed down to the eldest sibling," Ed said. "I guess we never really thought much of it."

"So the land goes to Brandon, but everything else is split between us?" Georgie asked. "How the hell does that work?"

It didn't. There was no way the farm equipment could be split or for him to afford to pay his siblings their equal share. His chest tightened and it was hard to breathe. "I'll call a lawyer," Brandon said. "Get everything clarified." He walked out.

Chapter 5

Brandon bypassed the phone in the kitchen and headed straight outside, his heart racing like he was under fire. He needed to breathe.

The heat hit him and the lazy breeze was like a hairdryer on low but he kept walking, distancing himself from the house, the accusations, the obligations.

His father had left him the Ridge. A mistake. Amy said the will hadn't been updated since the nineties, but Bill would have disinherited him straight after Charlie died. He'd said Brandon wasn't fit to run the station.

Had he not remembered to change the will? His father wasn't normally forgetful, not about things relating to the Ridge. He knew the history of the place by heart, like which Stokes had erected the windmill to the east of the homestead, and who had gathered the names of the ship passengers to inscribe on the plaque by the ocean. But when was the last time he'd actually spoken to his father? Brandon had never called home and Bill had never emailed or called him. Was it simply a matter of tradition? The eldest son always inherited the Ridge and his father was loyal to tradition.

Brandon remembered days with his father out on the station, just the two of them, and Bill would tell him about the land, and their history all the way back to the boat which gave Retribution Ridge its name. He'd felt like part of something so much bigger, a legacy, a dynasty with ancestry tracing to an English lord and he'd wanted to be part of it. He'd loved the land as much as his father had, as much as Darcy did, had dreamed of running it side-by-side with them. Had even pictured bringing up kids here. He and Darcy had chosen where they would build their own houses, far enough away from each other for a bit of privacy, but close enough that they were still in view.

Walking in that direction, he noticed the frame of a house on the spot Darcy had chosen. Darcy must have started building it when he married Sofia, but maybe she'd left him and Lara before Darcy had a chance to finish it. The marriage hadn't even lasted a year. Shame filled him. He should have been there for his brother, only eighteen with a newborn baby and a wife who'd left him rather than be stuck with a child on an isolated station.

A door slammed behind him and Darcy shouted, "Running away again?"

The accusation hit him like a punch, and he stepped back, biting his tongue to stop the retort. His brother's anger was understandable. He waited until Darcy was close before he said, "I needed air."

"Bullshit. You always run when things get hard."

Darcy had no idea the shit he'd seen, the number of times when running away was not an option. "It's not my fault Dad left the station to me."

"You don't deserve it. You've done nothing for this family."

"I know."

Darcy blinked rapidly, confusion on his face, still

clasping his anger. "Are you going to sell it to the highest bidder?"

Outrage rushed through Brandon so fast he lost his breath. "Hell no. Is that who you think I am? I would never sell this land. It's our legacy."

Darcy panted. "How am I supposed to know who you are now?" he demanded. "We've barely spoken in a decade. You didn't come to my wedding, didn't write when I got divorced, you've barely seen my daughter."

The raw hurt in Darcy's eyes twisted Brandon's gut into a knot. "I couldn't."

"Don't give me the military obligation bullshit, Bran. Tell me why you abandoned our family when we needed you the most."

No, he couldn't. He wouldn't put his deeds into words. Darcy would hate him even more than he did now. "It doesn't matter." He turned.

Darcy grabbed him and hauled him back. "Don't you dare walk away," he snarled, getting right up into Brandon's face. "You are not leaving here until you tell me the truth. One day we were making plans for the station, and the next you were joining the military."

The briefest flit of grief crossing Darcy's face prevented Brandon from pushing him away and continuing back to the house. He'd never considered how his absence might have affected Darcy. He'd figured they were all better off without him.

Disgust filled Darcy's expression. "Forget about it." He let go.

Brandon watched him walk away and panic swept through him. He couldn't let Darcy leave. He'd lost his parents because of his stubbornness, he didn't want to lose the rest of his family. Though his voice was low, it carried. "I killed Charlie."

Darcy stopped. Ever so slowly he turned, a frown on his face. "No, you didn't. A stampede killed

Charlie."

"I was the one who convinced Dad to try the cattle," he began. Before he could continue his list, Darcy shook his head and took a step back towards him.

"We *both* convinced Dad. We did the research and we approached him with our argument."

Brandon paused. He'd forgotten that, but it hardly mattered. "I was in charge of setting up the pens at muster time, making sure they were secure." So the cattle couldn't knock them down if they leaned against them. When Darcy opened his mouth to argue again, Brandon held up a hand and admitted his most heinous crime. "I caused the stampede."

Darcy flinched but came closer. "How?"

Revisiting that day was like reliving a nightmare. But his brother had a right to know, had a right to hate him for more than just leaving. "Charlie was going through a stage where he was trying to scare everyone, do you remember? He set up that fake spider to fall on your head as you walked into our bedroom."

Darcy scowled. "I remember."

"I figured he needed payback, so I bought a rubber snake and set it up outside the cattle yards. It was his job to encourage the cows into the yard with hay so I set a little trip wire up attached to the snake." He'd been so proud of his trap. He'd watched a few YouTube videos and tested it the day before.

"Something else set it off," Darcy guessed.

"Gertie." Their old blue heeler. He hadn't calculated her into the mix. "Charlie had dumped the hay inside the yard and then gone to close the gate behind the cattle. Gertie stopped for a drink at the leaking water pipe filling the trough and she tripped the wire. The snake actually flew over her head and landed in the yard with the cows and they stampeded." He still remembered the horror. He'd been on his horse encouraging the final cows to enter and hadn't seen the snake fly, but he'd heard the shrill bellow of the startled cow and watched as the entire herd turned almost as one and headed for the gate. The one Charlie was right next to.

The swell of the cows had been too much and the whole yard collapsed, the metal frame falling right on top of Charlie as the cows charged over him.

His gut convulsed and he placed a hand on his belly to calm it.

Darcy swore. "It was a freak accident, Bran. You didn't know what the cows would do."

"Dad's one rule was never do anything to startle the animals. I was so focused on getting Charlie back somewhere he'd least expect it that I didn't think of the consequences."

His brother pressed his lips together. "We didn't have a lot of experience with cattle."

That wasn't an excuse. "I still broke Dad's rule."

"Charlie broke the rules all the time." The understanding in Darcy's eyes almost did him in. "Did Dad find out what caused the stampede?"

Brandon still remembered every second of the following frantic minutes. The terror on Charlie's face as he fell backwards near where Brandon rode, the utter helplessness of being unable to reach him as cow after cow charged over his younger brother. He'd had to stop his horse from panicking and joining the stampede and by the time the dust settled and he'd dismounted, his father was already by Charlie's side. Together they'd lifted the fence from his battered and broken body. Darcy had ridden hell for leather for the house to call for an ambulance and his father had desperately tried to find a pulse. His scream of utter anguish when he couldn't find one would haunt Brandon all his days.

Then his father had jumped to his feet searching for

the cause of the stampede, looking for vengeance. And found the rubber snake.

Brandon nodded at Darcy. "Yeah, and he knew the snake was mine."

"What did he do?"

Brandon rubbed his eyes. "He called me a stupid, stupid boy. Said I wasn't fit to work the land. Then as you and Mum raced back in the ute he told me I was to never tell anyone what I'd done. He pocketed the snake and we never spoke of it again."

Darcy swore again. "So you left."

Brandon nodded. "Can't you remember Mum's screams when she saw Charlie? The devastation on her face. I couldn't be around her knowing I caused her pain. Every time Dad looked at me I felt his judgement and every time one of you cried over Charlie it tore into me."

"You should have told me," Darcy said. "We were best friends."

"I couldn't have you look at me the same way Dad did. Better I have a clean break." Somewhere in his mind he'd thought it would all be OK if he kept his distance.

"But you never gave a thought of how it was for me?" Darcy demanded. "I lost two brothers in the space of a couple of months and then I had to step into your shoes. Ed and Georgie slept in our room for months after you left and I had to constantly reassure them I wasn't going anywhere. Then Dad needed me to do all your chores on the farm as well as my own. For the first year I kept thinking you would come back any day and then life would get better." He shook his head. "Then I knocked up Sofia and knew life would never be the same."

The guilt threatened to drown Brandon. "I'm sorry."

"You should be," Darcy said. "Instead of facing up

to your mistake, you ran. We could have supported each other. Mum was a complete wreck until Lara was born and slowly she started living again."

Brandon swore. "I didn't know." Hadn't wanted to know.

They both studied the shell of Darcy's house. Darcy ran his hand through his hair and replaced his hat. "It's too late now."

He was right. It was all in the past. Brandon had to fix the future.

"When do you have to go back?"

The plan to leave straight after the funeral was no longer appealing. He wasn't leaving his family in this mess. "I can probably get a couple of weeks if I call my Lieutenant Colonel." Sam's words whispered in his head. Was it time to get out? "I won't go until we discover who killed Mum and Dad."

"And the station?"

"I'm not selling it," Brandon reiterated. "We'll figure out what to do together. You've got as much say, more so, than I do."

"That's right." There was a hint of a smile. "And don't you forget it." Without waiting for a response, Darcy headed towards the house.

A weight lifted from Brandon's shoulders and he stumbled, a little dizzy. The smile was an echo of the Darcy he remembered. Had he really forgiven Brandon so easily? No, it was foolish to believe it would be that easy, but for the first time, he thought they might have a chance to reconcile.

And Brandon wouldn't let him down again.

***

Amy held her breath as Darcy and Brandon walked into the lounge. Neither had black eyes, cuts or bruises so maybe their confrontation hadn't been as bad as she feared. Brandon was trained to kill and she'd been a little worried about Darcy. Though perhaps Brandon used her father's method and used words to wound instead.

"You two finished your tiff?" Georgie asked.

"I don't tiff," Darcy said.

"Men don't tiff," Brandon said.

Darcy grunted, but his small smile showed the tension between the two brothers had broken.

Amy exhaled. She hated conflict, disliked seeing the normally happy Darcy so angry.

"Whatever," Georgie said. "You don't look as if you're about to punch each other, so that's a win. We've got enough photos for the slideshow," she continued. "Why don't you sit down, and Ed and I can tell you what we're thinking?"

They sat on opposite sides of the couches and Amy smothered a smile. For all that Georgie was the youngest, she did know how to wrangle her brothers. Lara moved next to Darcy and he wrapped an arm around her. Lara was clingy, but the situation called for comfort. Amy wished Beth was here to hug her and tell her things would be all right. She stood. "I'll organise dinner." It wasn't her place to arrange the funeral.

"Thanks, Ames," Darcy said.

A small part of her wished they'd invite her to stay which was ridiculous. She wasn't family, she didn't know Beth and Bill as well as they did. Besides they didn't realise she'd had experience arranging a funeral. Her mother's had been long enough ago that things had probably changed anyway. She wandered down the corridor to the kitchen.

The house felt empty without Beth in it. She had been a presence either through the eighties music she listened to constantly, or the delicious scents floating from the kitchen because something was always baking or cooking.

Amy got ingredients out of the fridge for a soup and remembered the moment with Brandon earlier. He was an enigma—one moment gruff and stand-offish, and the next… well, pressed up against him had felt safe and arousing at the same time. He was such a presence.

A huff outside the kitchen door revealed Bennet lying in the doorway panting a little in the heat. Strange Matt hadn't taken him with him. She checked his bowl was full of water and let him inside the cool house.

As if she'd conjured him, Matt appeared from around the corner and climbed the steps. She held the door open. "Fix the fences?"

"Yeah. Is Darce around? I need to talk to him."

"They're all in the lounge finalising funeral arrangements."

Matt hesitated.

"If it's not urgent, why don't I make you a cuppa and you can have a scone first?"

"Yeah, that would be great. Thanks, Ames."

She filled the kettle and put two scones in the microwave to reheat. Matt lowered himself into a seat and kind of slumped over the table. This couldn't be easy for him. He'd known Bill and Beth his entire life. Was as close to family as someone could be without being related. When she put the mug of tea in front of Matt she asked, "How are you coping?"

He glanced up at her, his eyes redder than normal. "I'm OK." He sighed. "I told my parents and they'll tell the rest of the mob. They're worried about who's going to inherit the station."

Amy didn't know the details of the agreement the local indigenous group had with Bill, but from what she understood it gave them permission to access their traditional lands whenever they wanted. Some of them still chose to live on the station land. "Brandon inherited the Ridge."

"Really?"

She nodded.

Matt swore and his hands clenched around the mug.

"Do you think he'll sell?"

Matt shook his head. "I don't know him anymore. He might want to be rid of the place."

If only she could allay Matt's concerns. Instead she changed the subject. "Which fences did you check today?"

"The ones across the main road where the sheep are." He slathered strawberry jam on top of his scone and then topped it with a healthy dose of cream. He looked up at her. "I'm worried. One of them has been cut."

Her heart skipped a beat. "Cut?"

"Yeah. Someone's taken wire cutters to it and there were motorbike tracks nearby."

Dread filled her as she remembered what the police had said. "You need to tell Darcy. The police found the brake line was cut on Beth and Bill's four-wheel drive."

He swore. "You're kidding me!"

She shook her head. "They're trying to figure out who might have a grudge against them."

"Taylor was pretty angry when they fired him, but I can't imagine him doing anything like that."

Neither Taylor nor Bill had said why Taylor had been fired last month, and it had come as a shock to Amy. She liked the thirty-year-old stockman and had spent plenty of evenings chatting with him. He'd seen almost as much of Australia as she had, and they'd swapped tales of places they'd been and people they'd met.

Once she'd relented to play poker with him, but only after she set a limit of how much she'd bet. He didn't understand she didn't have money to waste. There'd been too many times when twenty dollars had been the difference between a meal and a bed, or sleeping hungry on the streets. After years of studying people, his tell had been easy to pick and she'd won money from him. "Do you know why he was fired?"

Matt shrugged. "Darce never said." He stood. "I'd better tell him about the fence."

He strode out. Amy gathered up the dishes and noticed a movement at the door. Lee stood there, his hand raised to knock. "What can I help you with, Lee?" She placed the dishes in the sink.

"I'm sorry to bother you, Amy, but there's no toilet paper in the bathroom." He screwed up his face in apology.

Shit. She'd forgotten to clean the bathrooms today. She hurried to the door. "I'll get some for you right now." The supplies were over by the shearers' quarters. "I'm so sorry."

Lee waved a hand. "You've got more important matters to attend to."

She nodded then entered the end room in the shearers' quarters and retrieved a roll of toilet paper. "Here you go. I'll clean it after you're finished in there."

"Thanks." He trotted away.

Amy brushed the loose hairs from her face and then stripped out the lackey band holding it back and redid her ponytail. She opened her own quarters and took a moment to freshen up. The hottest part of the day was always mid-afternoon but now with the sun sinking towards the horizon the temperature was dropping a little.

Maggie hopped onto the verandah and into Amy's room. Amy scratched her head. "Hey, Maggie May. Are you after a snack?" She kept a bag of almonds in her room after she'd learnt the kangaroo had a weakness for them. She gave her a couple, being careful to avoid her sharp nails and led her back onto the porch, closing the door after herself.

Lee was walking back to his campsite so she grabbed the cleaning gear from the store room and headed for the bathroom. With only two groups using it, it wasn't particularly dirty, so it didn't take her long to clean. As she did so she noticed a spare toilet roll on the top of the toilet partition. Maybe Lee hadn't seen it. She made a mental note to get a container to put the spare rolls in so they were within reach and easily found.

When she finished, she put her equipment away. Lee chatted with the retired couple who were also staying there. Amy wandered over. "The bathroom is clean and fully stocked. I'm sorry I didn't get to it earlier."

"No need to apologise," Jay said. "You've got other priorities."

She smiled. "What did you get up to today?"

"We went snorkelling at Turquoise Bay," he said. "It was beautiful. We even saw a couple of turtles."

"That's wonderful."

"Dear, please let us know when the funeral is," his wife, Cheryl said. "We'd like to come if we can."

"I will," Amy promised. "Darcy and his siblings are finalising the details now, so I should know tomorrow." Cheryl and Jay had been their first guests and had so enjoyed the experience they had decided to stay for the season. Jay had been a farmer before he retired and spent time helping Bill and Darcy on the station. "Let me know if you need anything in the meantime."

"We're all fine," Cheryl assured her. "We just invited Lee to have dinner with us."

"Great." Lee was travelling by himself, a keen photographer who ran a website with photography tips. She envied his ability to take his work with him and not have to find a new job at each place he visited. "Have a nice night."

Amy returned to the house to finish making dinner. She heard the others talking in the lounge but couldn't make out the actual words. She switched on the oven and kneaded the bread dough she'd made earlier which had finished rising. The soup she'd put in the slow cooker after lunch was nearly done. Beth had always said her pea and ham soup was comfort food and the family could do with as much comfort as possible right now.

She placed the bread in the oven and when she turned, Lara was at the doorway.

"Dad says I need to help you with dinner," Lara said.

"I think I'm done," she said and then caught sight of Darcy behind Lara mouthing, "Keep her busy." Right. They probably wanted to talk about the cut fence without scaring her. "But I haven't prepared any dessert yet. What should we make?"

Lara's face lit up and she pulled a recipe book from the shelf. "Let me take a look."

Darcy gave her a thumbs up and returned to the lounge.

Amy switched on the stereo and put on one of Beth's favourite eighties playlists, not too loud to be considered disrespectful, but loud enough so Lara couldn't hear anything from the lounge. "What have you decided?"

Lara held up the recipe book. "Can we make this?"

A triple-layered chocolate cake with cream and icing between each layer. Amy checked the ingredients. Yep, they had them all and it would keep them busy for a good hour. "Sure can, La La. Let's get to it."

She'd do what she could to protect Lara and this family.

Chapter 6

It was unsettling to sit in the lounge with his siblings and discuss their parents' funeral arrangements. The lounge was a room Brandon associated with warmth, family, comfort. He'd spent many a night watching television with his family, although they had all been much younger then. But the topic of conversation made his muscles tighten and unease bubbled in his stomach. Brandon wasn't inclined to argue with what his siblings wanted. He didn't have the right after being away for so long. It had been bad enough discussing the format and who would talk, but then Matt arrived to drop the bombshell about the cut fences.

Darcy returned and shut the door behind him. "Amy's got Lara making a dessert."

That would keep them both busy for a while.

Darcy sat on the couch next to Matt. "Only someone who didn't know the property would bother cutting the fence," he said. "There are plenty of access points and the gates aren't locked."

People trusted each other out here, but perhaps the culprit was trying to throw them off, or wanted an exit point for the sheep which wasn't as noticeable as an open gate. "How about you take us through everything that's happened in the past few months?" Brandon suggested.

"How far back do you want me to go?"

How long was a piece of string? "Did you notice anything strange before Stonefish contacted you?"

Darcy shrugged. "No. Things were normal. The only weird thing was when I found out about the company about a month ago. But when I checked Dad's computer earlier today it looks as if the emails go back to before Dad agreed to open the campgrounds."

Were the two connected?

"Whose idea was it?" Ed asked.

"Mine," Darcy said. "I've seen what other stations are doing, and I suspected the Ridge wasn't doing so well. Dad wouldn't spend any money on new equipment though we desperately need a new ute. Matt's been babying the Ridge one along for at least six months."

Matt nodded. "Bill's been making noises about not needing full-time station hands as well," he said. "When Taylor was fired, I wondered whether Bill grabbed any excuse to get rid of him."

"No, there was an excuse," Darcy said. "Dad caught Taylor in his office. Taylor said he was looking for a delivery invoice, but Dad said he had one of the old pearl hair combs which came from the Retribution in his hand."

"Taylor was stealing it?" Brandon asked.

"I don't know. Maybe he had money troubles, not that an old hair comb would have fetched much."

"Where's Taylor now?" He was definitely someone Brandon wanted to chat to.

"I'm not sure. He didn't leave a forwarding address."

"I'll call Lindsay later," Georgie said. "If anyone knows, it will be her. Pretty much everyone goes into her supermarket."

"Do that," Brandon said, his mind whirring. "Dad agreed to the campgrounds in what, February, March?"

"February," Darcy said. "Took a few weeks to get the necessary permissions and clean the shearers' quarters. Mum was adamant she didn't want to clean toilets and have to hang around the house for guests to arrive, so we agreed to hire someone."

"How many applicants did you get?" Could someone be disgruntled they hadn't got the job?

"Just Amy," Darcy said. "Georgie told her about the job and she was perfect, so we hired her on the spot."

Unease tightened Brandon's skin. He didn't want to consider the possibility, but it was an option. He asked Georgie, "How did you meet her?"

"She was on one of my tours. We got to talking and she mentioned she was new to the area and looking for a job. She'd done all sorts of hospitality work so I called Darcy and arranged the interview."

"That's convenient."

"What are you suggesting?" Ed asked.

Someone had to raise the possibility, if only to rule it out. "Amy knew to ask Georgie about work at the exact time the Ridge was looking for someone. Doesn't that seem odd to you?"

"No," Georgie said. "We get backpackers through all the time searching for work."

"She's a bit old for a backpacker."

"Don't be ageist. She's only a few years older than I am," Georgie retorted.

Brandon knew better than to argue with Georgie when she disagreed with him. She'd been stubborn as a mule since she was a baby, and he was pleased she was defending Amy. Still, he had to play devil's advocate, was the only one with enough distance to look at all the possibilities. "Where did she come from?"

"Are you really suspecting Amy of cutting the brake line?" Darcy asked. "She loved Mum and Dad. Mum had practically adopted her."

Great. He was going to put Darcy offside again. He leaned back, tried to appear less aggressive. "I'm investigating all the options," he replied. "What do we know about her?"

"She's great," Matt said with a shrug. "Friendly and always ready to help with anything. She's got a knack for fixing anything that's broken, and I've been teaching her how to fix the ute. She's picked it up quickly."

Not what he wanted to hear. "She's good with cars?" It wouldn't take much to slide under the four-wheel drive and cut a line.

"No!" Georgie shook her head. "I won't let you suggest that. Amy's my friend."

He kept his tone gentle. "What can you tell me about her then?"

"She was working in Karratha before she came to Retribution Bay. Spent six months working in a cafe there."

"And before that?"

"I don't know." Georgie threw up her hands.

"I've got her resume in the office," Darcy said. "I'll get it."

While he was gone, Ed said, "I was here when she was interviewed. She's smart and eloquent. She charmed us all."

And she'd charmed him, but con men were always charming. He took the paper Darcy handed him and flicked through it. No more than six months at any job, some even less. Much of it was seasonal work, vagrant work, fruit picking or hospitality jobs. No details of any education and no home address. His gut squeezed uncomfortably. It strengthened his argument rather than refuting it.

"This tells us she doesn't stick around long." He handed the resume to Matt.

"Bran, there's nothing nefarious about Amy," Georgie said. "She's a good person."

"How do you know?"

"Because I know her. She wouldn't hurt a fly. In fact I caught her moving a spider outside because she didn't want to kill it." Georgie shuddered. "I would have emptied an entire bottle of fly spray on the sucker."

He smiled. He'd forgotten about Georgie's fear of spiders.

"She rarely eats meat," Georgie continued. "And wanted to know more about my research on humpback whales. She supports the environment."

Which apparently meant you couldn't also be evil. "I'm not saying she's involved, only that we have to consider it. Maybe she told the wrong thing to the wrong person without realising the damage it would cause," he suggested.

Ed took his phone out. "She's not on any social media."

Neither was he, but most people were.

"I'll do a little digging," Ed said.

"Ed! Not you too," Georgie exclaimed.

"I don't like it either, Georgie," Darcy said. "But we have to explore the possibility. Amy arrived when Stonefish started sniffing around."

Georgie crossed her arms. "What about the campers? One of them could be a spy. Cheryl was pretty cosy with Mum."

Brandon straightened. "How long have they been here?"

"Cheryl and Jay were our first guests," Darcy said. "They loved it here and have stayed for months. Jay has been helping on the station. He owned a wheat farm down south and misses it."

"What do we know about them?"

Georgie rolled her eyes and sighed.

Annoyance filled him. "Someone cut the brake line on the four-wheel drive, Georgiana. We're not exactly in the middle of suburbia here. You can hear anyone coming from a mile away—literally. If it wasn't any of us, then we have to consider who else had the opportunity."

Georgie scowled. "What about motive?"

"We'll get to that. Anyone else been staying a while?"

Darcy shrugged. "Amy would know."

Involving her would only cause her to ask questions. "Can I look at the records?"

"They should be in the reception."

Great. He stood and then thought of something else. "We should also discuss safety. Everyone should check their car before driving anywhere." He glanced at his sister. She was the most vulnerable, the easiest to overwhelm. "You shouldn't go anywhere alone, Georgie. Can you move back home for a while?"

Her laugh was sarcastic. "I'm not the one who inherited the station," she said. "There's no reason for anyone to come after me if that's their aim. It's you who should have a bodyguard twenty-four seven."

Shit. She had a point. The others nodded their agreement.

He sighed. "OK. I don't have a car anyway and don't plan to go anywhere." Plus he could take care of himself.

"It will be interesting to see if Stonefish contacts us again," Darcy said.

"Yeah. We should all be alert in the meantime." He moved to the door. "We've finished the funeral arrangements, haven't we?"

Georgie nodded.

"Can you show me the records?" he asked Darcy. The sooner they got answers the better.

Ed also stood. "I'll see what I can find out about our current guests and Amy."

"Bring any info to me," Brandon told him.

"Us," Darcy corrected. "This is family business and we should all be part of it." He glanced at Matt.

"That includes Matt," Georgie said.

Matt smiled. "I'll ask my folks if they heard any motorbikes at night over the past few days," he said. "I'll tell you if I find out anything."

For the first time since Brandon got the news of his parents' death, he felt like he was doing something useful. "Great. Let's go."

He followed Darcy down the hall to the foyer by the front door. When he'd lived at the Ridge, they never used the area. Everyone went around to the kitchen door when they visited, even though there was a path from the front gate. Darcy had converted the area into a small reception with a desk and chairs set out in such a way that they blocked the way into the rest of the house. Darcy handed him a notebook. "Dad wouldn't approve the spend on a computer for the trial so everything is on paper. That's the guest registry."

His father hadn't been a fan of computers anyway, so it wasn't surprising. Brandon flicked through the first couple of pages. Names, addresses and dates of stay. A decent amount if they'd only been open a couple of months. He sat at the desk. "I'll go through it now while Amy's with Lara."

Darcy pursed his lips. "Just for the record, I agree with Georgie. I don't think Amy is related to any of this. If I had any concerns about the type of person she was, my daughter wouldn't be alone with her right now. But I get that you don't know her like we do and you need to check into her." With that Darcy walked away.

Brandon blew out a breath. He hadn't considered it from Darcy's point of view and hoped Amy wasn't involved. She had charmed him when she'd been so helpful in deflecting questions about his absence, but he had to consider all options. He grabbed a pen from the drawer and went through the list of guests, making notes of anyone who had stayed in the past week, as well as those who had stayed more than a week.

He had to start somewhere.

***

The chocolate cake layers were in the oven, the bread cooled on the bench and Lara stirred the cream filling. In the background Cyndi Lauper sang about girls just wanting to have fun. The cake would be enormous, but Lara was loving every second and Amy appreciated the distraction. It reminded her of Beth, felt as if they were honouring her memory together.

Her mobile's shrill ring caused her to jump. Very few people had her number so it had to be for the camp grounds. She'd agreed to use her number on the website which advertised the station. If the trial became permanent, then they'd get a separate number. "Retribution Ridge, Amy speaking."

"Hi! I want to book a camp site for next month," a perky female voice said. "Do you have any vacancies?"

They hadn't discussed what would happen with the campgrounds now. Amy opened the junk drawer for a notepad and pen and asked, "What dates did you want?"

The woman told her. "Is there a discount for long stays?"

"Yes," Amy said, writing the details. "I'm not in the office at the moment so can I get your name and number and call you back later?" Hopefully Darcy could give her an answer when he finished in the lounge.

"Sure." The woman rattled off her information.

"I'll call you back soon." She hung up as Georgie walked into the kitchen, looking a little tired. "How did things go?" Amy asked.

"The funeral is here on Thursday morning at nine," Georgie said. "Ed's in charge of food and I'll scan the photos."

She'd check the weather forecast, but it shouldn't be too hot. "Do you need me to arrange shade or seating?"

"I've already arranged chairs to be delivered Wednesday afternoon, but I guess we'll need a hand setting everything up." Georgie sniffed. "Something smells good in here."

"There's chocolate cake in the oven," Lara told her.

"And pea and ham soup for dinner," Amy added.

Georgie gave her a strange look. "Pea and ham soup?"

Amy nodded. "I know it's warm outside, but your mum always said it was comfort food."

Georgie gave a sad smile. "She was right."

The note in Amy's hand reminded her. "Do you know where Darcy is? I need to ask him about the campgrounds."

A flash of guilt crossed Georgie's face. "Ah, I think he was going through a few things with Brandon. He won't be long."

"The cream is ready," Lara said. "Can I start making the icing now?"

"Absolutely," Amy said. "Just let me put this note in the office." She hurried down the corridor to the reception and found Brandon seated at the desk with her guest book in front of him. Her steps slowed and she frowned. "Can I help you with something?"

He barely looked at her. "No."

Irritation flowed over her skin. Why was he going

through her things? This was her responsibility. "May I have the guest book for a moment? I need to check a few dates."

"I thought you weren't taking bookings."

"It's for next month. I need to talk to Darcy about it, but first I need to see whether we have a vacancy." She paused. "Or should I ask you whether the campgrounds are staying open?"

"Ask Darcy." He handed her the book and she flicked through to the calendar section. The reservation would be before the school holiday period, and they had a site free for the required dates. She pencilled the booking in and returned the book to Brandon. "Thank you."

"Have you had any repeat customers since you've been open?" he asked.

Surprised he was taking an interest she answered, "Most people are on their way up or down the coast. We've had maybe two who came back on their way home." She took the book from him again and pointed out the names. "These two."

"You've got a good memory," he said.

"Not really. Both couples rebooked before they left. Is there anything else?"

He studied her a moment, his gaze intense and something in her stirred. He was an attractive man, despite his often-sombre demeanour. His blue grey eyes held depth and mystery, but the buzz cut hairstyle reminded her he was military. Not going to happen.

"No, I'm good."

Crap, she'd been staring. She cleared her throat. "Dinner is almost ready." Hurrying back down the corridor, she almost bumped into Darcy coming out of Bill's office. "Sorry."

Darcy flashed her a smile, the first glimpse of the Darcy she knew since his parents had died. "No problem, Ames."

She stopped him from moving on. "I had a request for a reservation for June," she said. "We have space. Should I book them in?"

Darcy hesitated and then said, "Yeah. I'll chat to Brandon tonight about what we're doing going forward."

"Great. Dinner's almost ready, so you might like to wash up." Ed sat at the desk in the office behind him. "You too, Ed."

Ed waved a hand but didn't look up.

On her way back to the kitchen, Amy called the guest back and confirmed the booking.

Lara was getting the cakes out of the oven with Georgie supervising. Baking ingredients and utensils sprawled over half of the kitchen table so Amy quickly cleaned it. Her father had never tolerated mess and the habit had formed early. The chocolate icing sat in a bowl already prepared. Lara could put the cake together after dinner when it had cooled.

Darcy walked in and inhaled deeply. "What have you been cooking, pumpkin?"

"Chocolate cake," Lara said, beaming at him.

"Looks good." He stuck a finger in the icing bowl and tasted it. "Tastes good too."

"None of that," Amy told him, taking the bowl, covering it in cling film and putting it on the bench. "There'll be none left."

He grinned and reached into the fridge to get a jug of cold water, placed it on the table and then set out the cutlery. Brandon entered and helped without being asked.

Beth had raised her children right.

"Is Matt staying for dinner?" Amy asked as she turned off the slow cooker. He usually did unless he had plans in town.

"He went out to his room," Georgie said. "I'll go tell him it's ready."

Amy ladled the soup into the bowls. When she finished, Ed still hadn't arrived. "Lara can you tell Ed dinner's ready? He's in Grandfather's study."

She nodded and trotted out of the room.

Amy set the soup in front of Darcy and Brandon and then at the empty places around the table.

"It's pea and ham soup." The shock in Brandon's voice surprised her.

"Yes. Your mother's recipe. Is that OK?"

He was still a moment before he nodded. "We spoke about it today. Did you hear us?" The accusation in his tone made her step back, her heart racing.

"No," she answered carefully. Any wrong word might cause him to lash out. She forced a smile. "Beth always said it was her comfort food and I figured you'd all need some today." She waited for his slight nod of acceptance and then turned to get the loaf of bread that had cooled, willing herself to be calm. He wasn't her father. Punishment wouldn't follow angry words. Brandon was simply finding his way through his grief. She closed her eyes. They all were.

Lara returned with Ed and Georgie entered with Matt. Amy finished serving, placing butter on the table for the bread and pouring herself a glass of water before she sat next to Brandon.

Beth would want her to be patient with him, to get through to him. She had mentioned how serious he always was, how he felt the weight of responsibility for everyone. Perhaps he felt responsible for finding who killed his parents. Still, she wasn't sure what to say to him.

Lara spoke. "This soup is just like Granny's. It's like she's still here."

Amy's cheeks flushed and she ducked her head. "I'm

glad you like it." Beth had taught her how to cook after she'd discovered Amy lived on salads and sandwiches. With only herself to feed, it was cheaper and easier. But she'd been surprised to find she enjoyed cooking for more people, loved the satisfaction which came from feeding people who had been working hard all day. There was something a little primal about it.

"It is good," Brandon agreed. The compliment surprised her, but he smiled and gave a small nod as if apologising for his earlier snark. The smile hit her right in the gut and she blinked, not liking the warmth it brought with it. He was still someone who had hurt Beth deeply.

"Georgie, tell me about the boat you're working on," Brandon said.

Ed groaned. "You'll never shut her up now."

Matt flashed him a grin and Darcy smiled but both were too smart to comment. Amy leaned forward. Georgie's work was fascinating.

Georgie ignored them all. "I'm on a tour boat which runs whale shark, manta ray and humpback whale tours," she said. "Part of my job is taking the required statistics of the animals we swim with. I'm hoping a job will come up with Parks and Wildlife or the Aussie Institute of Marine Science though."

"It's a foot in the door," Brandon said.

"Yeah. We're learning more about the whale sharks in particular every year." Georgie continued to tell her brother about the majestic animals found off the coast for several months each year.

Amy had heard the spiel on her first tour. She'd saved for months to afford it and it had definitely been worth it. They'd found a whale shark almost as soon as they'd cleared the reef. Amy had been nervous getting into the ocean so far from land, but Georgie had encouraged her and they'd swum side by side to the location where the shark would swim past. Amy had stared into the blue and slowly the huge animal had appeared, gliding slowly through the water towards her. She'd gripped Georgie's arm as awe filled her. So majestic, so amazing.

Afterwards, Amy had sat with Georgie as they motored to a snorkelling spot, peppering her with questions. She'd hoped to get a job on one of the boats, but she'd been too late. Georgie had been filled with knowledge about the creatures, and had invited her for a drink at the local brewery where she'd met other locals, including Faith who was Lara's pony club instructor. She'd been so welcomed that when Georgie had mentioned the job at the Ridge, she'd jumped at it.

After dinner while Ed and Brandon did the dishes, Amy helped Lara put her monster chocolate cake together. Then they all sat down with a hot drink and had a slice.

"Pumpkin, this is amazing," Darcy said after he tasted a bite.

"Would Granny have liked it?" she asked.

He sobered. "She would have loved it. I would have fought Grandfather for the last piece."

Lara beamed at him.

Amy's greatest wish was to have a dad like Darcy. He cared about Lara and was genuinely interested in what she did. Amy couldn't remember a time when her father had complimented her on something she did, or asked her how school was. If he called while he was deployed, he only had time to speak with his wife, and when he was home there'd been no hugs, no reading bedtime stories and no encouragement to do anything creative. No, if there wasn't a purpose to it, a goal to further your standing in life, then it wasn't worth doing according to Major Hammond. She ignored the sting, which was more like a mozzie bite than a major hurt these days. Her life might not be the regimented routine her father had expected of her, but she enjoyed it.

When they finished eating Ed spoke. "Bran, can I have a word with you and Darce in Dad's office?"

"Sure." Both men stood and followed him out.

Georgie watched them go with incredulity on her face. "Oh hell, no they don't." She followed them down the corridor.

Matt chuckled. "Ed's been away from home too long if he thinks he can leave Freckles out of anything." The affection in his voice was clear. "Looks like the rest of the dishes are left to me."

"I'll help, Uncle Matt," Lara said.

"So will I." Amy loved how everyone pitched in. She finished wiping over the bench tops as Ed and Georgie walked back in. Georgie's eyes pinched together like they did when she was annoyed about something, but it was Ed who spoke. "Ames, Darcy and Brandon want a word with you in the study."

Her skin prickled and she wiped her hands on a tea towel. Perhaps they'd decided to end the campgrounds trial. She'd no longer have a job, and she'd have to find somewhere else to live. She wasn't ready to leave Retribution Bay yet, not when she had finally found somewhere she belonged, but it was unlikely there'd be many jobs in town. The tourist season was in full swing and the jobs were already taken.

Calm down. Don't jump to conclusions. She inhaled quietly and walked to the office. Brandon sat behind the desk in Bill's chair and suddenly she saw his resemblance to his father in the way he sat with his hands clasped in front of himself. Darcy leaned against the wall and he smiled and gestured her in. "Close the door behind you."

Yep, she was definitely getting fired.

The thunk of the door sounded like a head rolling

after the fall of the guillotine. She stood, hands by her side, feet together, as she would if she was facing her father—or a firing squad.

Brandon raised his eyebrows. "At ease."

The words made her flinch, but she clasped her hands behind her back and shifted so her feet were a little bit apart.

"Which branch?" Brandon asked.

She frowned. "What?"

"Which branch of military were you in?"

"None." She'd simply been indoctrinated another way.

Before he said anything else, Darcy spoke. "Amy you know Mum and Dad's crash wasn't an accident," he said. "We're trying to figure out who would want to hurt them."

No one. Beth and Bill were too lovely to have enemies. "Was it directed at them specifically? Anyone could have been driving the four-wheel drive. I took it to town last week to pick up some things Beth had ordered."

Brandon and Darcy exchanged a glance. Maybe they hadn't considered that. "It was unusual for them both to go into town together," she continued. "Usually Beth goes... went to catch up with friends. But I can't imagine anyone hated Beth or Bill enough to want to hurt them. Beth never mentioned upsetting anyone in town."

"When was the four-wheel drive used last?" Brandon asked.

Hell. He was testing her memory. The days all blended together here. "I drove to town on Wednesday," she said thinking back. "Darce, didn't you go to a school thing?"

He pushed off the wall. "Yeah, but I took my ute. Parent-teacher meeting on Friday afternoon and then

Lara and I went out to dinner."

Saturday had been her day off and she'd spent it reading in the hammock in the garden. "That's right, and then you and Lara went to the pony club practice day on Saturday and Matt was away for the weekend visiting his family."

"Someone's reopened the pony club in town and they're having a gymkhana next weekend to drum up interest. Lara's taking part," Darcy told Brandon.

Faith had been enthusiastic about the project when Amy had met her that first night at the pub with Georgie.

Brandon turned to him. "You took the four-wheel drive?"

"Yeah. Dad was out with my ute. It was running fine."

Which meant the line had to have been cut Saturday night.

"Which guests were on site Saturday night?" Brandon demanded, leaning forward.

Amy blinked. "Jay and Cheryl, but they really liked your parents. They asked me earlier when the funeral is." Surely they wouldn't have a reason to hurt Bill and Beth.

"What about Lee?" Darcy asked.

She shrugged. "Yeah, he was here too. He's obsessed with his photography, so I don't see him much." But he was always polite and she couldn't imagine him doing anything illegal. He'd asked permission for anything he did on the station.

"Where does he take photos?" Brandon asked.

"All over the place. He headed to Charles Knife Canyon today, but he's also been taking photos around the station. Matt drew a mud map for him so he could find the more interesting spots like down by the ocean and the caves in the gully."

"Did you know about him having free reign?" Brandon asked Darcy.

Darcy shook his head. "I guess Matt didn't consider it an issue. His family can go where they want and he would have kept Lee away from where we were working."

Amy didn't want to get Matt into trouble. "It's my fault. I called Matt over when Lee asked me if he could take photos on the property. I didn't consider you might not like it."

"Why not?" Brandon asked.

She narrowed her eyes as her gut clenched. She hadn't thought it a big deal. Sure, Bill had asked her to keep the guests in their area, but Darcy had wanted good reviews. "Darcy put me in charge of ensuring the guests were happy," she said. "Retribution Ridge has a quarter of a million acres of land, and I figured not all of it was being used at once. I didn't see what danger he could cause aside from getting lost, and we arranged for him to check in with me before he left and when he returned. He knew to leave any gates as he found them."

"It's fine," Darcy said. "Dad might have been a little cross if he'd known, but we would have sorted it out."

Which meant Bill wouldn't have been happy about it. She should have considered that. Rather than defend herself further, she said, "We had another two guests that night and they left after they heard about your parents."

"Can you get us their contact details?" Darcy asked.

"Sure." She turned to leave.

"What about you?" Brandon asked.

Amy frowned. "What do you mean?"

"What were you up to Saturday night?"

The implication took her breath away and she stumbled back, pain clamping around her chest. "Your parents were like family to me." She willed away the tears. "They treated me a damned sight better than my own family and I loved them. Beth was teaching me to cook, and Bill was teaching me to ride."

Darcy held up a hand. "What my brother is trying to say in a totally ham-fisted way is, we don't know a lot about your past. We need to rule out everyone we can even though we don't believe you're involved."

The very idea of it made her nauseous. She wrapped her arms around her to stop the shaking. "I don't have a permanent address so I must be dodgy, is that it?" She directed the question at Brandon.

He stared back at her with an edge of defiance—and maybe guilt.

She didn't want to get into her past. They couldn't comprehend what it was like when they'd grown up in such a supportive household. But if it stopped them suspecting her and made them look elsewhere towards the real culprit, she would answer their questions. She'd revisit her messy past for Beth and Bill. She focused on Darcy. "What do you want to know?"

Brandon answered. "Where are you from?"

Nowhere. That was part of the problem. "We moved a lot when I was a child, but I did high school in Perth."

"Why'd you move?"

"Father is a major in the army."

Brandon glanced down at her resume and his eyes widened. "Your father is Major Hammond?"

Shit. She should have known he would have heard of her father. She nodded.

Brandon swore. "You're Arthur's sister."

"You know him?"

"He's in my team."

Well damn. Did that count for or against her?

"You ran away from home. He doesn't know where

you are."

So that was the bullshit he was spouting. Anger sizzled over her skin. "He doesn't care where I am," she corrected.

Brandon frowned. "Yes, he does."

The idea Arthur gave a shit about her was laughable. "Just because you know my family, doesn't mean you're aware of all the facts," she spat. "So don't you dare judge me."

"Do you want to tell us about it?" Darcy asked quietly.

No. It was the last thing she wanted to do, but she also had to set the record straight. Let Brandon go back to the army and understand what type of person her brother really was. She rubbed her arms. "My mother was in a car accident when I was fourteen and was hospitalised for months. Arthur had just signed up to the army and was training somewhere, and wherever the major was, it was more important than coming home to support his wife and daughter." She'd spent hours alone on the bus each day travelling between home, school and the hospital. She'd lived on takeaway food, had barricaded the doors at night in case someone tried to break in and had cried herself to sleep. "When Mum came home, she became addicted to pain killers. I contacted the major and my brother, but either my messages didn't get through or they didn't care." She'd lost count of the number of emails she'd sent them both, begging for help.

Darcy stepped forward and placed a hand on her shoulder. "I'm sorry, Ames."

She stepped away from him. His sympathy would choke her up too much to go on. "On the last day of school in Year Ten, I came home to find my mother in bed. I tried to wake her but she didn't respond. I called an ambulance and they pronounced her dead when they arrived." She swallowed hard. "My father didn't attend the funeral. My brother stayed less than a week before he had to get back to training."

Darcy's expression was horrified, and even Brandon's gaze had softened. He shifted in his chair as if he was going to stand but didn't.

"I packed my things, took the last of the housekeeping money and left. I've been travelling ever since."

The silence stretched and Brandon eventually broke it. "I'm sorry." He sounded genuine.

She nodded, too choked up to speak.

Brandon cleared his throat. "I, ah, have to ask one more question," he said. He waited until she nodded before he asked, "Has anyone approached you about your job here?"

She took a moment to control her anger and reminded herself he was trying to find the person who killed his parents. Unlike her family, he cared they had died. "No," she said. "The only people I've spoken to are our guests, your family and the people who work here."

"That's all we need for now," Darcy said and shot his brother a look that said shut up.

Amy exhaled. "Thank you." She didn't look at Brandon as she walked out of the room. After she closed the door, she paused to control the nausea. Revisiting her past made her want to run and hide. So many days spent trying to find work so she could afford somewhere to stay the night. When she was lucky, the accommodation had been basic, with a hard or lumpy mattress, thin walls so she could hear everything in the next room, wondering whether someone would try and bash down her door. She'd felt so helpless, but the thought of going back to her father's controlling ways hadn't been an option she'd considered for long. She'd hitched a ride out of the city and headed east, finding a job in Kalgoorlie which had included accommodation. She had lied about her age for two years until she turned eighteen.

Life had quickly taught her how to read people's intent and she made friends with people who could help her. Survival was her only option, because she wasn't ever facing her father again.

Hearing sounds in the office behind her, she hurried down the hallway. Ed was the only one in the kitchen when she walked in. He looked a little concerned. "Everything OK?"

"It's fine. I'm heading to bed." She continued through the room and out into the cool night. The darkness swallowed her only metres from the door and she hugged herself as she walked back to the shearers' quarters.

The idea Brandon knew her brother and father didn't sit well with her. One of them must have mentioned her at some stage for him to know she was missing. Not that missing was the right word. She was certain her father would have the connections to find her if he was so inclined. She still had the same email address so they could contact her if they wanted to. And they never had.

Retribution Ridge was the first place she'd truly been welcomed, her only proper home since her mother's accident. And now her life here was at risk.

Somehow she had to make sure the culprit was found and ensure Brandon would keep the campgrounds going. She didn't want to lose her home. And the best way to do that was the way she'd dealt with all the haters in her life. Charm them until they forgot they disliked her.

It was time to befriend the enemy.

Chapter 7

Brandon groaned when his alarm sounded. He'd tossed and turned last night as he thought about how he'd treated Amy. Darcy had been right. He'd been a complete douche. But in his defence it had been such a shock to realise she was the missing sister Sherlock had told him about. He'd never mentioned his mother dying and his version of events lacked the detail of Amy's story. Who was he meant to believe? Sherlock would never abandon his team, so why would he abandon his family? Though Sherlock was one of those military for life types who lived and breathed its rules. He'd been on almost as many missions as Brandon, never home for Christmas, always the first to volunteer. Brandon should have guessed he had family issues. On the mission that had gone pear-shaped, Sherlock had confessed his sister had run away and begged Brandon to look for her if he died. Had said he'd failed her, but hadn't gone into detail.

Brandon opened his laptop. Should he email Sherlock and tell him he'd met his sister? Or was it a complete betrayal of Amy?

He sighed and shut his laptop lid. It was none of his business. He'd apologise to Amy for his behaviour last night and before he left, he'd ask her if she wanted him to tell Sherlock where she was. Darcy had reamed him for his lack of sensitivity after she had left.

But her story had clashed so violently with the man he thought Sherlock was and her emotions were so raw. He'd fought the urge to haul her into his arms and comfort her. The force of the emotion scared him, so he'd stuck to the mission. Getting answers.

He'd got far more than he'd bargained for. Unless Amy was a hell of an actress, he believed she truly cared about his parents.

What was it about Amy that got to him? He had spent little time with her, but somehow she always hovered at the edge of his awareness. Perhaps it was her nurturing way, reminding him what home felt like. Or perhaps it was his desire to explore what lay underneath her casual dress.

Whatever the reason, he shouldn't get too caught up in it. He wasn't staying long and he had to get to the bottom of who was telling the truth—Amy or Sherlock.

He glanced at his laptop again, and then his phone. Sherlock would be awake by now, and running laps around the base.

Leave it. He had enough of his own family issues to sort out.

He washed his face and then wandered over to the main house. The utes were already gone, so Darcy or Matt were probably off feeding the animals or checking fences.

As he neared the kitchen door, the scent of bacon wafted towards him and his stomach rumbled. Inside, Amy stood at the stove frying bacon. If nothing else, the woman could cook. He pushed open the door, determined to make amends. "Morning."

Her cautious smile made him feel like an asshole. "Good morning. Would you like bacon and eggs for breakfast?"

"Yes, please." He placed his baseball cap on the

hooks by the door. "Is there anything I can do to help?"

She didn't look at him as she responded. "You can make the coffee."

Yeah, he definitely needed to apologise. "I'm sorry about last night."

She raised an eyebrow. "Which part?"

He deserved that. "About prying into your life and then being so insensitive. I didn't mean to hurt you."

Amy sighed. "I get why you did it," she said. "And I'm used to men in the army being insensitive." She slid the bacon onto some paper towel.

Brandon flinched at being grouped with the major. His mother would be horrified, she'd taught him better. And he should have been understanding. He'd avoided questions about his family his entire adult life. "It must have been rough." She'd been all of fifteen when she'd left home.

"It was." She cracked a couple of eggs into the frypan and then put two slices of bread in the toaster.

It wasn't his place to pry, but maybe it would help to hear about her brother. "Arthur said you were tough and independent."

She glanced at him. "I had no choice."

Right. Had Sherlock realised? "How many years are between you two?"

"Four. Dad wasn't around often enough to get Mum pregnant."

Ouch. Not the way he wanted to envision the major.

The toast popped up and Amy buttered it, placing it on a plate with the eggs and bacon on top. "Here you go." She placed the plate on the table. "Darcy said to tell you he'll be back by ten. Asked for you to wait for him, whatever that means."

Damn. He wanted to get started. "Darcy and I have to finish going through Mum and Dad's papers."

"You don't think Ed and I are smart enough to help?" Georgie asked as she walked in.

He sighed. The last thing he needed was Georgie in a mood. "How much do you know about the Ridge's finances?"

She frowned. "Not a lot."

"Then you won't be much help. Darcy knows the business and until we get a lawyer to sort out things, I own the land. You're welcome to sit in, but it's likely to be boring as hell."

"I should go through Mum's address book and contact all her old school friends."

He winced. It wasn't a task he wanted. "If you feel up to it."

Georgie shrugged. "It should be done." She poured herself a coffee. "Where's La La?"

"She went with Darcy," Amy said. "She had a nightmare and doesn't want to let him out of her sight."

"Poor cherub," Georgie said, then she groaned. "I guess someone should tell Sofia."

"Why would she care?" Ed asked, coming in with his hair dishevelled, dark rings under his eyes.

"It's the polite thing to do."

"She wasn't polite when she abandoned Darcy and Lara." Ed sloshed coffee into his mug and sat at the table.

"What's up with you?" Brandon asked.

He yawned so widely Brandon almost saw his tonsils. "Didn't get much sleep. I was searching for information on Stonefish."

Brandon stiffened. "Find anything?"

"Not a lot. I traced the business name to Singapore, but that's as far as I got."

"So it's a Singaporean company?" Brandon asked.

"Singapore registered company but could be comprised of people in any country. A lot of companies register in Singapore but do business elsewhere. I don't know enough about it."

It was a start. "Thanks Ed."

"So what are we doing today?" he asked.

"Darcy and Brandon are going through Mum and Dad's papers," Georgie said.

Ed grimaced. "How about we take La La to the beach?"

"Sounds good to me. I'll phone some of Mum's friends before Lara gets back."

Amy dished up bacon and eggs for Georgie and an omelette for Ed. She was efficient and knew what they liked. Knew them better than he did. And that was perhaps another reason he'd made her a suspect— jealousy.

Amy poured herself a bowl of cereal, and Brandon topped up his coffee. "Can I get you a coffee?"

Her smile was warmer now, and washed over him like a sea breeze, invigorating him. "Yes, please."

Down boy. He poured her a cup and then refilled the filter machine.

"What are you doing today, Ames?" Georgie asked.

"The washing machine has been playing up. I told Beth I'd try and fix it."

"You can do that?" Brandon raised his eyebrows.

"Probably," she said. "Most of the time I can't afford new, so fixing what others are willing to throw out has saved me a bundle." She sipped her coffee. "The internet has taught me a lot."

Impressive. Brandon had been scared when he'd gone to the army, a whole world he knew nothing about. But at least he'd had guaranteed food and shelter, and someone to guide his way. Amy had none of that.

Georgie reached over and squeezed her hand. "You're the best."

What else needed to be done? Brandon hadn't given the work around the station much thought. Too many years away. At one time it would have been second nature, he would have known exactly what was required. Now he was out of practice. "Have the sheep been moved closer to the house?"

Georgie answered. "Yeah, I think Dad mentioned that the last time I was out here."

A deep longing settled into his gut. Work on the station was hot and dusty, but also honest and fulfilling. The type of work he could see himself doing for the rest of his days. He wanted to help Darcy and Matt. But would they want him around? He was an army man, he didn't know what—if anything—had changed.

The red dirt outside the window called to him. He'd have a few days leave still after the funeral and he could ask for more. It would make sense for him to help on the station.

He just hoped the reminder of what his life could have been like wouldn't be too painful.

When breakfast was over, Georgie excused herself to make some phone calls and Ed mumbled something about going back to bed. Brandon let them go, wanting some time alone with Amy. He ran water in the sink for the dishes.

"You don't need to help," Amy said. "I'm sure you've got a lot to do."

"You've been cooking and caring for all of us," he said. "The least I can do is help clean."

She flushed and continued to clear the table. "All right. Thank you."

Knowing more about her past explained things he'd noticed about her. Her posture was rigid straight, the same kind of posture drilled into soldiers from day one. Her movements were quick and efficient, grabbing all the cupboard items at once, before reaching for the fridge items. She had food on the table without anyone having to wait so her instincts and organisational skills were second to none. Had her mother taught her, or was it training from her father?

Major Hammond had a reputation for being a hard arse and a stickler for order. Sherlock had been much the same, not a thing out of place. His fastidious nature was one reason for his nickname. If that was Amy's upbringing, he didn't envy her.

He washed the dishes, placing them on the drying rack to drain and when the table was clear, Amy towelled them dry.

He was out of practice with small talk. Most of the past ten years he'd been surrounded by teammates and on the odd occasion he dated, talking wasn't what he'd got up to. His mother would be appalled at how bad his skills were. She'd always insisted they knew how to converse, from making them call and submit orders, to sitting at the table when her friends came to visit and volunteering them for various activities at the annual fund-raising events.

"Is cooking for the family part of your job?"

"No, but I used to help Beth. The guest liaison wasn't busy with only six campsites, so I wanted to do more to earn my keep."

Integrity. He liked that. "Did Darce show you around the station?"

She glanced at him. "Are you trying to figure out how well I know the property?" The accusation was light, a little uncertain and he grimaced.

"No. Just making conversation." He sighed. After last night he doubted she was the culprit. "I don't think you were involved in my parents' deaths."

"Good." She smiled. "Darcy showed me all the key areas, told me how to get to the beach, and Bill was teaching me how to ride since my car wouldn't handle some of the dirt tracks."

"Horses or motorbikes?"

"Both."

"I could take you out some time. Continue the lessons." What on earth possessed him to offer? He wasn't sticking around. Speaking of which, he needed to call his Lieutenant Colonel and ask for more time off.

Her hesitation was brief. "That would be lovely if you have time."

He'd make time. He dried his hands on the towel. "I need to make a couple of calls, but if Darcy isn't back by the time I'm done, maybe we can go riding this morning."

"Sure. Thanks for your help."

He grabbed his baseball cap from the hook and headed outside where the sun rose well over the horizon, warming the land. He ducked under the shade of the machinery shed and dialled his commanding officer.

"Brandon. How are things?"

"I'd like to request some more time off, sir," he said.

"Something wrong?"

Dobby would understand. "The police believe my parents' car was tampered with," he said. "I need some time to figure out why."

Dobby was quiet for a long moment. "Got any ideas?"

"A few."

There was some shuffling of paper in the background. "I can give you until the end of the month."

Three weeks. Hopefully that would be long enough. "Thanks, sir."

"Let me know if you need anything."

"Roger that." He hung up and tapped his finger on

his jeans. Amy's question last night resonated in his head. If his parents hadn't been the intended targets, what had been the point? He hated the idea of someone creeping around the station. They didn't have enough eyes to cover the whole area.

It was time to call in reinforcements. He dialled Sam's number.

"Wasn't sure I'd hear from you," Sam said as a greeting.

"Wasn't sure I'd call," he responded. "Funerals are on Thursday at Retribution Ridge."

"What's the sitch?"

"Police think the crash wasn't an accident."

His friend swore. "Why?"

"Cut brake lines and evidence they were side swiped."

"I'll be up tomorrow."

The wave of relief surprised him. He hadn't realised how much he needed to see a familiar face. And Sam was experienced dealing with bad guys. If Stonefish was behind his parents' deaths, he wanted someone who could help him protect his family. "Message me your flight details."

"Will do."

Brandon hung up, some of the weight gone from his concerns, and looked around the machinery shed. It had been years since he'd been in here. Feeling almost like an intruder, he moved past the water tank and into the workshop. Tools hung on one wall and other equipment was neatly packed on the shelves. His father had been organised, but it came from a place of necessity. If a tool was lost, there was no easy way to replace it. It was a two-hour round trip to town, and at worst it could take weeks for parts to come up from Geraldton or Perth. Everything had to be properly cleaned and the doors closed to keep out the dust.

Brandon frowned. The workshop door had been open when he came in. He couldn't imagine Darcy forgetting to shut it, but maybe Matt had been in. He'd have to ask him later.

A smaller room led off the workshop, a room which had always been locked when he'd been a kid. It was full of family heirlooms, some stuff going back to the Retribution. He'd been more interested in the station itself than going through mouldy trunks. Still, if Taylor had been stealing one of the hair combs, maybe there was something of value in there. The doorknob twisted in his hand and the door squeaked open.

The walls were lined with shelves full of boxes. Some were old wooden travel chests, the type featured in historical movies, but there were also more modern clear plastic tubs with labels on them. A thin layer of red dust coated everything, telling him someone must occasionally come in here to clean. He sneezed as the dust got up his nose and then strode over to read the labels.

Charlie's name on the bottom two containers caused his chest to squeeze. What things of Charlie's had his parents saved? No, lifting the lid would be far too painful. Ed's and Georgie's names were on the crates on top. He bent to get a better look and recognised one of Georgie's old teddy bears in the top container. Things left behind when they each moved out.

He spotted a box with his name on it. Well, shit. He'd never expected anything of his to be here. Had figured his father would have got rid of everything.

His hands a little shaky, he lifted it down. He'd taken only clothes with him when he'd left. What would his mother have kept?

His brown Akubra hat sat on top, brushed clean but still with the tinges of red dirt that wouldn't ever come out. He stared at it, turning it around in his hands to look at it from every side. He took his baseball cap off, and slowly replaced it with the Akubra. It settled snuggly, fitting perfectly as it always had. He closed his eyes and took a minute as a calm settled over him. Putting on the hat had always been like arming himself for the day's work. He'd felt prepared, ready to face whatever was thrown at him. Similar to the feel of strapping on a Kevlar vest.

What other treasures did the box contain?

Stacked underneath the hat were the well-worn copies of a thriller series he loved and had read at least once a year. He placed them on the lid to keep them off the dusty floor. Then there was his golden high school graduation sash which he'd worn with pride. He rubbed the satin and smiled as he remembered the graduation party afterwards, when he'd convinced Dot they should give their virginity to each other. It had been awkward in the back of his ute with only a sleeping bag for cushioning but a memorable and defining moment in his life. Did she remember the night as fondly as he did? Maybe he'd ask her one day when all this was resolved.

He pulled out a shoe box next and frowned. He had no shoes worth keeping. Most of his had been worn to within an inch of their life. He cracked open the lid and the glint of gold made his heart stop. His gymkhana trophies.

He hadn't thought about them in years, had pushed the memories as far back as possible. But he loved the gymkhanas. Retribution Bay held them a couple of times a year as another way of enticing visitors up to their remote location and he and Darcy spent the month leading up to it training together. He'd loved the speed and precision of the barrel race, and Darcy had been the king of the roping. At the last gymkhana he'd been asked whether he would take part in the rodeo circuit next year. And he'd been determined to, even though the adults were more experienced than him.

He sighed. Life had changed. He placed the lid back on the shoe box and returned all the items back to the container aside from his hat.

The urge to go riding hummed through his blood. Still an hour before Darcy was due back. He could take Amy out and Ed and Georgie could handle any people who arrived wishing to give their sympathies.

He longed to feel the wind rushing in his face as he galloped along the trail.

With a grin, he closed the door behind him, then hurried over to the house to see a woman about a ride.

**

Amy almost didn't recognise Brandon when he came in through the kitchen door. He wore a brown stockman's hat, and a loose chambray shirt with a white singlet underneath, looking every bit the cowboy. He brimmed with excited energy and his grin was as big as if he'd won the lottery. Something had happened in the past half an hour that had cheered him, and it was appealing as hell. "Good news?"

"Sort of," he said. "I've got another three weeks' leave, and I just found a bunch of my old stuff." He ran two fingers along the brim of his hat. "I loved this hat."

It must be nice to have those kinds of memories. She'd left everything non-essential behind and she doubted her father would have saved any of it. "That's great."

He glanced at the clock on the wall. "Want to go for a quick ride before Darcy gets back?"

The offer surprised her. She thought he'd been making platitudes when he'd offered to take her earlier. "What if we get guests?"

"Georgie and Ed can deal with them." He smiled,

annihilating her memories of his usual sombre expression as if it never existed. This was a Brandon who had swept all his troubles away for the moment. It connected with her deep-seated need to ignore expectations.

"Please," he continued. "I discovered my old gymkhana trophies and I have a sudden urge to go riding. Your company would be nice."

She laughed. "You won't get me doing any gymkhana stuff," she said. "I can barely trot."

"I can teach you."

"Teach her what?" Ed said. He was dressed for the day, his hair now slicked back and his clothes tidy.

"I'm going for a ride. Thought I'd take Amy with me."

Ed narrowed his eyes. "Why are you suddenly so cheerful?"

"Did you know there's a box of your old stuff in the shed?"

Ed blinked. "No."

Brandon grinned. "It's in the room off the workshop. I'm inspired to go riding."

"You always were the best rider of all of us," Ed said. "Though Darcy might be better now." He grinned, obviously stirring his older brother.

"Probably," Brandon agreed and turned back to Amy. "So you want to come?"

She'd enjoyed the few sessions she'd had with Bill and would have ridden more, but she wasn't confident enough to go alone. Besides she had decided to befriend Brandon. "Will you be all right if I go?" she asked Ed.

He nodded and waved his hand. "Go. Have fun. You deserve a break. I'll entertain anyone who drops by. Just don't let my brother push you around. If you're not comfortable, tell him so."

"All right. Thanks. I'll get changed."

"I'll meet you at the horses," Brandon said.

It took little time to change into a pair of jeans and a loose long-sleeved top. The day was already warm, and Bill had advised it was better to cover up and be a little warm, than to bake her skin in the sun's rays. Her light straw beach hat felt at odds with the rest of her clothing, but it would have to do. Maybe if she stayed, she'd get herself a hat like Brandon and Darcy's.

Over by the horses Brandon saddled Lara's bay horse, Starlight, and Bill's horse, Reg. Amy joined him as his competent fingers did up the saddle cinch and then he murmured to the horse as he slid the bridle over its head. Sure, but gentle movements. Unwanted attraction swept through her. In his current outfit it would be all too easy to forget he was in the army and wonder what his fingers would feel like against her skin.

He smiled at her. "What has Dad taught you?"

Focus. "He showed me how to saddle Starlight and take care of her afterwards. The last time we went out he said I was ready to canter." She wasn't certain she agreed with him.

"Don't look so concerned. We'll stick with what you're comfortable with." He turned his attention to Reg, hefting the saddle over his back and cinching it. For the first time since returning, he seemed in his element. Perhaps it was because his siblings weren't around.

Amy stroked Starlight's neck, murmuring to her. "Be gentle with me." Maybe she should go to the adult riding classes Faith ran on a Saturday afternoon. She'd definitely get more practice, and it would be nice to catch up with Dot and Faith in a social environment.

Brandon undid the halter ropes and slid them off both horses, handing her Starlight's reins. "Do you need a leg up?"

"I can manage." She mounted and directed Starlight away from the fence. "Where do you want to go?"

"How about over the ridge?" he suggested. "I haven't been that way yet."

The ridge which gave the station its name could be seen from the farmhouse and was probably a twenty-minute ride. "Sure." She nudged Starlight into a walk and they rode side-by-side down a path which led in the general direction. After a few minutes Brandon said, "You look comfortable on her."

"Walking is easy, especially when Starlight's so well behaved."

"She's of good stock," Brandon said. "Did you want to try a trot or canter?"

He was probably itching to take off. "Why don't you go ahead, check the path and come back for me?"

"Will you be OK on your own for a few minutes?"

She nodded, faking her confidence. "It's not like you can lose me." The flat land spread out for miles, with only the small sand dunes behind her interrupting the view.

"All right." He nudged his horse into a trot and then into a slow canter, dust floating in the air behind him. He rode well, sitting comfortably in the saddle like he was born to it, which, she supposed, he was.

Starlight tossed her head, snagging Amy's attention and then broke into a trot. Amy tensed, bouncing up and down, pulling on the reins. "Whoa." The horse ignored her and instead increased her pace, breaking into a canter as if trying to catch Brandon. Amy shrieked and grabbed the front of the saddle, gripping hard with her legs. Ahead, Brandon hadn't noticed her predicament.

The wind and the land rushed by as the horse's hooves set a rhythmic drumming on the ground. What if she stepped in a rabbit hole or something? Amy's heart pounded a much faster beat than the hooves.

The most important rule is not to panic. Bill's words echoed in her head.

Easier said than done. She loosened her grip on the saddle. The horse wanted to catch up with Brandon. Maybe Amy should let her. She forced herself to relax her clenched thighs and feel the rhythm of the canter, sitting into it rather than bouncing all over the place. It was rocking, kind of soothing if she let herself relax.

Brandon slowed to a trot and he glanced behind. Amy hoped Starlight would stop when they got near. Brandon waited for them to catch up and his expression morphed from a smile to concern when he realised she wasn't in control. About ten metres out, Starlight slowed, breaking into a jolting trot which jerked Amy about before coming to an abrupt stop in front of Brandon.

Amy's breath whooshed out of her and her hands shook on the reins.

"Are you all right?"

She nodded. Next time she'd remember to wear a sports bra. "Starlight decided she didn't want to be left behind." She swallowed to get the tremor out of her voice.

Brandon swore and the joy she'd seen in him vanished. "I'm sorry, Amy."

"Don't be. I managed OK." She smiled, relieved it was over.

"No, I shouldn't have brought you out here. I don't know these horses. I should have asked Georgie how they'd react."

She didn't want him beating himself up about it, so she reached over and squeezed his hand. "It's fine, really. No harm done. I got used to it at the end." She wanted to head up to the ridge and they were already halfway there. "Shall we continue?"

"Only if you're certain. I'm happy to go back as well." His concern was sweet and appreciated. Her father would have made her continue to ensure she improved.

"I won't race you," she said with a grin, "but I'd like to go to the top. The view is spectacular from there."

"It is." He nudged his horse back into a walk and Amy followed.

She wanted answers to questions like why he left, and what he would do with the station now he owned it, but they weren't questions she could ask. They wouldn't lead to befriending him. She should speak of something a little more light-hearted, but her mind came up blank.

Brandon broke the silence. "You must have lived in a lot of places."

She stiffened and then sighed. The best way to get someone to trust her was to let them in, share things with them. "Yeah, I travelled east first, crossing the Nullarbor eventually and exploring the east coast, but the west called me back."

"Where was your favourite?"

"Here. There's something about the landscape, the space, the air, the dirt so red you'd swear it was fake, that gets to me."

Respect shone on his face. "I understand."

She didn't know how he stayed away for so long. If Darcy could no longer hire her, she'd hunt high and low to find another job somewhere close by. It was the perfect segue. "Will you move back now that you own the station?"

His expression closed down. "I don't know."

Her own selfish fear about her job made her want to press him, so she changed the subject. "Is there a technique to being comfortable when cantering?"

He seemed surprised by the change of subject. "Not

really. You need to sit into it, relax." He shifted in his saddle as if making himself comfortable.

She followed his example and he laughed, the sound pure joy. Her heart fluttered. The lighter, friendlier Brandon was appealing. She pressed her lips together. "Could you help me try it?"

"Sure." He brightened as he explained what to do and she followed his instructions, kicking Starlight into a trot and then a canter. This time she was ready, and she settled into the saddle, letting Starlight set the pace. It felt amazing with the wind rushing past her and the ground a blur at her feet. She was cantering. She laughed, tossing her head back in glee and then pulled on the reins to slow back to a walk.

Brandon grinned at her. "You're a fast learner."

"Helps when I have a good teacher. Thank you."

She smiled. Their eyes met and she had no words for the pull she felt towards him.

Starlight tossed her head, shaking flies away and it broke the spell. Ahead of them the path narrowed. "You should lead the way."

He nodded and nudged his horse forward, but she still felt the thump of her heart.

Maybe she was doing too good a job at befriending him.

Chapter 8

Brandon and Amy arrived back at the house ahead of Darcy. Brandon dismounted, his legs a little achy from the unfamiliar exercise, but the tightness in his chest was gone and he could breathe again. Up there on the ridge, overlooking his land felt like coming home, a spiritual experience. Amy had stood next to him, silent, as if she realised he needed a moment to take it all in.

He glanced over to where she had already unsaddled Starlight and was brushing her with firm long strokes. She'd impressed him with her resilience, her desire to continue despite having been out of control. He hated that he'd been so wrapped up in his own ride that he hadn't noticed her in trouble and vowed to keep a close eye on her for the rest of the journey. But she'd picked up cantering quickly and he hadn't had to worry about her on the return trip.

"I can't believe I did it," she said as she came around to brush Starlight's right flank. Some of her frizzy hair had fallen out creating a cloud-like frame around her face. "Thank you so much!" Her grin was so wide it wiped away his self-recriminations, replacing them with a warmth in his chest. She was damned appealing.

"You did well," he said and carried his saddle into the tack room to distance himself. Darcy drove in as they climbed the porch and Bill's fishing buddy was just leaving. After he left, Ed said, "We should close the gate to keep people out."

Maybe he'd been selfish to leave Ed and Georgie to deal with visitors.

Darcy laughed as he pulled open the fly screen door. "It wouldn't stop them." He held the door open for Lara and Bennet.

That was a problem Brandon hadn't considered. "We're never going to get into Dad's study if they keep coming by."

"Georgie can deal with them," Darcy said.

His sister stood, shaking her head, her eyes a little red. "Georgie is taking La La to the beach with Ed," she said. "We've done our shift and it's your turn."

Lara perked up but glanced at Darcy as if unsure.

"Go on, pumpkin. You'll have fun."

She hugged him and ran to put her bathers on.

"How'd the calls go?" Brandon asked his sister.

She ran a hand through her hair and sighed, the exhaustion on her face obvious. "They weren't too bad. Simone offered to call the other friends in that group which left Mum's cousins. They can't make it to the funeral."

He gave into his instinct and hugged her. "Tell me if you want me to call anyone."

She squeezed him then rolled her eyes. "Now you offer, when they're all done."

He shrugged. "What can I say, my timing is impeccable." He got the laugh he was hoping for.

"I can entertain the guests," Amy said. "Most of them will understand you've got things to do."

Darcy placed a hand on her shoulder. "Are you sure? It's exhausting."

Her smile was sad. "I enjoy hearing the stories they tell about Beth and Bill, and it's more important you figure out who killed them."

Brandon wanted to hug her but was worried about overstepping. He was falling into the Amy camp with the rest of his family. He'd really enjoyed his time with her. "Thank you. Come get us if you need a break."

"Will do."

With the sound of another car outside, he and Darcy hurried into their father's office. The room smelled of old leather and whiskey. So like his father. "What are we searching for?" Brandon asked.

"Anything that mentions Stonefish, and I need to go over the finances to work out if we have anything we can spend." He glanced at Brandon. "How good are you at figures?"

"I manage."

"Then you look through the filing cabinet for taxes, balance sheets and bank statements and I'll go through the emails and invoices." He paused. "Keep an eye out for anything to do with Taylor as well. Or anything that could be a potential motive."

Vague.

"Did you get hold of the lawyer about being executor?" Darcy continued.

"Yeah, I put in an application to the court yesterday. I don't know how long it will take." It had been easy.

"So there's not a lot we can do until then. They'll freeze Mum and Dad's accounts."

"We might be able to do something with the business accounts." Brandon opened the top drawer of the filing cabinet and pulled out the bank statements. Shit. "Not much to freeze." He handed the latest statement to Darcy. Less than a thousand dollars.

"This is their joint account. There's got to be a station account as well."

Brandon dug through the files and finally found what he was looking for. His stomach clenched. It couldn't be right. He hadn't been involved in the financial aspect of the Ridge when he was younger, but his father had explained about the overdraft from the bank. "There's next to nothing in here."

Darcy swore. "Is that the most recent statement? We've spent the bare minimum this year."

"Yeah." Brandon dragged out the file and sat at the desk, flicking through each statement. "Here. There's a loan for over a hundred grand at the beginning of the year."

"Who to?"

Brandon read out the name.

Darcy stiffened. "Say that again."

"Livestock and Gear."

Darcy shook his head. "Surely Dad would have told me if he'd gone ahead." He pulled the keyboard towards him and typed in the details.

"Darce, you want to clue me in?" While he waited for an answer, he flicked through the receipts file and found one with the company name on it. The contents made him frown. "Looks like a purchase receipt for cattle."

Darcy swore and took the document from him. "Droughtmaster cattle. I've been telling Dad for years we need to switch back to cattle, but every time I brought it up he refused. This mob sent us information late last year and we had the discussion again, but he told me no."

Brandon wanted to be sick. "You know why he didn't want to go there."

Darcy nodded. "But so much of our flock was being taken by dingoes or wild dogs. We had to make the change."

"So where are the cattle?" Delivery date was last week.

"Not here as far as I know. I'll radio Matt."

While Darcy contacted Matt, Brandon typed in the

internet address on the top of the invoice. The site no longer existed. Odd. He went to the door and called for his youngest brother.

Ed wore board shorts and had a beach towel around his neck. "What's up? We're just heading out."

"What do you know about finding obsolete web addresses?"

"You mean finding who owned them? It's easy enough."

"Can you look up the details of Livestock and Gear?"

"Probably." He typed a few things into the computer. "It was registered in December to—" He swore. "Stonefish Enterprises." He looked at Brandon. "What's this all about?"

Brandon showed him the document. Ed's eyes widened as he read it. "Oh shit!" He typed again but shook his head. "It looks like it's a bogus company."

The unease in Brandon's stomach grew and he shook his head. "No way Dad and Darcy would be swindled."

Darcy came back in. "Matt knows nothing about any cattle."

"It's easy enough to put together a professional-looking website and trick people into thinking it's a legitimate business," Ed said. "Let me see if I can bring it up in the internet archive."

"The what?" Darcy asked.

"The internet archive. It's an organisation which crawls the internet taking snapshots to preserve it for future generations. They might have taken a snapshot of this site when it was up." While they waited, Brandon filled Darcy in. The blood drained from Darcy's face.

"No, it can't be." He ran a hand through his hair. "I checked all the details to make sure they were legit before I told Dad."

"Here it is," Ed said. The website appeared legitimate with a professional logo, contact details, an office address in Perth, plus lots of testimonials from satisfied customers. Brandon called the number but received a 'this number has been disconnected' message. "Nothing," he told the others.

Ed typed the address into Google maps and the street view showed a high rise building in the CBD. "Why would Dad purchase the cattle without telling anyone?" he asked.

Brandon looked at Darcy.

"Maybe he wanted to surprise me," Darcy mumbled, staring at the screen, his face pale.

The why didn't matter. Brandon placed a hand on Darcy's shoulder. "Is there anyone we can call to report this?"

"There might be some consumer protection." Ed glanced to the door as Georgie yelled for him from somewhere in the house.

"Go," Brandon said. "We'll look into it and if we get stuck, we'll call you in when you get back."

Darcy looked up. "Distract my baby girl for a while," he said. "She might seem OK on the outside, but she's struggling."

Ed nodded. "We will." He left, yelling at his sister. "Hold your horses!"

Brandon smiled as a pang washed through him. It was so reminiscent of when they'd all lived at home. Someone was always calling out for something. He'd missed it. Missed his siblings. Now he was back here he couldn't understand why he'd stayed away so long. Maybe if he hadn't, things wouldn't have turned out like this.

Darcy sank into the chair and lowered his head into his hands. "I've fucked all this up."

The protective urge was strong. "You did nothing wrong, Darce. We'll sort this out."

No matter what happened, he was sure of one thing. Brandon wouldn't let Darcy suffer the same kind of guilt he had suffered. This was all Stonefish's fault and Brandon would stay until it was fixed. "Let's figure out what we have to do next. What emails do we have about the transaction?" He clicked the email program open and waited for the latest messages to download.

The one at the top made him swear. He clicked on it.

Dear Darcy,

We were shocked to hear about Bill's death. Please accept our sincerest condolences. We would still like to continue our discussions about purchasing Retribution Ridge and hope you will be in touch at your earliest convenience.

Yours sincerely,

Tan Lewis

"You've got to be fucking kidding me!" Darcy said.

Brandon agreed, but at least the email distracted Darcy from his guilt. "Let's ignore it for now. Or maybe forward it to Dot."

Darcy nodded and clicked the forward button. "We need to stop them."

"We will," he promised. Somehow.

***

Amy dried the dinner dishes, her movements slow with fatigue weighing her down. Just a few more and then she could go back to her room and rest. She didn't begrudge how busy she'd been today, but she needed a few minutes alone. When she hadn't been comforting Beth and Bill's friends who visited, she'd cleaned the bathrooms and put on laundry. She'd also taken lunch to Darcy and Brandon who were up to their wrists in paperwork. Their grim expressions told her things weren't going well.

She had no idea what it would mean for her job, but the idea of having to leave added extra stress to her day.

When Ed and Georgie returned from taking Lara to the beach, Amy had sat down with Ed to finalise the food for the funeral and made a list of what they needed. She'd drive into town tomorrow to purchase everything.

She was just so tired. The walls seemed to crowd her and the chatter at the table behind her hurt her ears. She needed air and solace.

"Amy, are you going to play cards?" Georgie asked.

She forced a friendly smile as she turned. "Not tonight." She'd been on the go, surrounded by people non-stop since the accident. She hadn't had time to process everything. "I'm going to have an early one. I'll see you in the morning." She hung up the tea towel and hurried out of the kitchen, stepping over Bennet who lay by the door.

The full moon rose high in the sky and the evening had a hint of chill in the air. She moved towards her room, but before she reached it, she changed direction, moving away from the farmhouse, the sheds and her quarters. The four walls would cage her like she'd been caging all of her emotions. Without conscious thought, she travelled along the well-worn path towards the sand dunes, the moon shining enough to light her way, though the shadows were long.

A few creatures rustled through the undergrowth, but they would avoid her. The dingoes and wild dogs rarely came close to the yard, so she wasn't worried about them. She inhaled and tilted her head to the stars above. The Milky Way hung in the sky and the stars looked so close, so bright, like glitter scattered across the night sky. She hadn't realised how much the light pollution in the city caused the stars to fade until she'd come here. The universe was endless.

Bill had insisted she go with him and Ed to the dunes during her first week here. He'd carried a hefty telescope with him and set it up before he invited her to look. And the sight of the stars and planets took her breath away. Tears pricked her eyes. Bill had told her how Ed had got him into astronomy. He'd been so welcoming even though he wasn't enthused about the camp grounds idea. He'd showed her Jupiter, explained how to use the Southern Cross to navigate and pointed out several other constellations she'd heard of but never known where they were. Ed had told her about volunteering at the observatory in the city. The sky was his passion, not the land, but Bill accepted that, just as he accepted Georgie's call of the ocean. He'd never mentioned Brandon though.

She trudged up the small slope of the red sand dune.

They'd all welcomed her more warmly than any other place she'd been to in the past ten years. She hadn't felt like an outsider or a stranger, there'd been an instant comfort as if she'd known the Stokes her entire life. After only a few days of kindness from Beth, Amy had confessed her past, about her family life and running away—something she'd told no one else. And in turn Beth had told her about losing Charlie and her strained relationship with Brandon.

Tears flowed down Amy's cheeks as she sat on the soft, fine sand. Perhaps Beth and Bill were reunited with Charlie now. She wasn't sure if she believed such things, but it gave her comfort nonetheless. The idea of a twelve-year-old boy showing his parents around heaven made her cry harder for all that was lost.

Her shoulders shook as she cried for Beth and Bill, for her mother, for the family she wished she had and the abandonment of her own. Brandon's investigation into her past brought it back to the surface, as raw as it had been ten years ago. She'd thought she'd come to terms with it by now, but the idea that Arthur had mentioned her to Brandon upset her. He hadn't cared enough to contact her. She buried her head in her knees. At Retribution Ridge she'd found love and acceptance which she hadn't felt since before her mother's accident.

Her lungs burned and her throat was raw as the pain she'd kept inside stampeded out of her. She lifted her head to gasp in more air and the breath caught in her throat at the shadowy figure standing right in front of her. She scrambled back as the person said, "I didn't mean to startle you."

Brandon.

She placed a hand over her pounding heart and continued to gasp for air. She didn't want him to see her like this. It was one of the reasons she'd not gone into her quarters. He squatted next to her and rubbed her back. "I'm sorry."

Amy couldn't speak. The warmth of his hand making circles on her back helped to calm her heart and she sucked in air until she controlled her breathing. Then embarrassment flooded her. What was she supposed to say to him? She'd come here to get away from everyone, to grieve on her own. "What are you doing here?"

He lowered himself to the sand. "I saw you come this way. I was worried you might get lost in the dark."

She snorted. "More like you were worried I was some kind of spy." So much for coming to an understanding after the horse ride today.

The noise he made was no kind of confession. "My siblings trust you." He was quiet as he continued to rub her back. Then he sighed. "I trust you. You've done a lot for my family and you cared for my parents. I don't want you to feel as if you're alone."

She studied him. Had he really changed his opinion?

"Arthur would want me to look after you."

Disappointment and disbelief filled her. He was here for his teammate. Well, he was wasting his time. There was fat chance her brother cared. "I'm surprised Arthur mentioned me."

"Not often," Brandon admitted. "But we had a... situation once and he told me about you."

She could read between the lines. A situation in military terms meant things had gone bad. "Did he think he would die?"

"It was touch and go for a while."

It never really occurred to her that her brother could die and she wouldn't know. How was she meant to feel about that? They'd never been close and Arthur had tried to be the man of the house when their father was away, but the longer their father was gone, the nicer Arthur had been, as if he'd forget how strict the major was. Curious now she asked, "What did he say?"

"Asked me to find you if he died, tell you."

"But he survived."

Brandon nodded.

A near death experience hadn't been enough for him to contact her himself. Her eyes flooded again and she brushed away the tears.

"Want to talk about why you were crying?"

The ridiculousness of the question made her laugh. "Why do you think?" The annoyance was a far easier emotion than the grief and she gripped hold of it, using it to dry her tears. "I've spent the past few days listening to your parents' friends share stories of them, reiterating what kind and lovely people they were. They treated me as family—" her voice broke and she swallowed hard. "Beth reminded me so much of my mum before she became an addict, and Bill was the type of man I always wished my father had been."

"Major Hammond is uncompromising."

An apt description. She often wondered whether he was the same with his soldiers as he was with his children. "How well do you know him?"

"I serve under him."

Then he knew exactly what her father was like.

Brandon cleared his throat. "I'm sorry for the way I treated you last night," he said. "The accident was a shock, and coming back here... has brought back a lot of memories." He sat close enough for her to feel his body heat.

She shrugged, wiping her damp cheeks.

"I didn't follow you because I was suspicious, but because I was worried about you."

His confession made her turn to look at him.

"I realised when you left the kitchen that none of us have asked you how you're coping with Mum and Dad's death. Everyone's been telling stories about them, but we haven't asked you for yours."

Her chest ached. It was kind of him to ask.

"I'd love to hear them," he continued. "If you'd like to share."

Amy pressed her lips together, fighting to control the emotions swirling inside her. "You knew them better than I did."

He sighed. "I'm not so sure. We didn't talk much." The pain in his voice made her squeeze his hand. Maybe he felt as much of an outsider now as she did. He glanced at her and slipped his arm around her. "Why don't you tell me your favourite memory?"

It felt right to rest her head against his shoulder. "The first time I came to the Ridge I thought maybe Georgie had been having me on." She smiled. "I drove for ages before I saw the sign marking the driveway and it was close to sunset, so I was paranoid about emus and kangaroos."

"It's not so far out here when you get used to it."

"No, it's not," she agreed. "Georgie said to go around to the kitchen door, and I heard eighties pop blasting out of the speakers."

He chuckled. "Mum loved everything eighties."

"She didn't hear me knock, but Lara was at the table doing homework with Ed, and she let me in. Beth told me the men were caught up on something on the station and would be a little late, so I had to stay for dinner." There'd been no refusing her.

"So you arrived expecting a job interview and got dinner instead?"

She nodded.

"That sounds like Mum." Sadness tinged his amusement.

"Darcy, Bill and both station hands arrived about an hour later, filthy and wet, muttering about a bore. Darcy noticed me first and swore, apologising for being so late, but before he could shake my hand, Beth shooed them all out of the kitchen to get cleaned." She chuckled at the memory. It was the most bizarre interview she'd ever had. "By the end of the night they offered me the job and a place to stay. I didn't know what the job entailed, but I figured being surrounded by people like your family would be lovely, so I accepted."

"Mum and Dad always had a way of welcoming everyone. If we ever had friends out to play, they never wanted to leave."

"Retribution Ridge became home," she said softly, and her chest squeezed. "When Bill discovered I'd never ridden a horse, he took me out the next day and gave me lessons, told me I could ride the horses whenever I wanted. Then Darcy and Matt said I had to learn how to ride a motorbike as well."

"Can't have you stranded out here," Brandon said as he pulled her a little closer.

The weight lifted. "That's what they said." The evening was cool, but she was warm tucked into his side.

"Dad always insisted we learn how to do everything. Made us as self-sufficient as we could be. Even got Matt's family to teach us about edible and medicinal plants."

"It would have been interesting." She glanced at the sky. "Bill brought me out here with his telescope and showed me the stars. Told me how your ancestors had used them to navigate on their voyage here."

Brandon chuckled. "Didn't help them much. They wrecked the ship on an uncharted reef in the bay when they tried to escape a cyclone."

"Too busy looking skywards perhaps."

"There were rumours of a mutiny." His tone was conspiratorial.

"Really? That sounds fascinating."

"The stories have probably been exaggerated over the years," he said. "Maybe if I have time while I'm back, I'll go through the old stuff."

He'd mentioned he had three weeks. Longer than her father had ever taken from the military. "Will you visit more often afterwards?" He stiffened and the silence stretched. She sat up, leaning away from him. "Sorry. It's not my place to ask."

"It's complicated," he said. "I left after a difficult situation."

One thing Beth had wanted was to sit down with Brandon and discuss Charlie's death. She thought he felt responsible for it and wanted to ease his mind. Maybe Amy could do that for Beth. "Charlie's death was hard on everyone."

"What do you know about it?" There was a roughness to the question, almost a defiance, but under it all a vulnerability as well.

"Beth didn't tell me a lot," she said. "Only that Charlie was killed in a stampede. She thought you blamed yourself for it and that's why you never came home."

"I was to blame. I caused the stampede." The words were ripped from him.

Though shocked, she reacted instinctively, pulling him closer towards her. "It was an accident."

He said nothing, but Amy was certain it would have been. This family cared for one another, they wouldn't do anything to purposefully hurt each other. "Do you want to talk about it?"

Brandon raised his head and then looked away. "Do you hear that?"

In the distance there was a quiet rumble of an engine. "Yes. It'll be a car along the main road."

He shook his head as he stood and brushed the sand from his pants. "Wrong direction. That's on our land."

Quickly, she got to her feet, her heartbeat accelerating. "Could Darcy or Matt have gone out?"

"We would have heard them leave." He started down the dune towards the house and she hurried behind him, her muscles tense.

"What are you going to do?"

"Find out who it is." His tone was hard and fear for him swept through her. She didn't want him hurt.

"They might be dangerous."

He glanced at her. "So am I."

***

Anger simmered in Brandon's blood as he strode back to the farmhouse. Beside him Amy jogged to keep up. "Shouldn't we call the police?"

"It would take them too long to get here." And he wanted to deal with these bastards himself.

He flicked the light on in the shed and the

brightness made him blink. The gun safe was still in the corner, hopefully the code was still the same. As it clicked open Amy asked, "What are you doing?"

"They might be armed." He pulled the rifle out and loaded it with bullets.

Her face paled. She'd be safe inside. He eyed the motorbike and the ute, weighing up both vehicles. The bike would be more flexible, but it would be hard to carry the gun. He jumped in the ute, found the keys in the ignition and turned it on.

Amy called, "I'll tell Darcy. Be careful."

He nodded, not sure how he felt about the way his heart swelled at the worry on her face. Then she ran towards the house and he accelerated southwest towards the windmill, keeping his lights off. Whoever was out there would hear him, but maybe not realise it wasn't a car on the main road.

The two-way radio in the ute crackled to life. "What the hell are you doing?" Darcy sounded pissed off.

Brandon debated not answering but he didn't want Darcy to come after him. He grabbed the receiver. "Someone's at the windmill. I'm trying to catch them. Stay there until I contact you."

No answer and he hoped Darcy would listen to him. The road was bumpy, forcing him to slow. The windmill loomed in the darkness, a light shining at its base. The intruder was still there.

The light moved, bouncing away.

He'd been heard. The road smoothed and Brandon accelerated, switching on the headlights and pushing the rattling ute as fast as it would go. As he reached the clearing, he spotted a man in a helmet mounting a motorbike. Not someone he recognised, though it was difficult to make out the face with the helmet on, even with the headlights shining on him.

Brandon braked hard, pulling up in front of the bike.

He grabbed the rifle and leapt out, pointing the gun at the intruder. The engine roared to life and the back wheel skidded out as the man accelerated away. Brandon aimed for the back tyre and shot. The dust made it difficult to see if he hit it, but the man flinched.

Jumping back into the ute, he followed the bike along the track leading out to the main road. He reached for the radio. "I'm pursuing the intruder. Go check what damage he did."

"Be careful," Darcy answered.

Brandon wasn't letting the rider get away. He wished he had his pistol with him so he could continue shooting at the man—not to kill, but to stop him. The man rode straight towards an open gate. The bitumen road was up ahead. Brandon should be able to keep up with him there.

The ute's engine coughed and he glanced down at the display. Shit. The temperature gauge was climbing rapidly. Darcy had mentioned something about the ute needing replacement. It couldn't fail him now.

Steam or smoke came from under the hood and he swore out loud. If he kept going he was likely to damage the ute irreparably *and* lose the intruder.

He slowed, watching the motorbike turn onto the bitumen and race out of sight. He slammed his hand on the steering wheel and grabbed the radio. "Ute's overheated. I've lost him."

Matt answered a moment later. "Let it cool for ten minutes and it should be right. There's more radiator fluid in the tray."

Brandon turned the ute around and parked inside the fence line. He popped the hood and opened it, letting the steam waft into the air.

So close. He closed his eyes and pictured the man. About his height but slimmer, wiry. The jeans and checked shirt could belong to any farmer in the area, or indeed any local. He frowned. Was their saboteur a local? The idea was concerning.

Brandon wandered over to the gate and closed it. Glancing along the fence he noticed the wires were loose. Following the line, he found someone had cut right through the wire fence a hundred metres from the gate. Both sides curled away from each other, leaving plenty of gap for a bike to get through. Why? He'd left the gate open, unless they wanted to cause more damage… or make it seem as if the intruder wasn't familiar with the land.

Something to think about.

Brandon checked the back of the ute and discovered fencing materials in the tray and a torch. Matt must have left it in there after he'd fixed the fence the other day. He checked the heat coming from the engine. Still some time to wait, so he hefted the equipment from the back and went to fix the fence.

Finally the engine was cool enough for him to crawl back to the windmill. Darcy and Matt were both there, shining torches around the base and Darcy's ute was parked nearby.

"What did he damage?" Brandon asked.

Darcy stormed over to him, grabbing him by the front of the shirt. "What the hell, Bran?"

Brandon wouldn't apologise. Until he discovered who he was facing, he didn't want his family near this. "There wasn't time to fetch you." Brandon shrugged him off, ignoring his brother's fury.

"Bullshit. I was in the kitchen. I came outside as soon as I heard the ute."

"Sorry. Has anything been tampered with?"

Darcy swore and shoved past him. "The pipe between the bore and tank has been cut. Looks like you interrupted him before he could finish. I'll need to weld it."

Brandon walked over to check the damage. A definite line had been cut into the metal pipe and water seeped out.

Matt strode over. "Tank's fine, and seal is still on the bore."

Good. Damage to the windmill would have been serious, would mean moving the sheep to another location where they could get water. He gazed into the dark bush. "We can't monitor everything out here."

Darcy nodded. "I'll give Dot a call in the morning. Maybe she can suggest something."

"Why don't you two fetch the welder?" he suggested. "I'll keep searching, see if I can find some other evidence." He held his hand out for a torch.

Darcy narrowed his eyes and then gave it to him. "Don't shoot anyone. It would take too much to explain."

Brandon grinned. "We've got plenty of space to hide a body."

Matt put his fingers in his ears. "I didn't hear that." He slapped Darcy on the back. "Come on."

Brandon waited until the engine had faded before he slowly searched the surrounding area. The intruder's tyre marks weren't clear in the dust and he couldn't make out which footprints were Darcy and Matt's. He climbed the metal ladder on the side of the windmill, taking his time to make sure each rung held before moving to the next one. From a few metres off the ground, he could see for kilometres in any direction, the moon highlighting the different shapes on the ground. Aside from the lights over by the farmhouse, the land was dark. The intruder was long gone.

When he got back to the house, he'd sit down with Darcy and Matt and identify all the potential targets for sabotage.

Perhaps they could set up traps of their own.
He wasn't letting anyone scare them off the land.

Chapter 9

Nerves jiggled in Amy's stomach as she walked over to the farmhouse the next morning. She hadn't seen Brandon last night after he'd taken off in search of the trespasser. She'd waited with Georgie and Ed in the kitchen until Darcy had returned and told them about the cut pipe. Then she'd headed back to her room and stared at the ceiling until she'd heard Brandon return and enter the room next to hers. Only after she was sure he was safe could she sleep.

She could still feel the comfort of his arm around her shoulders. The way they'd leaned into each other and shared confidences in the dark. But now in the bright light of the morning she questioned how things were going to be between them. What was she supposed to say? It felt weird not to acknowledge last night, but she also didn't want Georgie or anyone else asking questions about what they'd got up to.

She huffed. She was making too big a deal about it. Everything would be fine. They were both adults. She braced herself and walked into the kitchen. Only Lara was there, making herself toast and wearing an oversized T-shirt rather than her usual pyjamas. Amy relaxed.

"Morning, La La. Where is everyone?"

"Dad went out with Uncle Matt and Uncle Brandon

and said I couldn't go with him," she said. "Georgie and Ed are still in bed."

They were probably looking for more evidence of the trespasser. Well, she could keep Lara busy for them. "Do you want a hot chocolate?"

"Nah, juice is fine." The young girl turned and Amy realised she was wearing Beth's favourite Michael Jackson T-shirt.

Her heart ached, but she didn't comment.

While Lara sat at the table and munched on her toast, Amy prepared coffee and poured herself cereal.

"Amy, what happens tomorrow?" The uncertainty in Lara's voice made Amy turn.

"You mean at the funeral?"

Lara nodded. "I didn't want to ask Dad in case it upset him. Are they burying Granny and Grandfather?"

The poor girl. They hadn't realised she would need everything explained. "No, sweetheart. They're going to be cremated." At Lara's frown she explained. "Remember that Viking movie we watched, where they put the soldier's body on a boat and set it alight?"

Lara nodded.

"It's the same kind of thing. After the fire, they'll collect Granny and Grandfather's ashes and scatter them on the station."

"So they are always part of the land?"

"Yeah."

Lara chewed thoughtfully and then smiled. "They would like that."

"The funeral itself is like a goodbye ceremony," Amy continued. "Your family will say nice things about your grandparents and some of their friends will too. Then we'll have a big party with food and drinks and celebrate what wonderful people they were." She choked up and glanced down at her bowl, blinking to stop the tears.

Lara slid her small hand over Amy's. "It's OK to cry."

The words made Amy laugh even as her eyes watered. "I know. I don't like to, though."

"Why not?"

She shrugged. "It makes me feel weak."

"Dad says crying makes me strong, because I can get out all the hurt and leave room for happiness."

Amy liked the thought. "Your dad is pretty smart. Mine never liked me to cry."

"Was he mean?"

Amy sipped her coffee. "He wasn't around much. He was in the army which is very structured, and he forgot the rest of the world isn't like that."

"Uncle Brandon is in the army. Don't they allow people to visit their families?" Lara asked. "Is that why Uncle Brandon never visits?"

The connection made sense. "The army allows visits." How much to say? "I think Brandon might have had some things he needed to work out on his own."

Lara frowned. "Dad says it's better to talk about things when they're troubling you. That way more people can help you solve the problem."

"That's good advice. Maybe Uncle Brandon will do that, now he's here."

Lara finished her breakfast and put her dishes in the sink. Georgie wandered in and Lara grabbed a mug from the cupboard. "Coffee?"

"Yes please, my sweet angel." She slid into a seat.

"Rough night?" Amy asked.

"Late night. After Darcy got back…" She thanked Lara as she put the coffee in front of her. "I couldn't sleep so I went into Mum's craft room to sort it out."

"Granny has lots of treasures in there," Lara said.

"Lots of something," Georgie agreed. "I don't know what to do with it all. Some of her friends might like the knitting gear, but she's got scrapbooking papers, fabrics, clay and ancestry stuff as well."

"You don't want any of it?"

Georgie shook her head. "I've got no room at my place."

Lara twisted her fingers together.

"What about you, Lara? Did you work on projects with Granny?" Amy asked.

The hopeful expression was so sweet. "She was teaching me to knit and to sew."

"In that case, keep whatever you want," Georgie said. "I don't think any of my brothers will want it."

"You should ask Ed," Lara said. "He was doing something in there with Granny the last time he visited."

"Ask Ed what?" he asked as he trundled in.

"Whether you want anything in Mum's craft room."

He paused with the coffee pot in his hand. "She helped me make some curtains for my place." His smile was sad. "But there's nothing in there I want."

"Are you getting rid of all Granny and Grandfather's things?" Lara asked.

"No, La La. We're just figuring out what they have."

According to the will, all the possessions were to be divided between the four children. Had they discussed it? It would mean Darcy would have to find his own furniture and maybe sell some of the farm equipment to pay out his siblings.

"We'll pass on some things though," Ed said. "Most of their clothes can go to another home."

"OK." The young girl seemed satisfied.

After breakfast Amy gathered her keys. "If you don't need me for anything, I'll head into town to get the groceries for tomorrow."

"Great," Georgie said. "We should get the delivery

of chairs this morning, so I need to stay here and tell them where to unload."

"Brandon's picking up a friend at the airport," Ed said. "Let me call them and ask how long they'll be." He went over to the kitchen radio and after a minute Amy had her answer. Ed turned to her. "You happy to wait for Brandon? You can give him a ride."

"Sure." The nerves from this morning came back with a vengeance. Over an hour alone in the car with him. Would they have anything to say to each other? "Is the friend staying here?"

"I guess so."

"I'll go make up a room." Unless the friend was female and would share Brandon's room. She didn't like the twinge of jealousy. When Ed didn't correct her, she headed over to the shearers' quarters. It contained a dozen basic rooms and it took her little time to make the bed in the room next to Brandon's, give it a quick dust and leave a clean towel on the desk. She placed a twig of rosemary in a vase to make the room smell a little fresher. Then she checked that the bathroom was clean before Brandon arrived back on a motorbike. He waved her over. "Give me five minutes to shower and we can go."

"What time is your friend's flight arriving?"

"It's supposed to be ten o'clock."

"I'll check it's on time." Most flights were, but the weather forecast for Perth was stormy, so there might have been a delay.

The website told her the airport baggage handlers were having a go-slow day in protest of working conditions. All flights out of the city had been delayed.

Brandon came into the kitchen five minutes later as promised, hair damp, wearing a T-shirt which clung to his chest and cargo pants which shaped his butt nicely. Her mouth went dry. The evidence of army training was clear in his fitness and muscles and now she'd experienced his softer side, he was far more appealing.

"Ready?" he asked.

She nodded and cleared her throat. "The flight's been delayed half an hour."

He glanced at his watch. "What are you getting in town?"

"Groceries for tomorrow."

"OK. I'll drop you at the supermarket and then go to the airport to pick up Sam. You'll probably be done by the time I come back to get you."

"All right." The name Sam didn't tell her if the friend was male or female, but she wouldn't ask.

She walked with him to the shed where her car was parked. Maggie was lounging underneath Jay and Cheryl's caravan, and Cheryl was reading under her awning.

Amy unlocked the small yellow Hyundai hatchback. If Brandon's friend was as large as him, it might be a squeeze, but the boot space should be big enough for all the groceries. Brandon examined the car and then scanned the shed.

"It's this or Georgie's car," Amy told him.

He sighed. "Maybe I should get a hire car at the airport."

"Up to you." She climbed into the driver's side. A moment later he got in next to her.

His broad shoulders exceeded the size of the seat, making Amy's car feel smaller than normal. Whatever soap he'd used in the shower was musky and manly, and she had to resist inhaling deeply. To get her mind off how attractive the man next to her was, she asked, "Did you find anything this morning?"

"No. Darcy and Matt are checking the other assets, but those closest to the yards haven't been tampered with."

The idea of someone out there making things difficult for the Stokes was creepy. Last night, for the first time since she'd been at the Ridge, she'd wished for a torch as she left the house to go to her room. She'd start leaving the shearers' quarters porch light on in future.

She turned onto the main road. What else could they talk about? Their conversation about Charlie had been interrupted but she wasn't willing to bring it up. The subject seemed too sensitive in the harsh light of day. "Who are you picking up from the airport?"

"Sam Hackett, an army buddy of mine." He tapped his finger on the hard plastic dash. "Though I guess not for long. He's getting out."

He. Amy relaxed. "That must be hard for you." Army teammates were like brothers.

He nodded. "Yeah. Said it was his time."

"You known each other long?"

"We went through basic training together."

So the bond would be strong. It was nice he was flying in for the funeral to support Brandon. "I look forward to meeting him."

Brandon glanced at her. "He thinks it's time for me to get out too."

Surprised he was telling her, she asked, "What do you think?" Her father would never entertain the idea of leaving the army. She'd once heard her parents arguing about it.

The tapping increased. "I don't know."

"You own an entire station now," she reminded him.

His lips pursed. "Yeah."

He'd encouraged her to talk about Beth and Bill. Perhaps she could repay the favour and listen to his story. "Did you like farming?"

He was silent and then let out a deep breath. "It was

my life."

Like Darcy and Bill. Her heart ached for him. "Did you enjoy it?"

"It was the only thing I ever wanted to do."

And yet he'd isolated himself, cut himself off from his passion because he blamed himself for his brother's death. "How much longer are you in for?"

"A couple of months. I'm due at the same time as Sam."

She wasn't certain how much notice he needed to give the army. "If you had no one to consider but yourself, what would you do?"

Brandon studied her. "That's a simplistic way of looking at things."

"No, it's a way of examining what you truly want. If you didn't have to worry about your loyalty to the army, or letting anyone down, or how your family might feel—what would you do for you?"

He didn't answer.

They passed a truck full of chairs and tables and Amy waved. "They must be going to the Ridge."

"Sam and I can set them up when we get back." He changed the subject. "How are you feeling this morning?"

The disappointment that he wouldn't confide in her was brushed aside as heat warmed her cheeks. "I'm fine."

"I'm sorry we were interrupted last night."

She shrugged. "It doesn't matter."

"Yes, it does. I enjoyed talking with you."

She glanced at him. "I enjoyed it too." She wanted to talk to him about Charlie, but if he wouldn't talk about what he wanted in a career, he would be even less likely to talk about his family. Instead she changed the subject to something neither of them should find difficult. "What do you like to do in your spare time?"

"Mostly I help new recruits or I'm on a mission. Sometimes I read."

She perked up. The cheapest form of entertainment for her was ebooks. "What genre?"

"Thriller and suspense."

"Me too." She grilled him about authors he liked and discovered they had a few in common which got them talking about plots they'd liked or didn't like. In next to no time she was parking in front of the supermarket. She handed him the keys.

"Have you got my mobile number?" Brandon asked.

"No." She withdrew her phone and typed it in. "I'll probably be a while. Lindsay will let me leave the trolley inside if you're not back by the time I have to go to the bakery."

"All right."

They both got out and she stood back as he adjusted the driver's seat. "The central locking button doesn't work on the key, so you'll need to lock it by hand." Not that it needed locking in Retribution Bay. "And reverse is sometimes temperamental so you may have to pump the clutch a couple of times before it goes in."

He smiled. "Got it. I won't be long."

Amy carried her grocery bags into the small independent supermarket, glancing at the community noticeboard by the entrance. No job vacancies. Hopefully she wouldn't need a new job. "Morning, Lindsay." The owner was behind the cash register as always.

"Amy. How are things out at the Ridge?" It was genuine concern rather than morbid curiosity on her face. Maybe news hadn't spread that the car crash wasn't an accident.

"They're as good as can be expected," Amy said. "You know the funeral is tomorrow?"

Lindsay nodded. "I've got one of my backpackers

covering for me. Do you need me to bring out anything?"

"No." She held up the list. "I'm buying what I need now."

"Is there anyone else to help you carry everything?"

"Brandon will be back. He's picking up a friend from the airport." Before she could get stuck in a long conversation she said, "I'd better get to it before he returns." She grabbed a trolley and hurried down the first narrow aisle.

Lindsay got caught serving a customer and Amy breathed a sigh of relief.

Checking her list, she strolled down the aisles adding what she needed. They had no idea how many people would turn up to the funeral so she erred on the side of caution and got plenty of everything. They could freeze what wasn't used.

In the final aisle she almost bumped into Taylor. The ex-station hand's clothes were a little grubby and he had that hadn't washed in a few days look and smell about him, the fish tattoo on his lower arm kind of grimy. Typical. She'd taken to throwing his clothes in with hers when she washed to make life more pleasant at the dinner table. "Hi, Taylor."

Taylor grinned at her and pulled her into a hug. "Ames, how's it going? I was going to call you. Do you still have the photo you took of me with that Spanish mackerel? I must have deleted it and wanted to prove to a friend how big it was." He glanced at her trolley. "Stocking up for something?"

She extricated herself, bemused by his rapid questions, but then the last question sunk in. Her mouth dropped open. "Haven't you heard?" Surely someone had told him.

He frowned. "Heard what? I've been fishing for the past week, just got back into town." He held up a filleting knife. "Lost my best knife so need a new one."

Crap. "I've got bad news." There was no way to say it gently. "Bill and Beth died in a car accident on Sunday morning."

Taylor's face blanched as his eyes widened. "Fuck. What happened?"

"The car rolled at Hangman's Bend."

His hand shook. "They were in the ute?"

"No, the four-wheel drive." She gestured to her trolley. "Their funeral is tomorrow at nine at the Ridge. I'm buying supplies."

He stared past her and then shook himself and blinked. "How are Darce and Georgie?"

"They're coping."

He nodded. "I'll bet. Ah, I've got to go. I'll see you tomorrow. Nine o'clock, right?"

"Yes."

He hurried out of the supermarket. Amy debated following him to make sure he was all right. Taylor had worked for Bill for over a year before he'd been fired, and they'd been friendly, though Bill had never approved of his gambling. She left her trolley and hurried to the entrance, but Taylor was gone. She texted him a message to call her if he needed to chat. Taylor had friends in town, but Amy wasn't sure how close they were.

Then she returned to the trolley and finished her shopping. She'd tell Darcy Taylor was planning to be at the funeral, in case there were hard feelings between them.

She paid for the groceries, packing them into her insulated bags and then left the trolley inside the door and walked across the mall to the bakery. Ed had placed the order the day before to ensure there was enough bread for them. The large box waiting for her would be a real squeeze to get into her car. She checked the time.

"I'll be back to pick them up," she told the server and headed outside.

The two men walking towards her drew her eye with their presence. Brandon's friend was slightly taller, with strawberry blond hair, and they both walked with a lethal grace, alert to everything around them. Brandon spotted her and smiled. "Finished?"

"Yeah, but I need two pack horses to help me carry it all."

He grinned. "I don't neigh, but I'll do in a pinch." He gestured to his friend. "This is Sam." To Sam he said, "Amy works at the Ridge."

Sam's smile was a little wicked. "Nice to meet you. What do you need?"

She stepped back into the bakery and directed him to take the box of bread. Then she fetched the trolley from where she'd left it in the supermarket. When Brandon saw it he said, "We should have brought the ute."

"It'll fit." She hoped.

It took a bit of creative thinking, but soon the car was full, and she squeezed in the back seat with Sam's bag and some of the bread. Her little car had never been so overloaded. Brandon drove slowly out of town. "You have any problems?"

"No, not really."

His eyes met hers in the rear-view mirror. "Explain."

"I ran into Taylor, the station hand Bill fired last month. He's been fishing all week and hadn't heard about your parents. He was pretty shaken."

Brandon pulled over. "He's in town?"

"Yeah, I saw him in the supermarket. He said he's coming to the funeral."

He dragged his phone out of his pocket and dialled a number. "Dot, Amy just ran into Taylor in town at the supermarket." He was silent a moment. "He's going to the funeral." Brandon stared out the window and then said, "Thanks," and dropped the phone in the front console of her car.

"Why'd you call Dot?" Amy asked.

"She hasn't been able to catch up with Taylor." He pulled back onto the road. "He's got a potential motive for tampering with the car."

She shook her head. "You should have seen him. He went as pale as a ghost when he found out."

"Guilty conscience?" Sam suggested.

She wanted to disagree, but didn't have the energy for an argument. Taylor had liked Bill and Beth. He wouldn't do anything so callous.

"Dot can ask him," Brandon said. "Did you catch where he's staying?"

"He didn't mention it. Darcy can probably get you his friends' numbers. He used to go to regular poker nights. He might even be staying in one of the caravan parks." There were enough of them. Retribution Bay was a popular tourist destination in winter with those living in the south escaping the cold.

"Dot's going to call me back," Brandon said.

Amy stared at the bush passing by. It was far easier to believe some faceless company had tampered with the brakes than to consider it could have been someone she knew. She sighed.

"You OK?" Brandon asked.

It sent a rush of warmth that he was attuned to her feelings. "I will be." She shifted to look at Sam. "How was your flight?"

"Uneventful. I had a woman next to me bitch about the delay for the first half an hour, but she finally shut up." He smirked.

"What did you say to her?" Amy asked.

"What makes you think I said anything?" He was innocence personified.

"You seem pleased with yourself."

"That's his general demeanour," Brandon joked and chuckled.

The sound heartened her. She had seen little humour from him, not that the circumstances called for fun, but it was nice to see the spark of humour.

"Lay off," Sam said. "I merely mentioned there were ways of making sure the baggage handlers did their job." He cracked his knuckles and the sound made Amy cringe.

She laughed. "So you terrified the woman into silence?"

"Hey, it wasn't just her who'd been affected, but the rest of us weren't complaining."

She liked his style, but it wasn't one she could pull off. When someone was annoying, she tried to focus their attention elsewhere. Like themselves. That usually worked. People loved to talk about themselves.

"You never told me Retribution Bay was such a pretty town," Sam said to Brandon.

"You never asked."

"This your first time up north, Sam?"

"We've done training around the place, but my folks live over east, so I visit them when I've got leave."

They chatted about what he was going to do when he left the army as they drove back to the Ridge. Brandon pulled up outside the kitchen door and they all unpacked the car. "I've given you the room next to Brandon," she told Sam.

"I'll show him to it," Brandon said. "Do you need a hand with the food?"

"Maybe. Ed was going to help. I'll see if I can find him."

"We'll be back shortly." His smile and the promise raised her spirits.

Amy nodded and went to find the others.

Chapter 10

Brandon tugged on the collar of his military dress uniform and stared at the man in the mirror. This was who he'd been for the past dozen years. He'd never felt comfortable in the dress uniform, but today it felt completely at odds with who he was. He glanced at the Akubra hat sitting on the bedside table. Was that his true identity?

He exhaled. He hoped Darcy wouldn't see his dress uniform as an affront, a reminder of Brandon abandoning them. It was the best way he knew of showing the proper respect to his parents, and Dobby had given him approval to wear it. He needed to believe the past twelve years weren't for nothing.

There was a knock on the door and Sam called, "You ready?"

No. He wanted the day to be over already.

He gave his collar a last tug before he opened the door. Sam was similarly dressed in khaki, his expression sympathetic. "Let's go."

They'd cleared out the machinery shed the day before and the chairs were set up in neat rows inside. They'd set up the television at the front so they could play a slideshow of photographs during the ceremony. Already cars lined the driveway and he joined his siblings greeting people as they arrived.

Amy was nowhere to be seen. "Can you see if Amy needs a hand in the kitchen?" he asked Sam. Everything was ready, but perhaps she was checking the urn was on or something.

He'd barely seen her yesterday after they'd arrived back from town as she'd spent all afternoon baking with Ed. He was glad they'd cleared the air during their drive into town. She was so easy to talk to, made him say things he hadn't been planning on saying. But it felt good to confide in someone.

The celebrant walked over to them. "It's time."

He swallowed hard. Was he ready to say goodbye to his parents?

"Give us five," Georgie said and gestured them inside the house. Sam was wiping over the bench, but Amy wasn't there. Sam smiled. "Ready?"

Brandon nodded. Lara clung to Darcy's hand, but she smiled back while Georgie sculled a glass of water, her skin a little pale.

"You OK?" Brandon asked.

She nodded. "Do you have pockets in that thing?"

"Yeah."

She shoved a whole packet of tissues at him. "You can be the dispenser then." She took two and then a third and stuffed them under her bra strap. The modest black shirt she wore hid them. "Is everyone here?"

"Take a look and tell me." The crowd milled around outside, and he recognised several people from his childhood. His heart swelled to see such love for his parents.

"I'll stay at the back," Sam murmured to him. "Keep an eye on everyone."

"Thanks."

Only Darcy knew what the man from Stonefish looked like, but it was doubtful he would turn up today.

Georgie scanned the crowd. "All the important

people are here." She glanced at the celebrant who was waiting for them on the porch. "I think we're ready."

No. They were missing one person. "Where's Amy?"

"She went to get changed when we did," Georgie said.

Then where was she? "I'll check her room." As he walked across the yard, he searched the crowd in case he'd missed her. No blonde woman with curly hair anywhere. He knocked on her door, his pulse a little fast. The door swung open and he stepped back.

Wow.

Until now, Amy had tied her hair back in a ponytail and dressed only in shorts and a polo shirt with the Retribution Ridge logo on it. Now she wore a black retro-style mini dress which ended just above her knees and clung to the curves he hadn't realised she had. She'd tamed her hair so the frizz was more like curls and it hung just below her shoulders.

She tugged at the bottom of her dress. "Is it all right? It's the only black thing I own. I don't remember it being so short."

"You look beautiful." Her eyes widened and he cursed himself. Probably not the most appropriate thing to say at a funeral. "Are you ready?"

"Yes."

He gestured for her to precede him. They joined the others and together they walked with the celebrant over to the shed. The crowd followed. Beside him Amy hesitated. They'd reserved seats at the front for the family. He held her hand and pulled her with him. "Come sit with us."

Her eyes shone and she pressed her lips together, nodding.

He sat at the end of the row next to Amy and the celebrant moved to the lectern to begin. Brandon let out a slow breath and Amy squeezed his hand. Her support gave him strength.

Brandon barely heard the words the celebrant said. He stared at the slideshow, the images all at once making what he was doing here real. His parents were dead.

His throat closed over, and his hand shook as he attempted to get a grip. Amy slid her other hand across his knee and he clenched the hand he still held, grounding himself in her. The shaking eased and he could breathe a little easier.

Darcy stood and strode to the front, placing a couple of sheets of paper on the lectern. He cleared his throat and looked at the attendees, tears already in his eyes. The sight of his brother upset only made things worse and Brandon gritted his teeth. He would not break down.

"Thank you—" Darcy's voice broke. He cleared his throat again and gripped the sides of the lectern as if it was a lifeline. "Thank you for coming. Mum and Dad would have been thrilled to see you all here, and I'm sure they're sad about missing their own party." His voice wavered. Lara ran to her dad, slipping her hand in his. Darcy's smile was tremulous as he continued. "They always did like a good party. Were always the first to invite people to stay for a meal." He bowed his head, squeezing his eyes closed.

Brandon shifted, wanting to go to his brother, but before he could stand, Georgie joined Darcy, sliding her hand around his waist. He leaned into her as she continued the speech they had prepared. "Dad loved this land and knew from an early age that he would never leave it. It would take a strong woman to join him here in such harsh country." She dabbed at her eyes and blew out a long breath, but she was struggling to control the tears.

Ed rushed to her side and she handed him the sheet of paper. "But Mum was the perfect match, strong and kind, ready for any challenge thrown at her. And she had to be, raising five children out here, often alone."

Brandon's heart clenched. Only four of them left now.

"We lost Charlie too young…" Ed faltered.

Shit. He couldn't stay seated, not when his family needed him. Brandon let go of Amy's hand and strode out to be with his family. He placed a hand on Ed's shoulder and scanned the speech on the lectern for where they were up to. "We once asked Mum what she saw in Dad, in this place and she smiled and said she'd seen her future." He blinked back the tears and Amy caught his eye. She smiled at him, dabbing her own eyes which were streaming with tears.

Before Brandon could continue, Darcy read the next line and together the four of them finished the rest of their speech. He handed the tissues out but kept a couple for himself. When he returned to his seat, he passed a tissue to Amy and wrapped his arm around her waist, wanting to comfort her the way she had comforted him. She leaned into him and her touch soothed his aching heart.

The next person to speak was one of his mother's friends but he zoned out, focusing on the woman by his side. Amy had only known his parents for a few months and her quiet sobs broke his heart.

It said a lot about who his parents were that she would feel so bereft at their loss after so little time. He should have trusted them, shouldn't have stayed away for so long. He'd lost his chance to make amends.

But he had a chance to make it up to his siblings. And he wouldn't let them down again.

The funeral ended and Amy dried her eyes and stood. "I'll go check the urn and the food." She hurried off and he hated that she felt she needed to be working at a time like this. He moved to follow her but Darcy grabbed him. "Taylor's here."

"Where?" He needed to get to the bottom of why the man had been fired.

"He's speaking with Matt and Matt's parents."

Brandon scanned the crowd and saw the group talking with a ropey man in his thirties who wore a white, short-sleeved buttoned shirt and black pants. The man was tanned from the sun and he kept glancing around as if he wanted to get out of there. Could he have been the man on the motorbike? It was too hard to tell. Many of the men here matched the description. "Let's go."

He found Sam and gestured for him to follow them. They would get answers.

Taylor's eyes widened when he spotted the three of them advancing on him, but he couldn't extricate himself from the group quickly enough. Brandon nodded to Matt's parents. "Good to see you."

Matt's mother smiled. "We're sorry it's in these circumstances."

"Amy and Ed have made a big spread over in the garden," Darcy said. "Why don't you grab a bite?"

They nodded and left. Matt stayed behind.

"Darcy, I'm so sorry," Taylor said in a hurry. "Amy told me yesterday. I've been fishing over the past week and only just got back to town." The instant grovelling spoke of fear and guilt.

"Whereabouts?"

Taylor hesitated. "Around the gulf near Onslow. Trying to get away from all the tourists in town."

A good excuse. Many of the locals avoided the popular camping spots at the height of the tourist season.

"I wanted to chat to you about something," Darcy

said. "We found documents that Dad bought cattle a couple of months ago. They were supposed to be delivered this month. Did he mention it to you?"

Taylor looked away. "Not that I can recall. Why would he be buying cattle? We're a sheep station."

"Might have been diversifying," Brandon said.

"Nah. Not Bill. He was a traditionalist through and through."

"He ever mention a company trying to buy the station?" Darcy asked.

A slight hesitation. "No. Everyone knew Bill would never sell."

Sam shifted closer, folded his arms in his patented intimidation stance. "They ever approach you?"

"No." Taylor looked him up and down. "Who are you?"

"Sam's a friend of Brandon's," Darcy said.

Brandon studied the man. Something didn't quite sit right with him. "You ever notice strangers around the place?"

He shrugged. "Only the campground guests. What's this about?"

Dot joined them. "Hey, Taylor. Can I have a word with you?" She raised her eyebrows at Brandon and Darcy and they both stepped back from Taylor.

"Yeah." Taylor walked away with her, glancing over his shoulder as he did.

"He's not telling you something," Sam said.

Brandon nodded.

"I don't like it." Darcy rubbed the back of his neck. "Taylor had been working with us for over a year."

"What's his background?" Sam asked.

"He came from another station a bit further east," Matt said.

They turned back to the gathering. "Any issues there?"

"Dad didn't mention anything, and he checked the references."

Maybe Brandon would have another word with Taylor after the funeral. See if he was willing to admit to something in private.

Amy caught his attention, carrying a tray of food, serving the guests. She didn't need to do that. Not on her own. "Let's discuss it later," he said. "Amy needs help." Ignoring Sam's smirk, he went to her.

***

People didn't know when to leave. Amy had been making small talk and handing around plates of food for hours and still they stayed, chatting about Beth and Bill. Her eyes stung from blinking back tears and her cheeks hurt from offering sympathetic smiles. She wanted to hide away and get some air, but her role was guest liaison and she figured this was exactly what she'd been hired to do. She would take as much work away from the Stokes family as she could.

Her eyes closed and her chest ached as she remembered the way they'd all stood up one by one to support each other. She craved to be part of something like that. But it wasn't likely. Yesterday she'd overheard Ed and Georgie talking and from the sounds of it, the station was almost bankrupt. They might not be able to afford to keep her. She'd have to move on. Again.

The thought added more despair to her day. The Ridge was home. She was used to the never-ending days of sun, the dry heat and even the red dust. The landscape was harsher but with it came a freedom to be exactly who she wanted to be. Even if one of the other stations in the area was hiring, it wouldn't be the same.

"Need a hand?" Brandon's voice tickled her senses. If she was honest with herself, he was another reason she didn't want to leave. Which was ridiculous. She'd vowed never to get involved with a military man and she could feel herself sliding from admiration into genuine attraction. She felt even more drawn to him when he'd included her in the front row of the ceremony and when he'd slipped his arm around her waist to comfort her.

Amy handed him the plate of mini sandwiches she was holding. "Have at it. I'll check our supplies."

The military dress reminded her of her vow, but Brandon looked so good in it, it helped to shift the bad memories. She hurried across the yard to the house.

In the kitchen, Lindsay and Cheryl were doing dishes and Amy plated up the last lot of finger food she and Ed had prepared. Maybe with no more food coming out people would leave. No, that wasn't fair. No one was here for the food. They would stay to catch up and commiserate, to unify the community in their sorrow.

Lee walked in from the interior corridor and winced when he saw Amy. "Sorry, I was busting for the toilet and the others were full."

She smiled at him, though she didn't like the idea of people wandering through the house. "It's fine. Thank you for coming."

"Bill and Beth were nice," he said. "I took a couple of photos of the funeral." He shrugged. "I wasn't sure whether the family would want them, but just in case..."

"Why don't you email them to me and I'll see they get them?"

"Sure. I'll see you later."

Lee left and Lindsay turned from the sink. "Strange man. Who takes photos of a funeral?"

"He's a keen photographer," Amy said. "I guess it's his way to capture everything."

She'd have to ask whether Dot had questioned him. He'd been all over the farm so perhaps he'd seen something or taken photos which might be useful.

She carried the tray outside and scanned the remaining people for Dot, but the sergeant had already left. Sam leaned against a tree at the edge of the garden with his phone out, but he rarely glanced at it. He was watching the crowd. Alert. Lara clung like a shadow to Darcy although there were a few other children in attendance. Darcy's shoulders slumped like they did when he'd put a long day in on the station. In fact all the Stokes children looked exhausted.

Brandon stood almost impossibly straight, overcompensating for his fatigue, Georgie's light laugh was a little shrill as she spoke with Beth's knitting group and Ed appeared as if he would like to be anywhere but where he was, talking with some of his father's friends. A small group caught her attention and she wandered over. Jimmy owned the tour boat Georgie worked on and he was there with some of his crew. She offered him some food.

"Thanks, Amy. How are you holding up?"

The tears were close to the surface today. "I'm coping."

"We'll all pitch in if you need a hand."

"There is something you can do," she said, hoping she was picking the right people. "Can you encourage people to leave?"

He raised an eyebrow and the women he was with smiled.

"Georgie and the others are exhausted," she explained. "They're too polite to ask anyone to go, but I can tell they need some quiet."

Jimmy watched Georgie. "You're right." He looked at the others. "Who wants which group?"

Amy left them to decide and carried the plate of food to the next group. When people asked how she was, she said it had been a long morning, and she was looking forward to some quiet.

Some people got the hint and began talking about making a move. Others needed Jimmy's groups' encouragement and Amy stacking the chairs ready for them to be picked up later, but within the hour they waved away the last of the guests.

Cheryl and Lindsay had done most of the dishes and Amy finished the last few as the siblings, Matt, Sam and Lara walked in. Ed sat at the table with a groan. "Anyone want tea?"

"No!" Georgie and Darcy chimed. "I think the past week has put me off tea for life," Georgie declared.

"Is it too early for beer?" Ed asked.

"How about Dad's whiskey?" Brandon suggested.

"We all deserve a shot," Darcy agreed. He left the room and a few minutes later returned with a whiskey bottle. Georgie got out the smaller glasses and Darcy poured.

"What about me?" Lara asked.

"You can have a can of soft drink," Darcy said.

She perked up and got it out of the fridge. When she returned, Darcy pulled her onto his lap. "How are you going, pumpkin?"

She buried her head into his neck. "OK."

"Is there anything you want to do this afternoon?"

She peeked out at the others. "Would Granny and Grandfather be upset if we went for a swim?"

The day had definitely been heating up.

The others smiled. "A swim sounds wonderful," Georgie declared.

"I should check the sheep," Matt said.

"They were fine this morning," Darcy answered. "We could all do with something relaxing after the week we've had."

"You should come, Matt," Georgie said, placing a hand on his shoulder.

"All right."

Everyone went to get ready. Amy stayed. Perhaps she could put together a picnic for them. She hadn't seen them eat much at the funeral.

"You joining us?" Brandon's voice made her turn. He stood at the outside door.

"Someone should stay here, monitor things."

"No one's going to visit this afternoon. They were at the funeral."

"What about Stonefish?"

His eyes narrowed. "They wouldn't dare today. Besides even if they did, you shouldn't be here alone." He glanced over her shoulder. "We'll lock the doors, and the camp guests will be around."

The idea of floating in the clear blue bay sounded luxurious. "I don't want to intrude."

"You wouldn't be. Without you, today would have been a lot harder for all of us."

"I was going to pack a picnic for you to take."

"We can do that together when we're all ready." He moved inside and tugged her hand. "Come on."

She ignored the thrill that went through her. "All right." He kept her hand in his as they walked over to the shearers' quarters.

She wasn't sure what was happening between them, but today she wouldn't question it.

She needed it too much.

Chapter 11

Brandon waited on the shearers' quarters porch for Sam and Amy. Across at the house Lara came out carrying a beach bag which was about the size of her and probably full of beach towels. She slung it into the back of the ute and went back inside. She was a real trouper and he wanted to get to know her better. Wanted to be a proper uncle to her, someone she could turn to if she needed help, like she did with Ed and Georgie. Though Ed and Georgie had still been in high school when Lara was born so it made sense they were close.

Sam joined him on the porch and spoke in a low tone. "You work fast."

Brandon frowned at him. "What?"

"You and Amy."

Crap. He tapped his leg. "It's nothing."

His friend grinned. "Didn't look like nothing to me during the ceremony."

He said nothing. It wasn't something he was willing to assess yet. All he knew was he was drawn to her. "I told you you should get out of the army. This is one reason." He gestured to the yard and sheds. "And she's another."

Not if they couldn't afford to keep her. He and Darcy had crunched numbers all day on Tuesday and they weren't certain how they could continue paying her.

Matt walked out, grinned at them and then moved over to the house. Georgie carried a beach shelter out and he helped her lift it into the tray. With the four-wheel drive destroyed, the only way for them all to get to the beach was in Darcy's dual cab ute.

"It's a little more complicated."

Sam grunted as if he disagreed. "Your family is nice."

Brandon nodded and Amy came out of her room wearing a white tank top and little shorts which barely covered her butt, exposing her long, luscious legs which seemed to go for miles. He definitely hadn't been paying enough attention to her. She tucked a loose hair behind her ear and slung her towel over her shoulder. "Are we ready to go?"

"Looks like," Brandon said. Ed placed an esky in the ute's tray which would be full of drinks and food.

It was decided that Matt, Ed and Amy would go with Darcy and Lara in the front, and the rest would ride in the tray. Bennet jumped in the back with them. It was a good half an hour's drive across a bumpy track on the property to reach the ocean which bordered their land. As Darcy drove over the final low hill, Brandon inhaled sharply. The ocean sparkled, a crisp pale blue that was so clear and pure it almost hurt his eyes. The rich red dirt blended with the white sand and the contrast between the colours was magical. This was where he belonged.

The feeling was so deep, so primal, he placed a palm against his chest.

"Had you forgotten how spectacular it is?" Georgie grinned. Darcy pulled the ute to a stop and she jumped out with the bag of towels before Brandon answered and ran towards the ocean, Bennet right next to her.

Sam clapped him on the back. "You all right mate?"

Brandon nodded. "I'll be there in a minute."

Georgie had already dropped her towel and stripped down to her bathers, urging Lara and Amy to hurry. His brothers were a little slower, but not by much. Across the bay lay Retribution Island and surrounding it was a reef which was seen only at the lowest of tides. His eyes were drawn to the left of the beach where a monument stood marking the place where the survivors of the shipwreck arrived after the cyclone. Where his ancestors had landed and made this their home.

Georgie was right. He had forgotten how spectacular the bay was, how the land called to him. And if his father's will was to be believed, this was all his now.

Not that he would take it from his siblings. This land was as much part of them as it was of him.

He wandered over to the plaque on which someone had engraved the names of those who had been on the ship, both those who died and those who survived. He traced his great, great, great grandfather Reginald Stokes' name, written next to his wife Lilian. They had started this, this connection to the land.

He turned to face the ocean. The mangroves rose out of the water close by, their green leaves adding another colour to the landscape. He used to snorkel around there looking for fish when he'd been a kid. Offshore, the island caught his attention, with its green shrubbery. It looked so close from here, but Brandon knew from experience it wasn't. Charlie once bet him he couldn't swim out to it and since winning the bet meant Charlie would do all his chores for a month, Brandon had taken it. About halfway out he'd admitted to himself that this was a really stupid idea. But he figured if his ancestors had managed it, then he could too.

A couple of turtles had swum by him as if wondering what was this strange creature splashing through the water. He'd even seen a dugong in the clear water below him. Then he'd seen his first shark. It was only a reef shark, but it reminded him tiger sharks also roamed this water. By that stage he was closer to the island than the mainland so he pushed on.

When the coral appeared, he had almost cried in relief. And finally he could stand again and staggered onto the shore.

He smiled as he remembered how the exhilaration of winning the bet was replaced by the realisation he had to swim all the way back. Across the water he'd seen Charlie and Darcy ride away on their motorbikes and he'd cursed both his brothers' names.

He'd sat down to get his breath back, waiting for someone to reappear but as the sun sank lower in the sky he'd worried. So, he explored the island, which took less than an hour, and found a couple of caves in the limestone to spend the night. He could be just like his ancestors, seeking protection from the elements. He'd gathered together some wood and tried to remember what he'd been taught about how to light a fire from scratch.

Just as he was reconciling himself to a lonely night on the deserted island, he'd heard a boat engine. He'd raced back to the shore to find his father and Charlie in the dinghy, coming for him. Elation swept away any concern and even his father's berating hadn't dampened his joy he was saved. His father had been there for him.

Like he always had been.

And now he was gone. The tightness in Brandon's chest made it difficult to breathe and he stared out at the island until the pressure eased. The bushes were a little bigger than he remembered. When he was sure his emotions were under control, Brandon returned to where the others had left their things. They were all in the water, his family splashing and playing, and Amy and Sam floating nearby chatting. The pull of jealousy was unwelcome. Sam didn't know anyone here and Brandon should be pleased Amy was talking to him. Still he quickly stripped off his shirt and joined them in the water. Both Sam and Amy looked at him with levels of concern. "I'm fine."

"Never doubted it," Sam said, and Amy smiled at him.

Below the surface of the water, she wore a simple black bikini and he wished he hadn't been so distracted when he'd first arrived so he could have seen it above the water.

"What's the island?" Sam asked.

"Retribution Island. No one lives there."

"So what's with all the Retribution names? Someone all fire and brimstone name the places?"

"Everything is named after the ship which brought people here," Brandon told him. "It wrecked off the island during a cyclone."

"An auspicious start."

He'd never thought of it that way. The stories his father had told him had been filled with hardship and dedication, the motto to work hard to fulfil your dreams.

Next to them, Lara begged to play Marco Polo. He hadn't played the game since he was a kid.

Georgie was the first to agree. "Come on, you three. Join us. The more the better."

"I'm in," Sam called and slapped Brandon on the back. "Come on."

Brandon wanted to be part of something normal like this, something which made him feel closer to his family. He needed it after today. He waded forward but when Amy hung back, he held out a hand to her. "You playing?"

"All right." She slipped her hand into his and joined the group.

Georgie set out the boundaries of the playing area from the mangroves on one side and the road on the other, so they didn't spread out too far and declared if a person was waist deep it counted as being a fish out of water. She went first, closing her eyes, and soon the air was filled with cries of Marco and echoes of Polo.

He smiled as Lara swam closer to Georgie and almost danced in her excitement at the game. She reminded him of Charlie who always pushed the edge of how close he could get without being caught.

The ache wasn't quite so painful this time.

He was so busy watching the others he hadn't processed Georgie getting closer to him. She was almost within touching distance when he realised and at his next 'Polo' call, she lunged and tagged him. With a grin she opened her eyes.

"I thought the army would have taught you to evade better than that."

He rolled his eyes and then scanned to see where everyone was before he closed them. As he called his Marco, he moved towards Amy. She was the only one he wanted to get his hands on. He could distinguish her call from the others and though she didn't stay still, he followed her easily enough. Frantic splashing told him he was getting closer and he lunged, his hand brushing soft, cool skin and he opened his eyes. "Got you."

She was eye to eye with him and her lips parted, water running down her breasts. Time stopped. He hadn't considered what he would do after he caught her. He tugged her closer and she pressed up against him, her breasts firm against his chest.

"Let her go, Uncle Brandon. It's her turn to be it," Lara called.

Amy blinked and pushed him away, her face flushing red as she glanced around. The others watched them with amused expressions.

Amy started calling and moved away from him. Sam sidled up. "She's worth coming home to."

Brandon glared at him.

Sam held up his hands. "I'm just saying. You've got a beautiful home here, mate. I might even consider moving up."

He glanced at his friend, but he seemed serious. "What about Izzy?"

"I'm not planning to move in with her indefinitely. Only until she gets a handle on being a single mum."

"What would you do?"

"There are a lot of outdoor tourist things. Maybe I'll chat to your cute little sister about work."

Shock filled him. "Georgie?"

"Come on, mate. I know she's your sister, but you've got to realise how hot she is."

He shook his head. "I don't want to know." Though Georgie could do far worse than Sam. He was a good man.

His sister swam over as if she knew they were talking about her. "Are you two playing or what?"

"I'll play any game you like." Sam winked at her and Georgie raised her eyebrows and grinned back at him.

"Come on then, soldier. Show me what you've got."

Brandon hadn't spent nearly enough time with his sister. It was hard to reconcile the cute kid with a ponytail with this blue-haired woman in front of him flirting with his best friend. He'd been gone too long. Even when she'd been at university in Perth, he'd barely made the time to see her, past helping her settle in and then the occasional visit when he was in town.

He glanced at the game. Matt watched Georgie and Sam with a scowl on his face and didn't notice Amy getting closer until she tagged him.

And so the game continued until Darcy called a halt and said they had to be getting back to the station.

Brandon waded out of the water with his family and déjà vu hit him of so many other times when the family had been to the beach together. Then, their father had called a halt to the games and told them it was time to go.

That wouldn't happen again.

With a sigh, he dried himself and took the snack Ed handed him from the esky. He was the last to climb in the ute before they headed home.

***

The machinery was still out in the yard when they returned, but Amy had already stacked the tables and chairs ready for collection. Brandon closed his eyes as the now familiar feeling of loss enveloped him. His parents were gone. He would have to get used to this feeling, the reminders which hit him when he wasn't expecting it. He followed the others into the kitchen and Amy filled the kettle.

Lara retrieved some biscuits from the pantry and placed them in the middle of the table. The swim had returned everyone's appetite. Darcy wandered out of the kitchen and as Brandon reached for a biscuit, Darcy yelled, "What the fuck?"

Not good. Brandon strode down the corridor to where his brother stood outside his father's study. The place was a mess. Drawers had been emptied, the bookshelf contents were now on the floor and the safe door was open.

Shit.

Darcy already had his phone out and was calling

Dot. The others crowded behind Brandon.

"Daddy, what happened?"

Darcy was still on the phone so Brandon turned to his niece. "It looks like someone had a look around Grandfather's office."

"Why would anyone do that?"

A good question. "I'm sure we'll find out."

"Lara, why don't you help me with the drinks while they tidy up?" Amy called. Quick thinking.

A deep frown on her face, Lara followed Amy back to the kitchen.

When Lara was out of earshot he asked, "Anyone come in here before we left for the beach?" There'd been plenty of opportunity for people to be in the house during the funeral.

"Darcy got the whiskey," Ed said.

Did that mean someone had been watching the farmhouse, waiting for them to leave? Amy had been right to be concerned. It took balls to do this on the day of the funeral—or cold-hearted malice. "We should ask the guests if they saw anyone."

Sam nodded. "I'll take over preparing the drinks and get Amy to check."

Darcy hung up. "Dot said she'll be out as soon as she can, and not to touch anything. Have any of the other rooms been searched?"

They went room by room. His parents' bedroom was the worst hit with clothes and items everywhere. Even the mattress was on the floor. The craft room was similarly a mess, but Darcy and Lara's was a little less turned over, as if the thieves had given up by the time they reached them. What were they searching for?

"I don't want Lara to see this," Darcy said.

"How about I take her out with me?" Matt said. "I can tell her I need to check the water troughs or something."

Darcy nodded.

"I'll go with you," Georgie said. "Maybe we can take the horses. It'll take longer."

Darcy picked up Lara's jodhpurs and a jacket and handed them to Georgie.

Together they headed to the kitchen. Lara was laughing at something Sam said and she glanced over at Brandon with a grin. "Did he really do that?"

Sam winked at Brandon. "He sure did, but he'll never admit to it."

Brandon didn't care what stories he told Lara, as long as she was happy.

"La La, I'm heading out to check the troughs. Want to come for a ride with me?" Matt asked.

Lara's smile faded and she glanced at her dad.

"I'm going too," Georgie said, handing over Lara's clothes. "I'd love you to join us."

"Hey, are you horse riding?" Sam asked. When Georgie nodded, he said, "I've never been on a horse. Is it hard?"

Lara turned to him. "It's easy. I could teach you."

"That would be great," Sam said. "Can I come now, or will I slow you down?"

"We've got four horses, so you can go now," Darcy said. "You'll want to put long pants on though."

"Yes, sir." Sam saluted and headed for the door. "Give me five." He glanced at Lara. "I bet I can get ready faster than you."

She laughed. "You have to go all the way over to your room."

"Yeah, but I'm army trained," Sam said. "We're fast."

Lara grinned. "Go!" She dropped her towel and reached for her jodhpurs as Sam sprinted out the door.

Brandon would thank his friend later. He seemed to know exactly what to say.

While Lara changed with no concern about who was in the room, Georgie and Matt went to dress in appropriate riding gear. Darcy followed Lara out as she finished dressing and Brandon heard her yell, "Beat you!"

"Sam's good value," Ed commented.

"He is," Brandon agreed. With Lara taken care of, they had to figure out who had ransacked the house and what they were looking for. But until Dot arrived to take prints, they couldn't touch anything. "We locked the house, didn't we?"

"I didn't," Ed said.

Darcy swore. "I know you said for us to, but we never do, and I forgot. This isn't Perth."

Which meant whoever it was didn't need to be an expert locksmith. Amy entered the kitchen. "None of the guests are in," she said. "They must have gone into town after the funeral. Probably wanted to give you a bit of space."

So no one was around to see the intruder. It wouldn't have been hard to watch the house and see them all leave. Brandon filled the teapot. At least everyone who went to the beach was off the suspect list. It was a relief to have confirmation even though he'd already taken Amy off the list, and Matt had never been on it.

"Think it might be Stonefish?" Ed asked, nibbling on a biscuit.

"Unless someone from town has a grudge against Mum and Dad." But most of the town had turned out for the funeral.

"I'll get my laptop and see what else I can find on them." Ed left the room and was back a few minutes later empty handed. The outrage on his face said it all.

"They took your laptop?"

He nodded. "They took all the computers."

Which meant they had to have come in a car, not on a motorbike. Amy placed a jug of milk on the table. "They might not have taken mine. Let me check."

She arrived back with her chunky, very ancient looking laptop. She handed it to Ed. "It's not much, but you can access the internet."

Ed shook his head. "Ames, how do you manage with this brick?"

Her cheeks flushed. "We're not all computer geeks like you."

He grinned at her. "When I get home, I'm sending you one of my old laptops. They were all made this decade."

"Not all of us need the latest tech, but thank you."

Brandon would bet she didn't have the extra cash to upgrade regularly. Not if she worked low-paying hospitality jobs. It was nice of his brother to offer. While Ed got to work on the laptop, Brandon asked, "Your room hasn't been touched?"

She shook her head. "I'd guess the others haven't been either if Sam and Matt didn't mention it."

Darcy entered the kitchen, his face a thundercloud. "I don't like this," he stated. "We have to discover who is targeting us quickly. Lara's going back to school next week and I won't have her coming home to an empty house if this is still going on."

"Won't Amy be here?" Ed asked.

Shit. Darcy must have decided. The guilt was written on his face, but it was Amy who spoke.

"You can't keep me on." Her voice was a little flat.

"We can't afford to," Darcy said. "There's no money. Mum and Dad were almost bankrupt."

Brandon wouldn't let his family suffer, couldn't let Amy be left without a job. "I've got money."

Darcy glanced at him. "Enough to get us out of this?"

"Maybe." Probably not, but he didn't want to make big decisions like firing Amy until they sorted out all the details.

"We won't find much with the computers stolen," Ed said.

Darcy swore. "What?"

"They've taken all the laptops," Ed told him.

He grimaced but Amy said, "Didn't Bill do everything in hard copy?"

Darcy grinned. "He did. Didn't trust computers." Then his face fell. "But all the paper is now strewn across his office floor."

"We'll sort it out." Amy hesitated. "If I can still get food and board, I'll stay for a few more weeks to help you. I can sort the paperwork and be here when Lara comes home from school. You don't need to pay me."

She really was something else. He didn't want to take advantage of her, but it would give them enough time to figure out where to go and hopefully find the money to keep her on.

"I can't ask you to do that," Darcy said.

"You didn't. I offered."

Brandon gave his brother a small nod.

Darcy sighed. "That would be amazing, Ames. I'll do everything I can to help you find somewhere else to work."

"Thanks."

And Brandon would do everything he could to enable her to stay.

When Dot arrived sometime later she was with her constable, Colin. Together they went through room by room, photographing and fingerprinting, starting with Lara's room at Darcy's request. When they were done there, Darcy and Amy cleaned the room, setting it back to rights. As the police finished the other rooms,

Brandon closed the doors to hide the mess from Lara. Finally they started on the study as Lara and the others returned from their ride.

Just in time.

Amy had started heating leftovers for dinner when Dot pulled Darcy and Brandon aside. "We've got a couple of prints, but they might be from your parents," she said. "There's not a lot of other evidence. Whoever did this was probably a professional. Can you think what they might have been looking for?"

Brandon shrugged. "There's nothing of real value in the house."

Darcy nodded. "There was some cash in the safe, but I moved it and they didn't find where I hid it."

Ed joined them. "We might be able to find them," he said. "I've got GPS tracking software on my laptop, but it only works when the laptop is turned on." He showed them the screen on Amy's laptop which had a map with a flashing dot.

"Where's that?" Brandon demanded.

"The Bay Caravan Park," Dot told him. "How accurate is the GPS?"

"To within fifty metres."

So it would narrow it down to a dozen sites.

"Can I take the laptop?" Dot asked.

"We'll go with you," Darcy said.

She shook her head. "You won't, and if I catch you at the park, I'll arrest you for trespass. This is police business and we don't know how dangerous these people are."

"Sam and I can go," Brandon said. "We're both trained."

"No."

Ed spoke. "This is Amy's laptop, but I can log you into my account on your phone."

Dot handed it over.

"Dot, do you and Colin want to stay for dinner?" Amy asked.

The sergeant shook her head. "Thanks, but no, I've got to get back to town." Ed handed back the phone and she tucked it in her pocket. "We'll be in touch."

After she and Colin walked out, both Darcy and Brandon turned on Ed. "Why didn't you mention the tracking to us?" Brandon asked.

"It only just switched on." He stared at them both with defiance. "Plus, Dot's right. They're dangerous."

"Sam and I are trained for dangerous situations," Brandon reiterated.

"You don't have any equipment or backup," Ed said. "It's safer for everyone if we leave it to the police."

Through the defiance Brandon saw a glimmer of fear on his brother's face and his annoyance faded. "All right." He and Sam could sneak out later tonight and go into town if Dot hadn't got back to them. His laptop was still in his room and maybe he could get Ed to log into his software on it.

He sat at the table and pretended he had nothing better to do than eat.

Chapter 12

After Lara had gone to bed, they began the long task of cleaning the mess. Amy was responsible for the campground reception area. She stared at the piles of paper and office equipment on the floor and rubbed her arms. The thought of a stranger going through her stuff, even if it was only work related, was all too creepy. She almost crossed over to the windows to close the curtains and prevent anyone outside looking in but she refused to be cowed. The curtains were never closed in this house.

Instead she crouched down and replaced all the stationery and equipment into the drawers and then straightened out the guest reservation book which had been bent out of shape. She flicked through it to make sure no pages were missing and when she was satisfied, she headed into the lounge. Brandon and Sam had already finished replacing the books and DVDs on the shelves and were standing close together talking in low tones. Sam looked irritated. They eased away as she walked in and Brandon smiled. "Are you done?"

"Yeah." They appeared as if they were plotting something. "What are you up to?"

"We've just finished here."

Perhaps it was none of her business. They were both highly trained military men, but then she remembered the fear on Ed's face. "What are you two planning?"

Brandon walked towards her. "Nothing." He tucked a stray hair behind her ear. "If you're not too tired, why don't you see if Georgie needs a hand?"

His gentle touch caused her heart to race. Sam's smug expression showed he could tell how Brandon affected her. She stepped back. "All right."

As she walked down the corridor, she glanced back. They were chatting again. Maybe they were going to set a guard on the house, though it was a little late now.

Georgie sat on the floor in Beth's craft room surrounded by fabric, wool, ribbons and glitter. She looked up at Amy with tears in her eyes. "Why?"

Amy's heart lurched. She sat and pulled Georgie into her arms. Georgie's sobs bit into Amy's defences and Amy rubbed her back. She'd been a trouper since her parents had died, getting things done and maybe this was the final straw. If Amy could, she'd take all of her pain away.

Someone stopped at the door. Brandon's gaze met hers, full of sorrow and uncertainty. She smiled and he hesitated for a moment, taking a half step inside before shaking his head and moving on. It had to be so difficult for him as well. Never sure how his family would react to him. Amy hoped he'd be more comfortable by the end of his stay.

When Georgie had finished crying and dried her eyes, she took a deep breath. "Lara wants to keep this stuff, but Mum was a hoarder so anything too old or crazy we'll chuck out." She looked at the mess. "It won't be missed."

"Sure." Amy picked up a box marked ribbons and sorted through the mess collecting ribbons of various colours and widths.

It was after midnight before things were tidy enough for Darcy to declare they'd done enough. Amy and

Georgie had stopped being so neat when stuffing things back in their boxes and the craft room looked more or less like it had that morning.

All Amy wanted to do was fall into bed and sleep. She reached the kitchen door and spotted Brandon speaking with Sam over by their quarters. She glanced at the table. "Does anyone know what happened to my laptop?"

Ed spoke. "Brandon said he'd return it to your room."

"Thanks. I'll see you in the morning." She walked back to her room, but there was no laptop on her table and her car keys which normally sat on the table were gone.

They had been there before dinner.

Her irritation gave her a boost of energy and she knocked on Brandon's door. When he opened it, he was shirtless and the sight of his naked chest made all rational thought leave her mind.

"Can I help you?"

She blinked, trying to get her brain to reboot. He'd changed into a black pair of cargo pants and held a black T-shirt in his hand. She focused on his eyes. "Do you have my laptop?"

"No."

"Ed said you'd taken it to my room, but it's not there."

"Ed was mistaken."

She glanced over his shoulder and he shuffled to the side to block her view but not before she noticed her car keys on his table. "Taking up a life of crime now?"

He frowned. "What?"

Matt walked up the steps of the porch, glancing their way. "Night."

She waved. "Night." When he entered his room, she lowered her voice. "Those are my car keys on your table."

He had the grace to look embarrassed. "I was borrowing it."

"Along with my laptop?" she said. "You're going into town to catch the intruder."

He said nothing.

"Ed doesn't want you to," she said.

"I can take care of myself."

She was sure he could, but the more she thought about him going into town, the more she hated the idea. "I'll come with you."

"No." His growl was low but no less full of authority. It reminded her of her father which stiffened her spine.

"Either I come with you, or I call the police and report my stolen car."

He glared at her as if he could change her mind. She crossed her arms and waited.

Sam slipped out of his room dressed in black, her laptop under his arm, and paused when he saw her there. He crept over. "What's going on?" His voice was barely a murmur.

"I'm going with you."

Sam shook his head. "It's no place for you."

An irrational part of her was certain as long as she had eyes on Brandon, he would be safe. "I'm coming, or I'll wake everyone and tell them what you're doing."

Brandon growled. "You've got two minutes to change into something dark and meet us at the shed or we go without you."

Elation and fear for what she was doing filled her. "I'll be there."

She had her shirt stripped off before she even got into her room.

***

Brandon seethed as he hustled over to the shed with Sam. There was no way they'd be able to push Amy's car down the drive far enough from the house to start it before Amy joined them, but he could hope. He didn't have time to waste arguing with her and Matt might hear and investigate.

"I don't like this," Sam said as Brandon unlocked the driver's door.

"Me neither but we don't have a lot of choice." He wasn't waiting around for the police to do their work. Dot had called earlier to say they hadn't been able to locate the laptop but were monitoring things.

He and Sam didn't have to worry so much about protocols.

Together they pushed the car out of the shed and down the drive. Soft steps behind as Amy joined them and helped push.

Damn it.

When they got far enough away, Sam took the front passenger seat, Amy climbed in the back and with Brandon driving, they headed into town. He flicked on the high beams which were pathetically weak and prayed there was no wildlife on the roads tonight.

"What's the plan?" Amy asked.

"Surveillance," Brandon told her. Next to him Sam had already closed his eyes. "Get some sleep if you can."

"Shouldn't I help you stay awake? Keep an eye out for 'roos?"

"No. I don't need help. I'm used to functioning tired."

"But surely it would be easier—"

"No." This wouldn't work if she kept arguing with him. "Sam, tell her how it is."

Sam didn't bother opening his eyes. "We're on a mission. Bran is in charge so we do what he says, when he says it. We should rest when we can, so we can take over when he needs to nap."

Brandon glanced in the rear vision mirror. She had pursed her lips, but then settled back against the back seat. "All right."

Relief filled him as she closed her eyes and he soon heard the rhythmic, steady breathing which indicated she was asleep. The hum of the tyres on the bitumen was the only noise he had for the drive to town and he had plenty of time to envision what he would do to the low-life scum who had hurt his family. Seeing Georgie in tears and the fear on Ed's face made him want to punish someone. Hadn't his family been hurt enough?

He sighed. He admitted to himself that this mission would probably be a bust, but he couldn't do nothing. The GPS app no longer showed the laptop's location which probably meant it had been turned off, but at least they had marked its last known location. Hopefully it would be obvious from the caravan set up as to who they should watch.

Brandon woke them as he drove into town and Sam opened Amy's laptop to the tracking app. "Still nothing."

It didn't matter. They'd get the lie of the land, figure out how many targets they had and then take photos of the number plates of all the cars. Dot had probably already done so but maybe Amy or Darcy would recognise one as a guest they'd had out at the Ridge.

He drove down a side road which ran between the caravan park and the beach. There were no streetlights and he doubted anyone would be out at this time of night. Switching off the car he made one last effort to keep Amy out of trouble. "You should stay in the car."

She had the door open before he finished his sentence and admiration filled him. He reassured himself she should be safe. Most people in the caravan park would be asleep and he doubted they would confront their target.

The caravan park had low pine fences which weren't meant to keep people out, but to demarcate the boundaries. They walked onto the property and over to the trees next to the ablution blocks. Sam checked his phone where he'd plugged in the GPS coordinates and then pointed. "Halfway along that road."

Not many empty sites here. A couple of heavy off-road caravans mixing with more luxurious options with expanding sides, as well as two four-wheel drives which had rooftop tents. He dismissed the sites which had children's bikes stacked against the caravan which left them with four options.

The lighting in the park was annoyingly good, with lit bollards every ten metres to illuminate the way to the toilets. As they stood under a tree on one of the empty sites, an older man came out of one of the caravans they were assessing and wandered along to the toilet without noticing them.

"Do we cross him off?" Sam asked.

Brandon nodded. The man shuffled along like he needed a hip replacement. No way he would have been able to search the farmhouse in the time they'd been away. But maybe the man could help them.

"Stay here."

Amy opened her mouth to protest and he pressed his finger to her lips. The warmth of them set a spark through his body. "I'm in charge," he murmured.

She nodded.

Brandon waited until the man exited the building and then moved out from under the tree, checking his phone and then the number of the site. The older man hesitated when he saw Brandon, so Brandon kept his steps slow as he approached him. "Mate, can you help me? I'm meant to be staying with a friend here, but my car blew a tyre just north of Geraldton and it took almost all day to get it fixed." He rubbed the back of his neck. "My friend said he was in site twenty-three but it's empty. He's not answering his phone and I don't know what rig he's in. I don't want to wake anyone I don't have to."

"Only guy travelling alone is an Asian bloke staying in the site behind mine." The man pointed.

Excitement simmered in Brandon's blood. If Stonefish was registered in Singapore it made sense it would have Asian workers. "Yeah, sounds like him."

"Not very friendly, is he?"

"He's not good with strangers," Brandon said. "Thanks, mate." He waved and walked towards the site the man had pointed out which had a four-wheel drive camper on it. Sam and Amy joined him.

"Good thinking," Sam said.

"Doesn't mean it's the right place, but it's a good bet." But now what? The bed was on top of the car with a ladder to reach it. "You think there's only one person inside?"

"Yeah. Unless Stonefish employees like to get cosy with each other."

"I'm going to look inside the windows." Make sure no one was sleeping in the car.

"We'll wait by the chalet," Sam said, indicating the building across from the camp site which had no car next to it.

Good call. He continued to the four-wheel drive as if it was his camp site. Soft snores came from the bed on the roof so he switched on his phone torch and scanned the interior of the car. A duffel bag, food and what looked like a gun lock box tucked under the seat. Not good. He moved around the other side and saw the edge of a laptop peeking out from under a blanket, the Milky Way skin on the front identifying it as Ed's.

Bingo.

The urge to drag the man from his bed was strong, but stealth would be better. He re-joined the others who were standing in the chalet's shadow. "It's him."

"Should we wake him?" Amy asked.

"No, he'll wake the whole camp." He looked at Sam. "You think it's better to leave him to the police?" Sam had argued against them coming, and now Brandon had seen the gun lock box he wasn't as keen to confront the man. Particularly not with Amy here.

"Police might not get here before he leaves."

So they would monitor him and call Dot if he made a move. Dot had been working hard the past few days and she deserved her sleep. Now he just had to get Amy out of harm's way. "Where's Georgie's place?"

"Across the other side of town, close to the harbour," she answered.

"We'll stay here until morning," he said to her. "I can take you to Georgie's so you can sleep and we'll pick you up when we're done."

She shook her head. "I'm staying with you."

Sam touched his elbow. "Chalet's empty. There'll be beds inside."

And an unobstructed view of their target. If they needed to move on him, Amy could stay inside, maybe she'd even sleep through it. He nodded.

"But that's breaking and entering," Amy whispered.

Her surprise made him smile. "What did you think we would do?"

She said nothing and Sam took a minute to unlock the door and then gestured them inside. Together they checked the rooms but it was empty with a clean, unoccupied vibe.

"I'll take first watch." Sam pulled a chair away from the table and set it up by the window overlooking their target area. Brandon didn't bother arguing. He was shattered and it only required one of them to keep watch. A couple of hours sleep was better than nothing.

"There's a double in the bedroom," he told Amy. "Get some sleep."

"What are you going to do?"

"I'll sleep on the couch." It was tiny but he'd slept in worse places.

She hesitated. "I'll take the other couch."

"Ames, you'll get a far better rest if you sleep on the bed." He moved closer to her, squeezed her hand.

"Will you wake me if you see anything or go anywhere?"

Hell no. He didn't want her anywhere near danger. "Sam and I are trained for these situations. You're not."

She glanced at Sam. "I know you are, but the idea of you at risk…"

His heart filled his ribcage. "I understand, but I feel the same way about you." He watched her for a long moment. Finally she rose on her tiptoes and brushed a kiss against his cheek. "I'll sleep on the other couch."

The kiss abolished his argument, and he was helpless to resist. The warmth of her lips spread heat through the rest of him. "Suit yourself." He stretched out on the couch the best he could and immediately fell asleep.

When Sam woke him, the horizon was lightening. "Anything?"

"Nothing, but I've got to tell you the grey nomads cannot hold their bladders. It was a constant flow of people to the ablution blocks."

"Something for us to look forward to." Brandon stretched and swapped places with Sam. Amy didn't stir.

According to the caravan park website, reception didn't open until eight o'clock so no one would need the chalet before then. He doubted any staff would check the place because it was clean, but as he monitored his target, he worked out a plan in case they were caught there.

As the sun rose, so did people, with a parade going to have their morning shower.

It seemed the only person not awake was whoever slept in the four-wheel drive across from them. Surely with the noise of the park, he would have to be awake. Even Sam stirred behind him. "How'd you go?"

"Waiting for him to emerge. Everyone else has."

"Think we should vacate the premises?"

Brandon could imagine Dot's expression if she was called out because he'd been trespassing. "Yeah. Let's sit on the patio." Was a nearby cafe already open so they could get a couple of coffees and at least pretend they were staying in the chalet? As he stood to wake Amy, the flap of the roof top tent opened. Brandon stopped Sam and whipped out his phone, his heart racing.

The man who climbed down wasn't anyone Brandon recognised. He took a couple of photos as the man trotted to the toilets.

"Search it?" Sam asked.

"Yeah." The man went into the building and Brandon gestured for Sam to move.

He closed the chalet door behind him and strode to the campsite. Sam climbed the ladder into the tent and Brandon checked the doors of the four-wheel drive. It was locked but inside he got a better look at the laptops. He took a few photos.

Now what? The toilet block was close to the edge of the property but not close enough that they wouldn't be seen dragging a resisting man into the bushes. And he wasn't letting the man get away. With a sigh he called Dot, shifting away from the site, while Sam knelt by the driver's side rear tyre and used his key to deflate it.

Good idea.

"You better have a good reason for calling me this early."

"Site twenty-five at Retribution Bay Caravan Park," he said. "Ed's laptop is sitting on the back seat of the four-wheel drive." He read out the number plate and then glanced towards the ablution block. The guy was exiting the building as a scowling Amy strode towards him from the chalet. Shit. "Target," he hissed, and Sam moved, heading away from the site. Brandon hung up. "Morning, honey." He grabbed Amy, and pushed her up against the nearby tree. "Play along," he ordered and covered her lips with his.

He caught her gasp in his mouth and she stiffened for a second before she melted in his arms. This was possibly the worst idea he'd ever had... and the best. Her lips were warm and soft, and tasted like honey. His surroundings faded away and all his focus was on her lips and the way her body pressed against his. Her small moan sent arousal straight to his groin and he struggled to keep his sanity. If the intruder had been spying on the Ridge, he might recognise either of them. They needed to move. But damn, he didn't want to.

He broke the kiss and moved Amy to his side, his arm around her waist. "Keep your head down." He shuffled them in the opposite direction from the man and ducked behind one of the caravan awnings. After a second he peered around the corner. The man was climbing back into his tent. He sighed. They hadn't been spotted.

When Brandon turned back to Amy, she was staring at him, her fingers brushing her lips.

The temptation to take her into his arms again was strong so he stepped further away. "I didn't want him to recognise us."

Disappointment flashed over her face. "Of course."

Hell. He tugged her closer. "But I want to kiss you again."

She leaned forward and her lips met his. The jolt of surprise was quickly followed by joy as he wrapped his arms around her waist and brought her body close to his. His tongue teased her lips and she opened for him, moaning a little as she did so. All of his worries faded away with the taste of her.

"If you two are finished, we should make ourselves scarce." Sam's amused tone was like a cold shower. "You're drawing attention."

Damn it. Brandon moved away and ignored Sam's huge grin. Amy's face was flushed and he slipped his hand into hers, needing to still touch her.

"We going to talk to him?" Sam asked.

He didn't want Amy anywhere near the danger. "I called Dot." And he'd hung up on her. Damn. He called the sergeant back.

"I'm on my way," she said. "If you're there when I arrive, I might arrest you on the spot."

"Gotcha." He hung up. "Dot's coming now." He moved so he could see the four-wheel drive. The guy was lowering the roof on his bed, packing up. Shit. Would he leave before Dot could arrive?

He glanced towards the entrance of the park. It was only a couple of minutes' drive from the police station, but Dot might have to wait for Colin.

Would the man notice the flat tyre?

One of them would have to risk recognition and point it out to him if he didn't. The man tested the latch and wandered around the car, checking everything was in place. He glanced at the tyres and swore.

Brandon let out a breath of relief as the man threw open the back and got a tyre pump out.

Where was Dot?

A car engine hummed, coming closer. Brandon

spotted the white police car crawling towards them. "This way." He took Amy's hand and moved into position in case the guy ran. Sam followed.

The guy hadn't noticed the police car.

Dot and Colin got out. Dot scanned the area and frowned as she spotted Brandon, but walked over to the man. Brandon couldn't hear what she said, but the man flinched, moved to run and Colin stopped him, pressing him up against the car.

Satisfied, Brandon said, "Time to go home." He shared a smile with Amy and kept his hand in hers as they headed back to the car.

Chapter 13

Had that just happened? Amy's brain held the fog of too little sleep combined with unexpected lust and struggled to catch up with what was going on. Brandon had kissed her and it had been supernova hot. Then she'd kissed him like some kind of starved fool, and now they were walking hand in hand back to the car. Like they were a couple. She was too tired to make sense of anything. Brandon was a hell of a kisser.

When she'd left the Ridge, she hadn't realised they would be out all night. Darcy would already be awake and probably out on the station and no one would know where she was. Lara.

She gasped and dropped Brandon's hand, scrambling to get her phone out of her pocket. "I've got to call Darcy. I'm supposed to be home for Lara."

"Georgie will be there."

That was beside the point. She'd promised to be there so Lara wasn't alone and then immediately broken the promise. She dialled the house and Georgie picked up.

"Can you keep an eye on Lara for a couple of hours?" Amy asked.

"Sure. Are you not feeling very well?"

Amy hesitated. "Ah, I'm not at the Ridge."

"What?" Amy winced at the shriek and moved away

from Brandon and Sam. "I'm at the caravan park in town."

Georgie swore. "By yourself?"

"Brandon and Sam are with me."

"I knew I should have kept a closer eye on them. Why are you involved?"

"They needed my car."

"Right. Did you find anything?"

"We saw the guy who broke in." She placed a hand over the phone. "Do you have a photo of the guy to send Georgie?" She assumed he'd taken one while she'd been sleeping. When he nodded, she said to Georgie, "Brandon sent you a picture. Do you recognise him?"

A pause before a quiet curse. "He might have been a customer on the tour boat last week."

Amy put the phone on speaker and told Brandon, then asked Georgie, "Did you speak with him?"

"What day, Georgie?" Brandon asked.

"Give me a second." Another pause. "He was excited about the tour. Kept going on about how he wished his parents could be there too, said he'd have to fly them out next year." Her voice broke. "I told him Mum and Dad were going out tomorrow and I couldn't wait for them to experience it."

Amy exchanged a glance with the men. It meant the people behind this knew Beth and Bill would be heading into town early.

"Oh, God," Georgie said. "Did I give them the information they needed to kill Mum and Dad?"

"No!" Brandon barked. "This isn't your fault, Georgiana. Dot's going to arrest the bastard and we'll get all the answers we need."

She sniffed. "When are you coming back?"

Amy glanced at Brandon. "Soon. We'll get coffee on the way."

"All right." She hung up.

"Lucky coincidence, or was he planted on Georgie's boat to get info?" Sam asked.

"I'd bet he was a plant," Brandon said.

Sam nodded and ran a hand through his hair. "I need coffee. Where's the best place, Amy?"

"Ningaloo Cafe," she responded. "Down at the town beach." She needed a decent dose of caffeine too. Her brain was running on empty.

Brandon handed over her car keys and she drove the short distance to the cafe. It was just opening. She didn't know the waitress, but she smiled and asked, "Any chance for a coffee?"

The woman returned her smile. "Of course. Machine's heated. Come in."

"Let's get take-away," Sam said. "We can walk along the beach and plan."

Less chance of being overheard. Brandon paid for the drinks and a few minutes later they discarded their shoes on the sand and wandered up the beach. The tide was low, exposing some of the rocky reef which rimmed this area of the shore.

Amy inhaled the salty air and it cleared some of the mugginess from her head. Maybe she should splash her face with water to relieve some of the heaviness in her eyes. She took a long sip of the coffee and her body celebrated the caffeine hit.

"We need to figure out if that guy's working with anyone else," Brandon said.

"He has a four-wheel drive which will get him anywhere he needs to go," Sam said. "Easy to get around your property."

"They also used a motorbike," Brandon said.

The sand was cool under Amy's feet. "Dot will get answers." She didn't know the process when someone was arrested. Did they get bail straight away, or were they held until a court date? There wasn't a courtroom in Retribution Bay so perhaps they had to travel to Carnarvon.

"She's not likely to tell us anything," Brandon said.

Sam rubbed the back of his neck. "Think Ed will be able to trace the guy's details?"

Amy looked at Brandon. "What exactly does Ed do?"

Brandon shrugged. "I don't know. Some kind of IT thing."

That didn't help.

"I'm supposed to fly out tomorrow," Sam said. "But I can always ask Dobby for more time."

"Dot has arrested him," Amy said.

The men exchanged a glance.

Realisation struck and her skin crawled. "He's not responsible for everything." She didn't need Brandon's nod to confirm that. There wasn't a motorbike at the caravan site and Stonefish were a big company. Her fatigue slowed her brain, had allowed her foolish hopes that this was all over.

"We're paid to be cautious," Brandon said.

She desperately wanted to put this all behind her, but facing reality was safer. Brandon's phone buzzed with a message and he glanced down at it. "Dot's taken him to the station. Let's get back to the Ridge."

That sounded like a wonderful idea. When she'd rested, she'd help them figure out the next step. They reached her car, she handed Brandon her keys and almost immediately fell asleep in the back seat.

***

Fatigue settled over Brandon as he drove into the Ridge. Across from the house, Lara was racing her horse around three barrels set up in a triangular shape while Darcy watched. "Barrel racing." The words fell from his lips as he watched Lara's technique. She was good. The longing in his chest was immediate, creating a powerful pull towards the yard, but Darcy and Lara were having a father-daughter moment. They might like to keep it that way.

"You ever do that?" Sam asked.

"I was junior champion at the last gymkhana I went to," he admitted.

Sam whistled. "That I've got to see."

Brandon shook his head. "I'm not interrupting them."

He parked and handed the keys back to Amy. "Thanks for the loan." His fingers brushed hers and desire filled him again. It would be impossible to get her out of his system now.

"You're welcome," she said. "You know, Lara has joined the new pony club that's opened in town. There's a gymkhana tomorrow. She could do with some tips."

He glanced over at the pair. "Darcy knows as much as I do."

"But was he junior champion?" Sam asked.

Brandon shrugged off the question and headed into the kitchen only to be faced with a wall of fury. Georgie and Ed stood side by side, arms crossed and unhappy. "What the hell do you three think you were doing?" Georgie demanded.

Next to him, Sam turned his laugh into a cough when Georgie glared at him. "You were supposed to be keeping him out of trouble." Then her gaze fixed on Amy. "And you, you're supposed to be the sensible one."

Beside him Amy shifted.

"It wasn't her fault," Brandon said. "I stole her laptop and car, and she was trying to get them back."

Amy flashed him a smile.

"I asked you not to." Ed's words were softer but

more painful because of the hurt in his eyes.

Shit. "I had to do something. I couldn't risk him getting away."

"And did he?" Georgie demanded.

"No. Dot arrested him this morning."

Both his siblings seemed satisfied by that. "I want to know what happened last night," Georgie said. "But first there's a young girl out there who is incredibly nervous about her first gymkhana. Lara knows Uncle Brandon was a champion and so you're going to march out there and give her some pointers."

"But Darcy's helping her."

"Lara even asked Georgie and me for tips," Ed said. "*That's* how nervous she is."

Ed had never entered a horse-riding competition in his life though he was a competent rider.

Georgie nodded. She pointed at Brandon. "You go to Lara." She pointed at Amy and Sam. "You two get some sleep because you both look exhausted. Then, after lunch, you're going to tell us what went on last night."

Brandon would have almost preferred facing more of Georgie's wrath and Ed's disappointment than going out to the horse yard, but he did what he was told. Before he left, Amy squeezed his hand. "You'll be fine."

Her faith in him dissolved some of his worries.

He flicked at the flies buzzing around his head as he strolled over. Darcy called out instructions to Lara and on his command, she kicked Starlight into a gallop and the horse barrelled around the course. She had good riding technique but wasn't directing Starlight close enough to the barrels. When she finished the course, Darcy called, "Good job, pumpkin."

Lara trotted over to him, spotting Brandon over by the fence. She ducked her head.

Crap. He didn't want his niece to be embarrassed around him. "Nice riding," he called.

Darcy turned and frowned. He gestured for Lara to walk Starlight around to cool her down and walked over to Brandon. "You're back."

Brandon nodded. "Dot arrested the guy this morning."

"You really think you should have taken Amy with you?"

"She didn't give me much choice." The anger in Darcy's tone concerned Brandon. "Is she... special to you?"

Darcy blinked. "Special? She's my employee and a friend, and I don't need you putting her in danger."

Given that he had kissed her and wanted to do it again, he needed more from his brother. "So she's not your girlfriend?"

Surprise washed across Darcy's face and he burst out laughing. "No, she's not." Then he narrowed his eyes. "Why do you ask? You're not sticking around, are you?"

Was he? He didn't know the answer. "Just checking." Behind Darcy, Lara circled her horse. "She rides well."

"Took to it like a duck to water," he said proudly. "She's been riding since before she could walk."

"So why is she so nervous about tomorrow?"

"The pony club has only just reopened. She's never competed against anyone, and all her friends will be there. She desperately wants to impress her instructor, Faith."

He remembered how big deal it felt whenever they had a gymkhana.

"Plus there's a girl in her class who's been trash-talking her." Darcy shook his head. "I'd forgotten how mean ten-year-old girls can be. Saying she can't be any good at riding if her mum didn't stick around."

Indignation filled Brandon. "Then I guess we'd better make sure Lara wipes the ground with the little bitch."

Darcy grinned at him. "You want to give her some advice?"

"You sure?"

"You were always better than me with the barrels." Darcy gestured Lara over. "Uncle Brandon's got a couple of tips for you."

Lara perked up and smiled at him. The hope on her face wrapped around his heart, in a hold that would never break.

"Let's get started." He wouldn't let her down.

***

Amy woke as footsteps crossed the porch outside her door. The light was bright outside, and her room was hot. With a groan she rolled over and checked the time. Eleven o'clock. She'd slept for two hours and every inch of her being wanted to close her eyes and go back to sleep. But she had work to do and it was her own fault she was so tired.

She dressed, tied her hair back in a ponytail—the frizz she'd tackled out the day before was back with a vengeance—and headed over to the house. Lara no longer rode in the paddock and the rest of the yard was deserted. Only Jay and Cheryl sat under the awning of their van reading. Cheryl glanced up and waved, and Amy returned the greeting. She'd have to clean the guest bathroom after she'd checked in.

Everyone sat in the kitchen and a fresh batch of scones christened the table. Her gaze immediately found Brandon who smiled at her and then turned his attention back to Lara.

"I beat my best time!" Lara crowed. "After Uncle

Brandon showed Starlight what she had to do, she was like a bullet."

Darcy clapped Brandon on the shoulder. "Told you he was the best."

Brandon's expression was priceless. Shock, embarrassment and also deep pleasure shone on his face and he ducked his head. "It was all La La," he said. "She just needed a couple of tips."

"I can't wait to see Natasha's face when I beat her tomorrow. Faith's going to be so impressed."

Amy smiled as she moved around the table to put the kettle on. Lara loved her pony club instructor, was always filled with stories of what Faith had done during the class.

"There's a fresh pot of tea," Brandon said. He shifted down the table to make room for her next to him. Heat rushed to her cheeks as she remembered the kiss.

"Feel any better?" he asked, pouring the tea for her.

"A little. Did you get any sleep?"

"No, but I don't need any." He handed her the plate of scones and she took one.

He seemed at home. In fact there wasn't any tension around the table as Lara chatted happily about the gymkhana tomorrow. "Everyone's coming, aren't they?" Lara asked.

"I'd love to, La La, but I'm flying back to Perth tomorrow," Sam said. "I'll get Brandon to send me some photos."

She pouted for a second and then said, "You'll have to come and visit when you get out of the army."

"I will," Sam promised.

"When do you have to leave, Ed?" Lara asked.

"Sunday," he replied.

With Georgie going back into town this afternoon and Lara back at school on Monday, soon she'd be out here with only Matt, Darcy and Brandon. The place would feel empty. Amy pushed away her concern as the phone rang. Darcy answered it, shot a look at Lara and then walked out of the room. Almost as one, Brandon, Georgie and Ed followed him.

Lara glanced at them. "What's going on?"

"They're probably being nosy," Amy told her.

"Yeah, Brandon always has to know everything," Sam said.

"And Georgie never likes to be left out," Matt added.

Satisfied with the answer, she took a huge bite of her scone and whipped cream dotted her nose. She laughed as she wiped it off.

It was heartening to see Lara more cheerful. The week had been long and hard, but things were getting back to a new normal. Amy spread a generous layer of jam and cream on her scone, keeping an ear out for conversation from the siblings, but she couldn't hear anything.

"What time's your flight?" she asked Sam.

"Nine-thirty."

"That's when my barrel race is," Lara said.

"I'll get Amy or Brandon to drop me off early so they don't miss it," Sam said.

"I can take you," Amy told him. Darcy's ute would tow the horse trailer and Brandon, Matt and Ed could ride with them so they didn't miss any of the excitement of Lara's first gymkhana.

"But you'll come and watch, won't you Ames?" Lara asked.

"I wouldn't miss it," she promised as the others came back into the room. "But we won't all fit in the one car."

She studied Brandon's face. He didn't seem particularly impressed. As he sat, he leaned closer and murmured, "The guy's no help. He ransacked the place because he owed a guy a favour and isn't naming names."

Would the sabotage stop now he was in gaol?

"What are we doing this afternoon?" Lara asked.

Darcy sat next to her. "You are going to catch up on the schoolwork your teacher sent out for you."

She pouted. "Do I have to? I'll be back at school next week."

"And you've missed an entire week. Everyone's been working on a big project and you need to pick a topic."

"I can help if you need it," Brandon offered.

"Cool!"

Brandon seemed to expand at Lara's excitement. Amy's heart squeezed. He really was a sweet man. She was glad he and Darcy were on better terms.

"Well, my lovelies, I've got to be going," Georgie said, standing and placing her plate and mug in the sink.

"Do you have to?" Lara asked.

"Yeah, La La. I can't remember what state I left my house in."

"I can help you clean it."

Georgie hugged her niece. "Thanks for the offer, but I'll be fine. The place isn't big, so it won't take me long. Besides, you'll see me tomorrow at the gymkhana." She hugged her brothers and then Sam. "Next time you're up this way, let me know and I'll get you on one of our tours."

"Sounds great."

Georgie turned to go and Lara said, "You didn't hug Uncle Matt."

Georgie scowled at Matt. "That's because Uncle Matt thinks I've got girl germs."

Lara laughed. "No, he doesn't."

What was going on? Georgie and Matt were normally good friends, always teasing each other, but friends nonetheless. Matt rolled his eyes and stood. "Don't miss me out, Freckles." He opened his arms.

She hugged him quickly. "There. Now I'm off. I'll see you tomorrow."

Amy got to her feet. "I'll walk you out." When they were clear of the house, she asked, "Did you and Matt fight?"

Georgie crossed her arms. "He told me that flirting with Sam was inappropriate given the fact my parents just died." She growled, "How dare he try and shame me!" Her anger disappeared and she added softly, "He's so clueless, he drives me crazy sometimes." The misery in her friend's voice made Amy study her.

"You like him."

Georgie shrugged. "Of course I do. Everyone likes Matt. He's likeable."

"No, you *like* him."

She scowled. "You mean like how you *like* Brandon?" She raised her eyebrows.

Amy pressed her lips together. Did she like Brandon that way? "Yeah."

Georgie's defiance vanished. "Ames, I've *like* liked Matt since I was about ten, but I've resolved myself to the fact he doesn't see me as anything but a kid sister. It's a hopeless cause."

Amy hugged Georgie. "Matt might surprise you one day."

"Doubtful." Georgie opened her car door. "You, on the other hand, might have better luck with my brother. Maybe you can convince him to move back home. Having him back at the Ridge would be awesome."

Amy laughed. "I don't think I have that much influence." Though the idea of Brandon staying shot a thrill through her.

"Give it a shot." Georgie started the car's engine. "Take care of everyone for me and call me if you need anything."

"Will do." She waved as her friend drove away and then went to clean the bathroom. When she was finished, she wandered over to Lee's tent where he sat under the shade with his laptop on a table. "How's things?"

He smiled. "Great. I've got some fantastic photos while I've been here."

"I'm pleased for you. There's a gymkhana in town tomorrow if you want to get some action shots."

He straightened. "Sounds like fun. Where is it?"

She explained how to get there while he wrote down the details.

"Thanks, Amy. I'm sorting out my photos from the past few days, so I'll send you any good ones I've got of the station, and those of the funeral."

"That would be great." The others would appreciate them as well. She waved and headed inside where the aircon was blasting. Someone had cleared the table and Brandon and Lara were hunched over the homework outline, debating which topic she should choose. Ed had her laptop open and looked up as she walked back in.

"I don't know how you handle the speed of this thing. I could process the information faster."

She smiled. "Patience is a virtue."

She didn't quite catch his grumbled response. Darcy, Matt and Sam were heading out the door, all looking like they were on a mission. Everyone had things to do. "I guess I'll organise dinner," she said. "You got any requests Lara?"

"Can we have a barbecue?"

"Sure." Though that meant there was nothing for her to really prepare. Amy retrieved some sausages and steaks from the big freezer and set them on the sink to thaw. She'd make a couple of salads closer to dinner time.

She hovered at the sink. Brandon and Lara were deep into something to do with Australian history, and Ed muttered to himself over her laptop. She wasn't needed. The reminder that she would have to find a new job soon was unwelcome and painful. How would she leave this place without her heart being broken?

Brandon looked up and his smile made her heart beat faster. "Why don't you take a couple of hours for yourself?" he suggested. "You still look tired and we've got everything here under control."

The idea was appealing. With Ed using her laptop, she couldn't do any promotional work for the Ridge. "All right. Come get me if you need me."

His eyes darkened. "I will."

A shiver of lust ran through her. Was he thinking about their kiss too?

She licked her lips and headed back to her room.

Chapter 14

It took a few minutes for Brandon to block thoughts of Amy from his head after she left. He'd wanted to follow her to her room and resume their kiss, but he wasn't going back on his promise to help Lara.

In the end, he had far more fun than he expected helping Lara with her history project. She was smart and creative and her opinions were well considered for one so young. Occasionally Ed added his two cents but mostly he swore over Amy's laptop. His frustration was kind of amusing and Brandon debated for a while whether he should mention he had a much better laptop in his own room, but after another muttered curse from Ed, he took pity on his brother. "Do you want to borrow my laptop?"

Ed glanced up, his eyes wide. "You've got a laptop? Was it made this decade?"

"Bought it last year."

"And you've been letting me suffer on this hunk of junk for the past day?"

Brandon chuckled at his brother's outrage. "Is it that bad?"

"It's worse!" Ed stood. "Where is it?"

"I left it on the desk in my room."

Ed stormed out and Lara laughed. "That's so naughty of you, Uncle Brandon. Ed's so good with computers that he fixed Grandfather's the last time he was here."

"He's pretty smart," Brandon agreed.

Ed arrived back and sat, his fingers flying over the keyboard and a look of deep concentration on his face. Yeah, maybe it had been naughty of him. Ed was obviously very skilled.

A little over an hour later, Lara put down her pen with a sigh. "Have we done enough now?"

"Yeah, I think we have," Brandon said. Ed had disappeared somewhere and it was nearly afternoon tea time. "Is there anything you have to do to prepare for tomorrow?"

Lara's eyes flew open. "I have to plait Starlight's mane and tail."

He used to help Georgie with her horse, though he had never bothered with his. "All right. Have you got the ties?"

"Dad put them in the tack room."

"Then let's go."

As they walked across the yard, Lara slipped her hand into his. "Do you really know how to plait, Uncle Brandon?"

The ache in his heart feeling her small hand in his was real. He swallowed and kept his tone light. "Sure do, La La." How was he going to leave at the end of the month, not knowing when he would be back?

Sam's voice echoed in his head. Maybe it *was* time he got out of the army.

Going back was becoming less and less appealing.

They found the elastic bands and Lara fetched Starlight while Brandon gathered the rest of the equipment they needed. Hopefully he would remember what to do. A few minutes later he was splitting Starlight's mane into sections and plaiting them alongside Lara.

By the time Darcy returned they were finishing Starlight's tail. His eyebrows raised. "Nice job, pumpkin."

"Uncle Brandon did most of the work," she said.

Brandon wrapped the last band around the tail. "Done."

"Did you thank him?" Darcy asked.

"Thank you, Uncle Brandon." Lara hugged him and he felt like a hero.

"My pleasure, La La."

"Lucky he was here," Darcy said taking his daughter's hand. "I'm hopeless at plaiting."

"I know." Lara's matter of fact tone made Brandon laugh.

He was going to slap his brother on the back but realised how oily his hands were. "I'm going to wash my hands."

"Take a shower," Darcy suggested. "You smell like horse. Lara and I can make salads for dinner."

Where was Amy? "Is Amy in the house?"

Darcy smirked. "No, she might be in her room. You should check on her when you've showered."

Had Sam mentioned the kiss? "I will." He didn't need any other excuse.

He stopped in his room for his towel and a fresh change of clothes and had a cool shower. On his way back to his room he spotted Matt and Sam in deep discussion over by the sheds. He'd have to ask them what they'd been up to all afternoon. Before he went back to the house, he hesitated outside Amy's door. It was only polite to see if she was OK.

He wasn't kidding himself. He wanted to see the frizzy halo of her hair, wanted to kiss her soft lips, and touch her smooth skin, hear her sigh for him.

He knocked and when she answered her eyes were heavy and her hair stuck out at all angles. Sexy, sleepy woman. "Sorry, did I wake you?"

She ran a hand through her hair. "I must have dozed off. I was reading... what time is it?"

"About five."

"Oh. I should be making dinner." She moved forward.

He placed a hand on her arm to stop her. "Darcy and Lara have it sorted. There's no rush." He smiled. "You might want to brush your hair before you leave."

She moved over to the mirror and gasped. "Why can't I be one of those women who wakes up looking sexy?"

Brandon stepped inside. "You look sexy to me."

She glanced at him, wide-eyed. "Really?"

The disbelief in her tone amused him. "Really. I've been thinking about our kiss all day."

She turned and in the small room she was so close he could feel her body heat. "Me too." Her breasts pressed up against his chest. It was all the sign he needed. He pulled her against him, and his lips met hers. Instant inferno, like an oxygen-fed fire. She moaned and his hands roamed down her back to her soft, luscious arse. He was so hard. All he wanted was to taste her entire body. He kicked the door shut.

Amy stepped away as the door clicked closed. Her chest rose and fell with her heavy breath.

"Amy..."

"Yes." She stripped off her T-shirt, exposing her bare breasts and his brain short-circuited. She pulled him towards her, shoving his T-shirt up and finally his brain clicked into gear again and he stripped his shirt off, throwing it to the floor.

His shorts were painfully tight, but Amy made quick work of the button and zip and released him.

She was so damned hot. He pulled her close, needing to taste her again and she slipped into his arms as if she fit there all along. Her hands were busy touching his skin, running down his back, slipping under his underpants and pushing them down. His penis pressed against her shorts and before he could, she was stripping them off.

There wasn't anything sexier than a woman taking charge.

She pushed away from him only for a second to grab a condom out of the desk drawer.

He took it from her and slipped it on.

"Now, Brandon." She tugged him towards the bed.

No, it was his turn to take control. He dragged her against him and lifted her, her legs wrapping around his waist. He gripped her butt, sliding one hand between her legs. She was so wet.

With one thrust he filled her and her moan was full of desire. He pressed her against the door and she gripped him tighter, riding him. He could barely think, barely breathe. Brandon kissed her neck, running his teeth over her soft skin and she groaned. "More."

The ecstasy built and he thrust harder and faster, her groans of yes spurring him on. His orgasm was close, but he wasn't coming until she did. He adjusted his thrust and she moaned, clenching around him as she came. She clutched him, trembling as his orgasm overtook him, his heart pounding in his chest.

"Yes." She opened her eyes, looked at him with such intensity. His heart shifted and fell at her feet.

This was the woman he wanted in his life.

∗∗

It took a good minute for Amy's heart rate to decrease and for her brain to switch back on. The bedroom door was hard against her back and she was wrapped around the man she'd been having very sexy dreams about before he'd woken her. Maybe that was why she'd been so wanton. She'd thought she was still dreaming.

But damn, she was glad she wasn't. She didn't want to let go and that scared her. She hadn't needed anyone for years.

Her face flushed to match the heat in her body as Brandon lowered her to the ground. She stepped away as he cleaned himself and disposed of the condom.

This was awkward. "Ah…" She had no words. She'd basically thrown herself at him.

"I'll say." He laughed, the sound relaxing the sudden tension in her. He pulled her towards him and gently kissed her lips. "Was it all right for you? I didn't hurt you, did I?"

"No." At the concern on his face she clarified, "You didn't hurt me, and it was more than all right." She might ache a little later, but it would be a good ache. Amy couldn't stop herself from pulling him closer, running her hands down his muscled back to his butt. She met his blue-grey gaze. "You OK?"

"More than," he assured her. "I wasn't expecting it when I knocked on your door, but I'm not complaining."

"I'd been dreaming of you," she admitted.

"Must have been a great dream." His grin lightened her heart. "Want to tell me about it?"

How could she fight her attraction when he was this happy Brandon? "We kind of just re-enacted it," she admitted.

"Then I hope you dream of me more often." He kissed her again.

Someone knocked on the door. "Amy? Dinner will be in ten." Matt.

"Be right there," she called.

"Bran, you hear that message?" Sam yelled, laughter in his voice.

Great. They knew Brandon was in here.

"Roger that," Bran called. He'd already slid his shorts back on.

Outside the two men chuckled and their footsteps faded.

She pushed away her embarrassment. They were both unattached adults, there was nothing to be embarrassed about. She slipped on her underwear.

"Amy."

Brandon's tone was serious, and she turned to face him, pulling a shirt on.

He rubbed his head. "That meant something to me. It wasn't just sex. I care for you."

His vulnerability drew her closer and she slid her arms around him. "I'm pretty fond of you too," she admitted and brushed a kiss against his lips.

He stepped back but took her hand. "I've been thinking about a lot of things since I came home." He tapped his thigh. "I hadn't realised how much of a hole I had in my life until I came back and this place filled it." He smiled. "I was jealous of you when I first arrived."

She leaned away from him. "Why?"

"Because you were more part of my family than I was. The Ridge was your home and I wanted it to be mine."

"It's always been yours," she said. "Beth knew you'd come back one day."

Grief filled his face. "I couldn't face her after what I did."

She finished dressing and pulled him down to sit on the bed next to her. "You shouldn't blame yourself for Charlie's death."

He shook his head. "I should. A prank I set up caused the cattle to stampede and Charlie to be crushed." His hand trembled a little in hers and she squeezed it. "I thought it was best for everyone if I stayed away, but only by coming back have I seen how I've kept hurting them. I've been punishing myself for over a decade, missing this place, missing my family."

She couldn't imagine how hard it must have been for him—a fun prank with tragic consequences. No wonder he hadn't come back. "So what are you going to do?"

He was silent for a long moment. "I want to get out of the army and come home."

Her heart pounded. "That's wonderful."

He shrugged. "I need to talk to Darcy about it. This is his place now, even if I technically own it."

"I'm sure it will be fine."

"Maybe. We've still got some things to work out. I have a lot to make up to him."

"But you're family and the four of you are the strongest family I've ever known."

He nodded and smiled. "We will be." He squeezed her hand. "I know you don't have a job any more, but I was hoping you might stick around Retribution Bay."

It was all she wanted to do. "Until you finish in the army?"

"Yeah."

"I want to," she said. "But if Darcy can't pay me, then I'll need to consider finding a new job." Though she loved it here, being reliant on someone's goodwill still made a part of her uneasy. She'd had too many issues when goodwill had changed overnight. She hesitated and thought about all the ideas she'd put together for the campgrounds. "I had some ideas I wanted to run past Darcy, ways of bringing in more income to the Ridge, but this past week hasn't really been the right time."

"I'd love to hear them, and Darcy will too. Maybe we can find some more funds to keep you on." He smiled. "I'd like it if you were here when I returned."

"I'd like that too."

His kiss was long and sweet, a promise of what was to come. "Good. I'll chat to Darcy tonight." He stood and pulled her to her feet. "Let's go eat."

They held hands all the way across to the house.

Maybe finally things were improving.

***

After dinner, Brandon pulled Darcy aside. "Can we talk?"

Darcy nodded and Brandon walked down the corridor into their father's office. It seemed as good a place as any for this discussion.

"What's up?" Darcy asked perching himself on the edge of the desk.

Brandon studied his brother. He'd always been a cheerful teen, but the cheerfulness had grown into confidence and surety. He knew who he was and what he wanted. Brandon wished he'd had that knowledge when he was younger. He drew a deep breath. "I'd like to move home."

Darcy's fingers twitched, but it was the only sign of surprise. "To the Ridge?" he asked. "Into this house?"

He nodded. "For the short term," he said. "Until I can build something on the spot we picked out all those years ago."

Darcy studied him. "Why now?"

"Because now I've come home, I don't want to leave. I've missed so much of life here, Ed and Georgie growing up, Lara—" His throat closed up. "I don't want to miss any more."

"Charlie would have said you were an idiot for not coming home long ago." His lip twitched in a smile before he became serious. "The station might not survive, you know," he said. "I don't want you to lose everything."

212

Shit. Darcy was really worried. "Stonefish won't win," he said. "I'll invest the money I've got saved, and Amy has a list of ideas about how to bring more tourists in and earn more income."

His eyebrows raised. "She tell you this?"

"Yeah," he said. "She was going to approach you about it but then Mum and Dad died. Maybe the guests will bring in regular money while we sort out the livestock and machinery."

"It's a lot of work," Darcy warned.

"Work hard to fulfil your dreams." He quoted their father.

Darcy closed his eyes and breathed deeply. "All right. We need a new station hand now Taylor's gone. You can move into Mum and Dad's room if you want."

Relief washed over Brandon. He would have camped with his swag if that's what it took. "Thanks." He held out his hand.

Darcy looked at it and rolled his eyes. "That's not how we do it here." He grabbed Brandon's hand and pulled him into a hug. "Welcome home, Bran."

The words took a moment to come. "Thanks."

Brandon was home.

Chapter 15

The next morning saw a flurry of activity. Amy hadn't seen such an uproar since she'd arrived. Lara was in a total panic. "Where are my jodhpurs?" she yelled, racing through the kitchen into the laundry and tossing clothes from the hamper. "I'm going to be late. Faith said we can't be late!"

"I folded them and put them in your room yesterday," Amy told her.

Lara ran past with a "Thanks," and a wide-eyed expression on her face. Poor girl.

Brandon stood. "I'll go hitch up the float and check the gear, you calm her."

Darcy nodded his thanks.

Amy made sandwiches to take with them and Lara ran back in, this time dressed but her hair in disarray. She glanced between her father and Ed and then handed Ed the hairbrush. "Can you do my hair?"

"Burn," Ed joked as he shifted so Lara could sit in front of him while he brushed her hair.

"I could never get the hang of the braid," Darcy said. He held Lara's hand. "You're going to be fine, pumpkin."

She jiggled in her seat until Ed told her to stop moving. "What if I fall off?"

"Then you get back up and try again," Darcy said.

"No matter what, I'm proud of you."

Amy's heart clenched. She wished her father had said something like that to her.

Outside the kitchen door, Sam dumped his bag on the porch and chatted to Matt who had returned from seeing to the animals.

Finally all was ready and they climbed into their cars. Lara paused before she got into the ute. "Uncle Brandon, will you come with us?" Her hopeful expression was so sweet.

Brandon glanced at Amy and she nodded. "All right."

He gave Sam a bear hug. "Thanks for coming."

"Any time. I'll see you back at base in a couple of weeks." He got in the passenger side of Amy's car and she waved at the others before leaving the property. She'd drop Sam at the airport a little early so she'd make it in time for Lara's first event.

"Have you enjoyed your time here?" Amy asked. She liked Brandon's best friend, but she hadn't spent enough time with him to get to know him.

"I did. Brandon's family is great. I get why he was so miserable being away from them."

"He ever talk about them?"

"Only once." Sam peered at her. "You know about Charlie?"

"Yeah."

"Then you understand. He's got a stubborn streak, but I reckon it's focused in the right direction now. He won't let Darcy keep him away now he's decided to come home."

"I don't think Darcy will."

"Yeah, you're probably right," Sam conceded.

Amy didn't want to talk about Brandon behind his back. "Have you booked your flight to Melbourne for when you get out?"

"Not yet. Izzy's telling me she doesn't need any help with the baby."

"Be patient with her. She might be fine, or she might see you coming as being a failure."

"She's never a failure."

"Then tell her," Amy said. She would have loved her brother to have been kind to her. "And if she's adamant she doesn't need you, I'm sure you'll always have a bed at the Ridge if you need it."

He nodded. "Darcy and Bran both mentioned that. They're good people."

"They are," she agreed.

At the airport she parked and got out, hugging the large man. "I hope I see you again."

"Same." He slung his bag over his shoulder and entered the small terminal.

Amy's phone beeped with a message from Lee to say he'd emailed through the photos and asking her to check them. She got back into her car and flicked to her email. Even on her small screen the photos were spectacular. There was one of a sunset over the ridge, the farmhouse in the foreground, and another contrasting the turquoise ocean with the red sand. Brandon and Darcy would love them.

She continued to scroll through. The last one was of the machinery shed, but nothing interesting. A couple of people were chatting. She frowned and zoomed in on the photo. It was Taylor, so it must have been taken a while ago. The other guy stood side on but it wasn't Matt, Darcy or Bill. She enlarged it further and her mouth dropped open. It was the guy who'd broken into the house, the one they'd seen at the caravan park. Why was he talking to Taylor, and when had the photo been taken?

She couldn't see the photo properties on her phone to get the date. But she wanted answers.

She checked the time. Still an hour before Lara's event. The others would be unloading Starlight and calming Lara. She had time to drive into town and find Dot.

Amy drove as fast as she dared, though if she was pulled over for speeding at least she'd find the person she was looking for. When she arrived at the police station, the closed sign on the door made her swear. Saturday. Damn it. It had a generic phone number to call, but she didn't want to deal with someone who didn't know the situation. She wasn't sure where Dot lived, but Lindsay would know. She drove to the shopping centre and headed inside the supermarket. Lindsay stood at the cash register.

"Hi, Amy! I thought you'd be at the gymkhana today."

"Just heading there, Lindsay," she said. "I wanted to take Dot a gift for all her help with the crash, but I forgot the station is closed on Saturday. Do you know where she lives?"

"Yeah. The station has a house behind it for the officer in charge. But she's probably at the gymkhana. She mentioned she liked horse-riding."

Of course. Half the town would be there and Dot took the adult lessons with Faith. "Thanks."

"I'll see you down there. My staff should arrive soon, and I'll pop over to watch."

"Great!" Amy returned to her car and drove back past the police station to knock on the door of the house, but there was no answer. Hopefully Dot was at the gymkhana.

The pony club was on the edge of the town and cars had already filled the small car park and were lining the road. Amy joined the line and got out, hurrying down the road to the entrance. Inside the fence were a bunch of horse floats and people unloading horses. The Ridge float was opposite her and Starlight was tied to a nearby railing. Both Brandon and Darcy were by Lara's side as she got ready. Only ten minutes until Lara's event. Damn it. She didn't want to miss it.

A car door slammed across the road and she glanced across.

Taylor.

He smiled at her. "Hey, Amy. Shouldn't you be in there already? Isn't Lara competing?"

She narrowed her eyes, her anger at his casual greeting catching her by surprise. She wanted answers, but was it wise to confront him herself? There had to be a logical explanation for the photograph. They'd sat across from each other at dinner almost every night until he'd been fired. They'd laughed and played cards together. Still the lessons she'd learnt as a teenager on the street urged her towards caution. "I had to go into town for something." Her phone was a comforting presence in her pocket.

"Hey, I never got that photo from you," Taylor said. "The one of me with the mackerel I caught. Can you send it to me now?"

She had no decent excuse to refuse. They were about a hundred metres from the gate into the pony club and people stood collecting an entrance fee. "Sure." She retrieved her phone and Taylor stood next to her, looking over her shoulder. Too late, she realised she still had Taylor's incriminating photo on the screen. She tilted her phone away from him and flicked past it, but not fast enough.

"What's that?" He snatched the phone. Fear widened his eyes. "Where did you get this?" He looked both ways down the road and moved so he was between her and the gate into the pony club.

She stepped away from him. Her best chance was to go on the attack. "When was it taken?"

His hand shook. "Who has seen this?"

She didn't answer. She should have forwarded it to Brandon or Darcy.

He pressed buttons on her phone. Deleting the photo. She tried to grab it back from him but he pushed her away and she stumbled back, losing her balance on the slope that ran off the road and falling to the ground. Her palms stung and she brushed them together. "What did the man want?"

Taylor shook his head as he handed the phone back to her and helped her to her feet. "Nothing."

"Bullshit." Her mind whirled. The photo had to have been taken at least a month ago, way before the accident. But what could the intruder want of Taylor? "Did he ask you to tell him about the station?"

"No."

What then? "Taylor, it's important you tell the police. That man broke into the house and ransacked the place. Anything he said might be useful for getting a better conviction." This photo proved the intruder had been around longer than just this week.

"It was nothing." He glanced at his four-wheel drive which had a dinghy on the top. "I've got to go."

"You're not watching the gymkhana?"

He reached for the door handle, his hand shaking. "No, I have to leave."

He was scared. But the only reason to be scared was if he had something to hide. The answer came to her with a bolt of lightning. "He asked you to sabotage things."

Taylor flinched.

She stared at him. "You cut the windmill water pipe."

"No, I didn't." He rubbed his thumb and forefinger together.

Taylor's poker tell. He did that when he was

bluffing. "You did."

His face screwed up in pain. "You don't know what you're talking about!"

She was fairly certain she did. Horror and fury mixed to fuel her. "What did you get in return?"

He pressed his lips together.

"Money?" No, Taylor had never been interested in material possessions. As long as he had his swag and his car he was happy. But he did like to gamble. "Do you owe people money?"

Taylor's eyes widened slightly, but he didn't confirm it.

The son of a bitch. He'd damaged the windmill for his own gain. But that wasn't the first bit of sabotage. She froze. "You cut the brake line on the four-wheel drive."

At her shout Taylor stepped closer. "Shut up! You don't understand."

He was right. She didn't. "You were in debt so you sabotaged the people who gave you a job and a home?"

"Bill fired me over nothing!"

"Bill and Beth are dead because of you!"

"No one was meant to get hurt," he said. "It was just meant to put the car out of action for a while. A minor inconvenience, an extra cost."

Dot would have a different opinion on it. Asshole. "Go to hell, Taylor." She turned but Taylor grabbed her ponytail, yanking her back. Tears of pain stung her eyes as he wrapped his arms around her waist, trapping her arms.

"Wait. You can't tell anyone. I'm not going to gaol."

Fear struck her and she struggled, but his arms gripped her tighter, squeezing the air out of her lungs.

Across the road at the pony club the crowd cheered as someone did their turn at the barrel race. Even if she screamed, no one would hear her. "Let go of me,

Taylor."

Taylor kicked her legs out from under her and she fell to the ground, landing hard on the dirt. Before she could get up, his fist came flying towards her face.

***

Brandon checked his watch. Amy should have been here by now. The airport was only ten minutes down the road and even if she'd walked Sam in, she'd had plenty of time to get back. Lara's race was about to start. He rang Amy's mobile, but it went to voice mail. His gut churned a warning. Something wasn't right.

Lara had already gone to join the line of riders waiting for their turn and Darcy was with her, chatting to the cute pony club organiser Faith Arnold.

"Did I miss it?" Sam's question made him jump. His friend stood behind him puffing.

"What are you doing here?"

"Flight was delayed two hours. The baggage handlers are having another go slow day, so I figured I'd take my chances and try to catch Lara's race. I bummed a lift from the airport."

"Where's Amy?" He glanced behind Sam.

Sam frowned. "Isn't she here yet? She left as soon as she dropped me off."

"No." The churning became alarm. He scanned the crowd. Ed and Georgie had nabbed front row seats by the arena and there were other familiar faces in the crowd, including Dot, but no Amy. Georgie spotted him and waved. He held up his phone and then messaged her to see if she'd seen Amy.

No.

Damn it. Don't panic. She couldn't have crashed, because Sam would have seen it on his way here. So what else? Darcy joined them. "Sam, aren't you going to miss your flight?"

"Was delayed. Have you seen Amy?"

"No." He frowned at Brandon. "Something wrong?"

"I don't know. She should be here by now. I need to ask Dot if they let the intruder out on bail." He dialled her number and a few seconds later he had his answer. "Prisoner is still in gaol."

"Hey, Darcy. Would you like me to take some photos of Lara racing?"

They all turned to the speaker. He was the Ridge's campground guest travelling alone—the photographer.

"That would be great, Lee. Have you seen Amy?"

"No. Did she show you the photos I sent her of the Ridge?" His hopeful expression spoke of an artist needing praise.

"When did you send them?" Brandon asked.

"About an hour ago."

The timing lined up. "Can you show them to me now?"

"They're on my laptop back at camp," he said. "Oh, hang on. I might be able to access them in the cloud."

Brandon waited impatiently as the man flicked through his phone.

"What's happening?" Dot asked. She was dressed in jeans, her black hair tucked under a baseball cap.

"Amy's not here. She wouldn't miss Lara's race."

The crowd cheered as another child raced the clock.

"I just ran into Lindsay," Dot said. "She mentioned Amy had been looking for me earlier."

Not good. Something must have happened to her.

"Here they are." Lee handed over the phone. Brandon snatched it, flicking past gorgeous landscapes of his land and ending on the shed. He zoomed in and swore, handing the phone to Dot. "Why did you send her this one?"

Lee blinked and stepped back. "I didn't know I had it until I went through my photos yesterday. The sergeant had asked questions about Taylor and whether I'd seen strange people around so I sent it to Amy in case it meant something. I was going to talk to her at the gymkhana."

"Where's Taylor staying?" he asked Dot.

"At the caravan park. We can take my car."

He was already moving, Sam by his side. "Tell Lara I watched from the stands," he yelled back at Darcy.

"Yeah. Be careful."

As he manoeuvred through the crowds of people and horses in the stable area, he kept scanning faces, hoping Amy would appear before him. The woman at the gates called, "Wait a second and I'll stamp your hand so you can get back in." She held up a hand but jumped out of the way when they didn't stop.

Dot's car was about halfway along the line of cars. He scanned the road and noticed a bright yellow hatchback parked at the far end. "Wait. That's Amy's car." He took off at a run, but before he reached it, a ute backed out, almost running him over. It had an aluminium dinghy on the top. He glanced at the driver.

Taylor. And in the passenger seat was Amy, slumped down, her eyes closed. "Amy!" He lunged for the door handle.

Taylor flinched and accelerated away.

Shit. What had he done to her?

Dot and Sam pulled up next to him in a blue sedan and he jumped in the back seat. "Taylor's got Amy in the ute." He pointed.

Dot slid her phone out of her pocket and thrust it at Sam. "Call Colin."

When the man answered, Dot told him what was going on and where they were headed.

The ute pulled away from them. "Can't you go any faster?" Brandon demanded.

"I don't have a V8 like him," Dot snapped. "And he

doesn't have two hulking big men in his car weighing it down."

Brandon swore.

"There's nowhere he can go anyway," Dot continued. "There's no turn off until your road."

The ute proved her wrong when it bounced off the road heading towards the ocean on a barely-there track. Dot swore as she slowed to make the turn. "Colin, we're heading off track."

No response. Sam checked the phone. "We've lost connection." He unstrapped. "Drop me here. I'll direct him. You want to be as light as possible taking that road."

He was right. It was rutted red dirt, the type only a four-wheel drive should attempt. Dot peered at Brandon in the rear-view mirror as Sam jumped out. "I'm staying," he said.

She accelerated, the car lurching over the bumps. Brandon shifted into the middle of the seat to even out the weight. The ute was a dust cloud in front of them. Where was Taylor going? There was nothing out here. Another couple of kilometres and it would be Stokes land, so there'd be a fence to cross.

Unless things had changed since the last time he was here.

Their progress was painfully slow but thankfully the track was hard enough that they didn't get bogged.

They reached the fence line and the track turned to run alongside it. The dust floating in the air indicated Taylor had turned north. Towards the ocean. And he had his dinghy on the roof. Would he leave Amy behind if he launched the boat in time?

"Dot, he's heading for the bay and he's got his boat."

She nodded. "We got any mobile reception?"

"Nope."

She swore. "I should have brought the patrol car. It's got satellite."

Brandon exhaled, calming the tension. Think. Taylor couldn't be a violent man or Bill never would have kept him on for so long. So why would he have taken Amy? Maybe she'd asked him about the photo.

Taylor had panicked.

The image of Amy slumped in the front seat made him mission-focused. He refused to believe Amy was dead. She had to be unconscious or he'd kill Taylor himself. He pushed down the anger. It couldn't have been a simple conversation with their intruder. Taylor must have done something which would get him into trouble.

They ridged a hill and the ocean spread out before them. The ute was parked on the beach, the dinghy on the sand and Amy and Taylor fought over the boat's engine. Taylor hit Amy and she sprawled back over the sand.

Brandon growled.

"You take my lead when we stop," Dot told him. "If you attack him, I will arrest you both."

"Yes, ma'am." She knew the man better than he did. He'd follow her lead unless Amy was in real danger. Then all bets were off.

Taylor spotted the car and grabbed something from the dinghy. Then he hauled Amy to her feet and held her in front of him like a shield.

The sun glinted off the item Taylor held.

Brandon's blood ran cold. He was holding a knife to Amy's throat.

Chapter 16

Amy had been more pissed off than scared right up to the moment when Taylor pressed a razor-sharp filleting knife against her throat. Then terror flooded out every other emotion. She froze, her body tense as Taylor gasped, "Do exactly what I say."

"Yes," she murmured.

A blue sedan bumped its way towards them but it was too far away for her to recognise the occupants. It had to be the cavalry, but the pressure of the knife across her windpipe took all her focus. One jerk from Taylor and she was dead. She didn't even dare speak in case she moved the wrong way.

"Convince them to let me go," he said. "I don't want to hurt you, I just want to get in my dinghy and leave, got it?"

"Yes." Perhaps he hadn't considered they'd have planes in the air looking for him the moment he left, but she wouldn't point it out to him. She realised he was desperate when she'd come to in the front seat of his ute. After her mind cleared, she'd tried to talk sense into him, but he hadn't listened. All he repeated was he wasn't going to gaol.

She should have run away while she'd had the chance, but she hadn't really considered herself in danger. This was Taylor. Her aim had been to prevent him from escaping and she'd tried to stop him from unhooking the dinghy from the roof, but he was well practised and she'd barely got in the way.

The car pulled up before the track became beach sand and Dot and Brandon climbed out. Definitely the cavalry. Brandon's expression was like a snake about to strike. Mean, focused and angry. Her heart leapt and chills went down her arms, even though the expression wasn't for her.

Taylor wasn't getting away.

She just hoped he didn't hurt her in his desperation.

Dot had a word to Brandon and he nodded once, his gaze not leaving Amy's. Then Dot strolled across the sand. "Going fishing?"

Taylor loosened the knife on Amy's neck. "Something like that. You going to let me go?"

"Let you go?" She sounded intrigued by the idea.

"Yeah. I'll take my dinghy and disappear."

Brandon shifted where he stood.

"Tell Brandon to go back to the car," Taylor said.

Amy almost laughed. No way was he leaving.

"Brandon, go back to the car," Dot said.

"No."

Amy didn't dare speak as Taylor tightened his hold on her again, the sharp point of the knife pressing into her skin. She felt a warm drip of blood run down her neck.

"Taylor, the knife!" Dot pointed.

Taylor swore and adjusted his hold, moving the knife hard against her back instead. "Sorry," he murmured. To Dot he yelled, "I mean it! Let me go."

Dot held up her hands. "All right, I'll let you go. Do you want me to push the dinghy into the water for you? Connect the engine?"

Taylor pulled Amy away from the boat, down the beach away from Dot and Brandon. "Yeah. Good idea."

He was a fool. How did he think he'd get away? The closest town to Retribution Bay was Onslow, over three hundred kilometres away by car. The rest of the coastline was isolated and unfriendly. The dinghy's tank of fuel wouldn't get him back to civilisation, but there was plenty of land to get lost in.

Still she kept her mouth shut as Brandon attached the outboard motor to the boat and then he and Dot pushed it into the water. They were only ten metres away.

A movement in her periphery towards the dunes made her shift her head slightly.

"Don't move!" Taylor cried, and the knife pierced her shirt, pricking her skin.

She froze.

Swallowing, she tracked a body along the dunes. If she didn't know better, she would swear it was Sam, but he should be flying somewhere over Carnarvon by now.

"The boat's ready." Dot stood ankle deep in the water, holding the boat while Brandon stood on the shore.

"Join Brandon," Taylor called.

"Taylor, please let me go," Amy murmured.

"Not until I'm in the boat." He pushed her forward as Dot backed away from the dinghy.

The ocean was cool and calm and the dinghy bobbed in the shallows. Amy waded through the water, shuffling her feet, hoping no stingrays basked in the shallows this morning. Brandon was tense, ready to pounce. But Taylor wasn't a vicious criminal. He simply wanted his freedom. Surely Brandon realised that.

"Hold the boat steady," Taylor ordered as they reached it.

She gripped the warm metal side while he shifted next to her.

"Start the motor."

"I don't know how."

"It's a rip cord." He reached around her with his left hand, the right hand still holding the knife to her lower back. He leaned against the edge of the dinghy and the boat shifted away. Taylor lost his balance and the knife sliced a deep cut across her back. She twisted and grabbed his hand, yelling, but it was too late. The pain was excruciating. She stumbled away, falling to her knees in the water.

"Amy!" Brandon bellowed and charged towards her.

Taylor twisted, and dropped the knife, his face pale. "Shit."

She pressed both hands across her lower back and her hand came back covered in blood.

***

Time stopped. It must have, because Brandon couldn't get to Amy fast enough. The rich red ballooning from her back came faster and turned the water pink. She swayed. If she fainted, she could drown. Taylor scrambled for the boat, terror on his face but Brandon couldn't give a shit about him.

To his right, Sam charged across the sand, always his backup, and Colin was right behind him. Which meant there was another vehicle, hopefully better suited to the terrain, out there. Amy needed a hospital.

He dropped to his knees and pulled Amy's shirt up to examine the wound. It was nasty, deep and torn. "I've got you, Amy." He pressed his hand firmly across the wound. Sam reached him and stripped off his T-shirt, and handed it to Brandon to use as a bandage.

"How bad is it?" Amy gasped. "It hurts so much."

"The salt water's got to sting like a mother-fucker," Brandon agreed. "I've seen worse injuries than this on the battlefield. Hold this in place for me, as tight as you can." He guided her hand to Sam's shirt. The blood seeped through almost immediately. They needed a hospital. "What's the vehicle?" he asked Sam.

"Four-wheel drive patrol car's parked a hundred metres behind Dot's."

"Let's go." He lifted Amy, being careful to avoid the wound. She placed one arm around his neck while she continued to hold the bandage in place.

"Colin," Sam called. "Keys."

Dot and Colin had wrestled Taylor into submission. With arms handcuffed behind his back, tears poured down his face. "Is she all right?"

Brandon ignored him as Colin threw the keys to Sam.

"There's a radio inside," Dot said. "Contact the hospital and tell them you're coming in."

Brandon nodded, already jogging behind Sam. The sand sucked at his feet, but it barely slowed him. Sam opened the back seat of the patrol car and Brandon put Amy inside. He shuffled next to her and closed the door.

Amy's face was white, and her eyelids flickered closed. Sam's shirt was soaked in blood.

"Amy, stay with me," Brandon said, tapping her cheek. "Step on it, Sam."

Brandon cushioned Amy the best he could during the rough ride, keeping pressure on the wound. "I feel woozy," Amy said.

He nodded. "That's my overwhelming personality. Women feel faint around me all the time."

Sam snorted and Amy cracked a smile before closing her eyes again.

"Come on, honey. I need to see those beautiful eyes of yours."

Her eyes flickered and he could tell it was a real effort for her to keep them open. Her pulse was light, thready. As they reached the bitumen road, Sam hit the sirens and the accelerator.

Brandon continued to talk to her, but she didn't respond, her eyes opening and closing before staying closed. "Amy!" Her pulse slowed. "Faster, Sam."

It was the longest ride in Brandon's life. He kept pressure on Amy's wound, and monitored her pulse. At the hospital, a group of nurses waited with a gurney. He lifted Amy out of the car and placed her on it. "We've got her," one nurse said as they pushed the bed into the hospital.

Brandon trailed after them. "I'm an army medic. I can help."

A second nurse placed her hand on his arm. "We've got this. Take a seat." She ran after the others.

He moved forward but Sam clapped him on the shoulder. "Leave it to them."

Brandon spun around, the frustration and fear colliding inside of him. "She can't die."

Sam said nothing. They both knew hope wasn't always enough.

Brandon paced the corridor while Sam answered the questions Tracy asked him.

People survived serious injuries like Amy's all the time. He couldn't lose her now.

He stopped pacing. He couldn't lose her *ever*. That's what he wanted. A life with Amy. How had he fallen for her so fast?

He pictured the brightness of her smile, the quiet way she got things done and her joy when she laughed. He loved her.

His legs trembled and he stumbled into the nearest plastic chair of the waiting room. Sam was by his side in an instant. "You, OK, mate?"

"I love her."

His friend immediately smiled. "Took you long

enough to figure it out. You'd better tell her when she comes out of surgery."

"I will." The positive attitude was what he needed right now. Because he wouldn't consider anything else.

"She got any family you should call?" Sam asked.

Shit. He hadn't even considered it. "She's Arthur's sister."

Sam's eyes widened. "Sherlock?"

Brandon nodded.

"But wasn't she missing?"

"Long story. Amy might not want me to call him." She could decide when she came out of surgery—if she got out of surgery. Shit. He couldn't think like that. "He won't get to Retribution Bay before the surgery is over anyway and from what she told me, Sherlock might not be interested."

Sam frowned. "How about I call him, suss out the situation?"

Brandon closed his eyes, remembered how serious Sherlock had been when he'd spoken about his sister. He'd seemed sad, but would Brandon be betraying Amy's trust? "I don't know. I can't think about it at the moment." All he could do was pray she would be all right.

"Go wash up." Sam patted his back. "I'll wait here but you can't see her with hands covered in blood."

Brandon looked down and shuddered. He headed for the bathroom.

Time passed. The outside doors opened and Dot strode in.

"She's in surgery," Brandon said to her unasked question. "Where's Taylor?"

"Gaol," she answered. "He's confessed to sabotaging the four-wheel drive and the windmill on the drive back. He told us he owed large gambling debts to the intruder, who said he'd wipe the slate clean if he did a few things. Taylor doesn't know much else and neither one can point the finger at Stonefish." She sighed. "We'll transport both to Carnarvon tomorrow. Taylor's not likely to get bail given how much of a flight risk he is."

Brandon thought he'd feel more of a sense of satisfaction knowing his parents' killer was caught, but he was numb. All that mattered was Amy surviving.

Dot hugged him. "I've got to get back. Call me when Amy gets out of surgery." She nodded to Sam. "Thanks for your help today."

He nodded back. "Any time."

As she left, Georgie and Ed raced in and Georgie hugged him hard. "How is she?"

"No news." He tapped his thigh. "Is the gymkhana over?"

"Lara's done all her events. She came first in the barrel racing and Darcy's taking her to the cafe for an ice cream sundae. He hasn't told her about Amy yet, wanted to wait until we had more news."

Losing Amy would devastate the girl and she'd been through too much lately. "Go celebrate with her," he said. "Where does she think we are?"

"We told her you had to take Sam back to the airport."

Good.

"Brandon Stokes?" A doctor stood by the door they'd taken Amy through.

He lunged to his feet, heart pounding. "How is she?"

The doctor smiled. "She's doing well. The surgery was a success and she's awake but light-headed."

Georgie squealed and hugged him. Brandon slumped against her as the fear and tension melted away.

She was alive.

*****

The drugs in Amy's body made her drowsy, but at least she felt no pain. She lay in the recovery room, her only thought of Brandon. Her memories of the trip to the hospital were hazy, but the one certainty was that Brandon had held her the whole way. Her heart thumped in her chest. It was impossible not to love him.

Movement at the door made her turn her head and her spirits lifted seeing Brandon there. Then horror filled her. His shirt was covered in blood... her blood.

His eyes were wide, expression concerned. "Amy." The relief in his voice pulled at her.

"Hi." Her voice was croaky and she cleared her throat. "Thanks for saving me."

He entered the room. "I didn't. The doctors did."

"He said your fast thinking saved my life. I lost a lot of blood."

"I know." His hand trembled as he slipped it into hers.

She squeezed it. "Taylor?"

"Dot arrested him. He won't be going anywhere but gaol," Brandon said. "He confessed to the sabotage; he slit the brake line." Anger flitted over his face before he hid it.

They'd found the culprit, but it didn't bring Bill and Beth back. "I'm sorry."

"Dot said he's already pointing the finger at the guy who broke into the house. I hope with the police focusing on Stonefish, they'll stop bothering us now."

Amy shifted, wanting to sit up.

"What do you need?" Brandon asked.

"A hug."

He gently wrapped his arms around her, and she

inhaled his musky smell. "It's over." She let go and winced as she shifted into a more comfortable position.

Brandon growled. "I'm not letting you out of my sight ever again."

Her body warmed at the sentiment. "That's going to be hard from the army."

"I'm going to ask to be released early. I might get it on compassionate grounds, but if not, I still want you to be at the Ridge when I return."

Her heart fluttered.

His thumb rubbed the back of her hand. "I've fallen in love with you, Amy. I want to share my home and my family with you."

Her mouth dropped open. Perhaps the drugs were making her hear things she wanted to hear. "Say that again?"

He smiled. "I love you. I want to marry you and share my life with you."

Her chest swelled. He was giving her everything she ever wanted. "Are you sure?"

"Never been more sure of anything in my life." He hesitated. "I know it's fast, so you could move in first. We don't have to marry immediately."

The emotion made it difficult to speak. His love and fear was clear on his face. She swallowed and took a deep breath. "I love you, Brandon. I would love to marry you and share your home and your family."

"It's our home," he murmured. "Our family. Always."

Chapter 17

Amy waited impatiently in the reception area for Brandon to pick her up from the hospital the next morning. Though she was still sore, the hospital environment reminded her too much of when her mother had been injured. She would recover far quicker in the comforting surroundings of the Ridge.

He drove her car into the carpark and love filled her as he strode across to her. His eyes lit up. "What are you doing out here?"

"Waiting for you." She kissed him and pulled him out of the building, waving goodbye to the receptionist.

He chuckled. "Slow down, Ames." At the car he stopped her and took both of her hands. "There's something I have to tell you."

Concern zinged along her skin. Had he changed his mind about the proposal? Had something else gone wrong overnight? "What is it?"

He sighed. "When you were in surgery, Sam asked me whether you had any family we should call."

Her stomach sank. Did she want to hear this?

"I mentioned you were Arthur's sister and Sam called him."

Every muscle in her body tightened and she winced at the pain in her side. She didn't want to know the answer, but she gazed into Brandon's stormy eyes and asked, "What did he say?"

Brandon squeezed her hands. "He wants to visit you."

Her mouth dropped open. "Are you sure?"

"Yeah. He was pretty upset when he heard about the attack, but he can't get leave for another month."

Hope and defiance warred within her. It took her being stabbed for her brother to show any interest. Was he doing it for appearances' sake? Perhaps he didn't want his team mates to look at him badly.

"Do you want to see him?"

She shrugged. "Why does he care now?"

"I can chat to him about it when I go back to Perth if you want." He smiled. "I'll support whatever you decide."

It was a scary concept. She didn't know how she would react seeing her brother again. Part of her worried she would release all her anger and pain at being abandoned and ruin any chance of reconciliation. The other part worried he wouldn't really care and she'd be devastated again. "Let me think about it."

He nodded and opened the car door for her.

Back at the station everyone was waiting for her, including Sam and Ed. "Aren't you two supposed to be on a flight?" she asked.

"We switched to the afternoon one," Ed said. "Couldn't miss welcoming you home."

"Besides, it's probably going to be delayed anyway," Sam said.

Lara flung her arms around Amy. "I'm sorry you got hurt."

Amy winced at the pull on her wound but hugged her. Brandon had mentioned they'd skipped the details of how Amy had been hurt when they'd told Lara. "I'm sorry I missed your race. Congratulations on winning."

She beamed. "Faith says I'm even better than she was at my age."

"Miss Arnold's a popular topic at the moment," Darcy said.

"Sexy too," Matt murmured and Darcy elbowed him.

"She said we could call her Faith," Lara said. "Dad filmed my race so you can still watch it."

"I'd love to," Amy said and Lara grabbed her hand and started pulling her towards the house. Amy laughed. "Let me put my things in my room."

"Uncle Brandon said you're getting married. That will make you my aunt. Will you be staying in Granny and Grandfather's room now with Uncle Brandon?"

"Ah…" It was hard to keep up with Lara's excitement.

Ed and Sam laughed while Darcy placed an arm around his daughter's shoulders. "Come and help me set up the recording."

The others followed them in and soon it was just her and Brandon. "You've moved inside the house?"

He nodded. "Darcy invited me to when I told him I wanted to move back. I figured it made sense." He slipped his hand into hers. "I'd love for you to be in my bed, but I understand if it might feel a bit weird."

She had three weeks with him until he had to go back to the army to finish his commission. She wasn't wasting a second of it. "I'd love to move into your room."

He beamed and kissed her. "Thank you. Come on. Let's go watch Lara's ride. Then we can move your stuff into the house."

A blanket of belonging settled over her as his arm wrapped around her waist. He was her family now. This was her home. She realised with startling clarity that it didn't matter how Arthur reacted when he visited.

She'd found her own family, her own love and a permanent place to call her own. "Tell Arthur he can visit if he wants."

Brandon glanced at her. "You sure?"

She nodded. There wasn't anything he could do to take this away from her.

She was home.

Hello Dear Reader,

I hope you enjoyed Return to Retribution Bay. There's something I wanted to address before you go. My editor's comments on finishing were, 'You haven't fully addressed Amy and Arthur's situation and we don't know why Stonefish Enterprises want the station.' So in case you had the same complaints...

I was going to add a small scene towards the end where Amy actually chatted to her brother, but then I added Arthur to the first scene in the bar with Brandon and Sam, and he came alive for me and demanded his own book. He told me I couldn't possibly do justice to his side of the story in a short conversation with Amy, and I agreed. So Arthur's story will be told in about book 6 in the series, so I'm sorry, but you're going to have to wait for the full reconciliation.

The other issue is what Stonefish wants with the Ridge. Well, they're being super secretive about that and won't even tell me. I'm fairly sure some of the explanation will come out in book 3, Escape to Retribution Bay, but I promise, by the end of the series, all will be explained. I hope you'll stick with me to find out.

I was also going to have a scene at the end with Faith and Darcy at the pony club, but it was a little jarring, so I've added it as a deleted scene for those who are part of my reader group. To sign up and read it, go to

https://www.claireboston.com/reader-group/

Anyway, Darcy's story will be out soon in Trapped in Retribution Bay.

Happy Reading!

Claire B

Acknowledgements

Starting a new series comes with a bunch of new challenges especially when the setting is completely different from the series before. Retribution Bay is based on Exmouth, a town on the north-west peninsula of Western Australia. I got many of my ideas from a couple of holidays I took in the area and was able to interview people for my series. So I want to thank Jimmy Small from Ocean Eco Adventures who spoke to me about running a tour boat. Much of what he told me will be used in future books, but I wanted to thank him here anyway.

Thank you also to Edwina Shallcross who owns Bullara Station. I based the Ridge off Bullara and my husband and I stayed there a couple of nights. Edwina was able to answer a number of questions about station life which made this story richer.

Toni Roe from Gwoonwardu Mia answered my questions, enabling me to make Matt an indigenous man from the area.

As always I'd like to thank my editors, Ann Harth and Teena Raffa-Mulligan and my cover designer, LJ from Mayhem Cover Creations.

Trapped in Retribution Bay

Aussie Heroes: Retribution Bay

Coming in 2021

Printed in the USA
CPSIA information can be obtained
at www.ICGtesting.com
LVHW091927260924
792260LV00010B/45